Sinful Illusions

SINFUL DUET | BOOK ONE

MORGAN JAMES

About the Book

EVA

Revenge.

It's been the only thing driving me for the past six months since my sister was murdered—and he's the one responsible. I want to break him the way he broke my family. But to get what I want, I'll need to get close to him, win his trust. He stirs a dark need inside me that I never knew existed. My attraction to him is a distraction I can't afford. I'll give him my body... but he can never have my heart.

FOX

The first time I set eyes on Eva, I'm entranced. When the brazen young woman breaks into my home, I take it as a sign —she's meant to be mine. She's hell-bent on revenge, but the more I'm with her, the more I want to keep her.

I'm the devil... and she's my fallen angel.

Sinful Illusions is the first book in the Sinful Duet, a dark romantic suspense. It ends on a cliffhanger and depicts some situations that may be uncomfortable for some readers, which includes kidnapping, spanking, humiliation, etc.

CHAPTER One

VILLAINY WEARS MANY MASKS; NONE SO DANGEROUS AS THE MASK OF VIRTUE.
~WASHINGTON IRVING

EVA

As far as stupid ideas went, this one definitely took the cake. I crouched next to the stone pillar at the corner of the estate and glanced around one last time before tossing the large stick over the metal fence. I cringed, closing my eyes to narrow slits as I waited for lights to flash, sirens to blast the air, men to come running.

None of those things happened. I cracked open my eyes, and my eyebrows shot toward my hairline. So, maybe tonight was my lucky night. I'd watched the black car pull out of the driveway just over fifteen minutes ago, so I knew he was gone. I was fairly certain the fence surrounding the property had trips of some sort, but maybe he only activated them when he was home. I hoped to God that was the case, considering what I was about to do.

Still, I waited another five minutes. When all remained quiet and tranquil, I rose from my place concealed behind the pillar. The fence encircled the entire five-acre estate, a small fortune in itself. But that didn't really surprise me. A man like Fox had enough money to buy whatever he wanted—whether it was some material object or someone's life.

A combination of sadness and anger surged through me at the reminder of my sister's death. It was a never-ending cycle these days. Cry, rage, cry all over again. The past four months had been exhausting, fueled intermittently by hope and despair. Tomorrow would make one hundred and thirty days since my sister disappeared. No matter how long I lived, I would never forget the sound of my ringing phone piercing the air, the shaky sound of my father's voice telling me she was gone.

I didn't know if it was intuition or something else, but I knew the moment I saw Daddy's name lighting up my screen that something had happened to my sister. Elle had been married for nearly two years, and I hadn't gotten to see her as often as I would have liked between my schoolwork and her obligations as a senator's wife. The last time I'd seen her was around Fourth of July, when she and Spencer stopped by my family's annual party at the lake. They hadn't stayed long, and I cursed myself for not going out of my way to spend more time with her.

A little over a month later, she'd disappeared. A hiker had discovered her phone first. Thinking nothing of it, he'd pocketed it to turn it in. A few hundred yards later he'd found her. Or, rather, the place she'd died. The authorities found a significant amount of blood and trace evidence at the scene to believe with certainty that she'd been attacked and couldn't have possibly survived.

Authorities had spent several days scouring the woods, searching for any sign of her. Her purse containing her identity had been found more than a mile from the crime scene, and a knife covered in her DNA was found near the edge of the river just beyond that. They'd searched the riverbank for miles upstream, but her body had never been recovered. I'd held out hope for months that they were wrong; she would come back to us. We would find her. Part of me felt like she was still alive, and I couldn't possibly let her go until I knew for sure. If she was truly gone, I wanted to find her and put her to rest. I needed the closure—we all did.

Each day that passed without word of her return dug the knife of pain and despair a little deeper. Finally, we could wait no longer. Daddy insisted we move on with our lives— what was left of them. We had finally laid her memory to rest just a couple weeks ago, lowering an empty coffin into the ground two days after Christmas.

I still couldn't believe she was gone. Or maybe I just refused to accept it. Even though Elle and I had lived apart and were busy with our own lives, she was still my sister, and a part of my heart died with her. Justice needed to be served —and I was going to ensure that happened.

While I'd been staying with my family over the holidays, Elle's husband, Spencer, stopped by. I'd overhead him speaking with Daddy late one night while I eavesdropped outside his office. Spencer believed a man by the name of Fox was responsible for Elle's death. For years I'd only heard whispers of the man who lived in the shadows and ran an underground crime organization. Daddy had protected Elle and me from everything growing up, but when Elle was murdered, the rose-colored glasses had been ripped away, revealing the ugly truth of the world around me. Our family had been torn apart, and I'd sworn I would exact revenge on the man who'd done this to us.

I glanced through the bars of the heavy-duty wrought iron fence and glared at the mansion, mentally cursing the man who owned it. A puff of air escaped my lips, curling in front of my face in the frigid evening air. A shiver worked its way down my spine, but I closed my eyes, drawing on my strength and tuning out the cold that penetrated my bones. It was a perfect night. Not too bright, and the snow that we'd gotten around Christmas had melted off several days ago and the cold front that had moved through yesterday had left the ground frozen solid—no chance of footprints.

Spring semester had just started a week ago, and I was back in the apartment I shared with my roommate, Rose. She was headed to the club to relax and unwind with a few of our friends. Though they'd invited me along, I'd declined. My mission tonight was revenge.

The note I'd left for Rose said that I was staying with my parents tonight. If tomorrow rolled around and I was still gone, I knew she'd reach out to my parents, who would then contact the authorities. Not that I would allow that to happen. I would be in and out before anyone was the wiser—just as soon as I found what I was looking for. Unfortunately, I wouldn't know exactly what I was looking for until I saw it.

What was his weakness? I needed to find whatever it was that would hurt him the worst and exploit it. So far, though, I hadn't been able to dig up much on the mysterious man everyone called Fox—due, no doubt, to his cunning and ruthless nature. His business was never mentioned directly, though he moved in the upper echelons of society. The information on Fox was infuriatingly scarce, but I'd never been a quitter, and I wasn't going to start now.

My plan was to get into the house, find any information that would help me formulate a strategy, then get back out. What I really needed to do was find his office, his private domain. I assumed that he, like all men, would keep any pertinent documents safely tucked away on computers or—better yet—filing cabinets. Unfortunately, that meant I would have to search the whole damn house to find the right room before I could even start. But that was fine with me. Gauging from his recent activity, Fox wouldn't be back for hours yet.

I'd spent the previous three nights parked one street over, watching the house, studying his routine. Each evening, Fox had stepped out the front doors of the mansion, then climbed into the back of the black Mercedes. Though I'd continued to watch the premises, he still hadn't returned by the time I left around one. Tonight would be the same. The car had pulled out of the garage just over twenty minutes ago now, so I was safe for several hours, at least.

During my time watching the house, I'd seen only the same two men: the driver who never returned without Fox, and the second man who remained at the house, occasionally stepping outside for a smoke. I wasn't naïve enough to believe those were the only guards he had, but I was confident that I could elude the others once I was inside.

From the position of the thin crescent moon high above me, I judged it to be about ten o'clock. That meant I would have about three hours to get what I needed and get out. I'd be home right around the same time as Rose. No harm done. Now, I just needed to get inside. I didn't know how to pick locks—not well, anyway. I'd researched it but had quickly given up. With a house like this, Fox surely had high end security, including more advanced locking mechanisms that couldn't be easily breached. I could break a window, but I really didn't want to leave behind any evidence of my brief foray into his home. My plan was to create some kind of diversion the next time the guard stepped outside for his break. I would slip inside undetected so I wouldn't have to worry about the alarm system or missing my window of opportunity.

Tonight, I'd left my car behind and instead taken the bus to Oakmont Street. From there, I'd walked the rest of the way. Though I hadn't encountered anyone on my previous trips, I couldn't risk anyone discovering my empty car while I was gone and calling it in. Once I'd gotten into the house and retrieved what I needed, I would walk to the gas station a mile down the road and contact an Uber to pick me up. Worst case, I could hike over to the L and ride the subway home. In the middle of the night, it wasn't safe or smart, so I sincerely hoped a driver would be available. I'd have made arrangements earlier, but I wasn't sure how long I would be. I needed to get moving.

Looking around the darkened grounds again, I took a deep breath. Grasping the top rail, I braced my feet against the smooth iron and scaled the fence. Cautiously avoiding the spindles at the top, I hoisted myself up. The spiky point of one caught the back of my thigh as I swung it over, and I grimaced as my leggings ripped and the sharp metal cut into my skin. Shoving the pain away, I balanced my weight and swung my other leg over, then dropped to the ground on the other side.

Crouched low, I took a moment to inspect my leg. I couldn't see it in the near-dark, but it didn't appear to be too bad. I pressed against the wound, rubbing away the slight stinging sensation as I climbed to my feet and gazed around. Still nothing. Moving quickly, I ran to the copse of trees on the east side of the yard, taking care to stay low. Blending from shadow to shadow, I crept closer to the house. From my spot concealed behind a thick tree trunk, I eyed the well-manicured landscaping surrounding the house. There were plenty of places to hide within the bushes and topiary trees spaced around the mammoth brick home. To get there, though, I'd have to cut across the open lawn, up the slight knoll at an angle away from the front door.

Glancing up through the mostly bare limbs, I glanced at the sky. Wispy clouds dotted the navy expanse, and I prayed one would cover the moon, temporarily blotting out the light. Turning my attention back to the house, I withdrew further into the trees. A twig snapped quietly beneath my feet, and I froze, the hairs on the back of my neck lifting as a second sound reached my ears.

My breath caught in my chest as I spun around, and my gaze collided with the form of the hulking man standing only a few feet away. I had no idea how he'd crept up on me, but suddenly he was there, his dark pupils standing out against the whites of his eyes. A chill raced over my skin, and my heart slammed against my ribcage, stealing my breath.

Oh, God. It was him.

Fox.

CHAPTER Two

FOX

I stared at the screen, unable to believe my eyes.

"Boss?" Rodrigo glanced at me over his shoulder. "Want me to take this one?"

"No." I gave a brief shake of my head as I watched the kid scale the fence and drop to his feet, sweeping the lawn with his gaze as he crouched there for a minute. "I'll take care of it."

Still dressed all in black, the dried blood in the fibers of my sweater making it stiff, my lips settled into a thin line. I'd just fucking walked in the door, and all I wanted was a whiskey and a hot shower to relax my sore muscles from my altercation with Malikov earlier this evening. Instead, I had to deal with another asshole tonight who thought he could take something of mine. Sometimes a man had to take care of his castle, demonstrate his strength and power to his enemies. Now was one of those times.

I spun on a heel and left the security office. A combination of adrenaline and anger coursed through my veins, and my pace quickened as I stormed down the hall and headed toward the den. Keeping the lights off, I moved across the room to the doors that exited onto the rear patio. I slipped outside, closing the door softly behind me. Sliding along the brick façade of the house, I paused at the corner, leaning against the wall and allowing my eyes to adjust to the darkness.

A hundred yards away, I watched the kid slip between the trees, drawing closer and closer to the house. The moon was a narrow sliver in the sky, barely enough to light the way, but I knew every inch of my estate like the back of my hand. Cutting to the left, I gradually worked my way around the copse of trees until I was directly behind him. He froze as his foot landed on a twig, and it snapped under his weight. That's when I made my move.

I stepped forward, and a dry leaf crunched under my shoe. Fuck. The kid whirled toward me, eyes huge in his pale face as they landed on me. Half a second later, he was spinning away again, darting toward the east side of the property where he'd scaled the fence. Lunging forward, I snagged the back of his thick hooded sweatshirt and dragged him back. One arm around his waist, I slapped the other hand over his nose and mouth and yanked him against my chest, lifting him right off his feet. Surprised at the lack of weight dangling from my arms, it took me a moment to recover. The kid kicked and squirmed wildly as he thought to get free, and I grimaced as the heel of one booted foot connected with my shin.

Taking two steps forward, I pinned the kid to a tree, pressing all of my weight against his back to keep him in place. "Who the hell are you, and why are you sneaking around my house?"

I slowly lifted my hand so he could talk. Instead, a set of sharp teeth sank into my hand, and I hissed in breath as pain shot up my arm. "Motherfucker!"

I yanked against his hold, and the kid released me.

Wrapping one arm around his bicep, I jerked him backward, throwing him to the ground. He clambered to his feet, but I kicked out with my right foot, sending him rolling into the dirt with a cry of pain. I dropped to my knees, straddling his waist, and wrapped one hand around his throat. A pair of light-colored irises stared up at me in the moonlight, filled with fear. He writhed and twisted, trying to throw me off, but I fisted one hand in his black shirt, halting his progress. As the fabric bunched beneath my fingers, it immediately became obvious that I'd severely miscalculated. He was actually a she—and a grown one at that.

Damn. This was a complication I hadn't forseen.

As I loosened my hold, my fingers brushed the side of her breast, and the woman recoiled further. "I won't hurt you," I promised.

My words were drowned out by her shriek of indignation, and she bucked her hips in an attempt to throw me off. I lifted my weight off her hips, ready to stand when one knee came up, slamming into my balls. "God*damn* it!"

She threw herself away from me, then scrambled to her feet. Oh, hell no. She was out of her mind if she thought I was going to let her get away now. It was no accident that she'd ended up here; I needed to know what had driven her to break onto my property in the middle of the night.

Just as I grabbed her shirt again she yanked away, and her feet slipped from underneath of her, sending her stumbling backward. She let out a little cry, her eyes going wide as her arms windmilled wildly, fighting for balance. She went sprawling backwards, and a moment later, silence fell as she crumpled to the ground in a dark, ungainly heap.

Still on my knees, I crawled forward cautiously, inspecting her as I did so. She lay with her eyes closed, her head turned slightly to the side. I lunged forward, snatching up her wrists and securing them together before she had a chance to fight back. She made no movement at all, and my brows drew together. It was almost impossible to see anything in the near-dark, so I tugged off one glove and swept my hand along the ground behind her head. The dark hat she wore had come loose during our struggle, and long strands of what could only be blonde hair fluttered around her face. I swept them aside, and my fingers brushed against the cool, hard surface of the rock behind her head.

Sifting through her hair, I felt along her skull until I encountered something sticky and damp. In the moonlight, a dark substance that I recognized as blood coated the tips of my fingers. I let out a sigh. Sliding one hand gently beneath her shoulders, I looped the other under her knees and lifted her to my chest and stood. Her head lolled back as I carried her toward the house. I took my time, walking cautiously so as not to jostle her and exacerbate the injury to her head.

Xavier threw open the front door before I even crested the last step, and his eyes narrowed in concern when they landed on the girl. "What's this?" he asked in heavily accented English.

I dipped my chin toward the young woman in my arms. "Our fugitive."

He snorted softly, then closed the door behind us. I turned slightly to face him, still walking backwards toward the staircase. "Call Dr. Marlowe. Tell him we've got a head wound."

Xavier gave a concise nod and pulled a slim black cell phone from his pocket. I was already disappearing around the curve in the staircase before I heard him speaking to the doctor. Halfway down the hall that led to the guestrooms, I halted midstride. I had no idea who this woman was or what the hell she was doing trying to break into my home. She could be dangerous, not only to me, but to herself. No fucking way was I giving her free rein to wreak havoc. Judging from the way she'd fought back outside, she was probably tempted to kill me in my sleep.

I changed directions, heading down the set of stairs at the back of the house. They deposited right around the corner from my office, and I nodded to Callum as I approached the door. His eyes dipped to the young woman in my arms before meeting mine again. Without a word, he opened the door to my office, and I maneuvered past him. I shifted her in my arms as I approached the far wall.

Lightly pushing the dark wood paneling, I stepped back as it swung toward me, exposing the thick steel door to the panic room. I pressed my thumb to a small pad discreetly mounted on the door near the handle, and the lock disengaged with a nearly silent click. Turning to the side, I maneuvered us through the doorway and into the small room.

Until I knew who the woman was and what the hell she was doing sneaking around my property, it was better to keep her here. I settled her on the small bed tucked against the wall and flicked a glance around the room to make sure there was nothing that could be used as a weapon. She was small, but she most certainly wasn't helpless—the fight she'd put up outside told me that much. I returned my gaze to the woman lying silently on the thin mattress.

Blood had matted her hair, and it sent a pang of unease through me. I was no stranger to blood and gore, but seeing it on a woman—regardless of the fact that she'd been caught trespassing—was unsettling. Moving to the sink in the corner, I pulled down a washcloth, then dampened it and carried it back to the bed. Lifting her head slightly, I pressed it to the wound. The bleeding had slowed, but it would undoubtedly need stitches. Through it all, the woman never stirred. My lips flattened into a firm line as I regarded her. Pulling off the remaining black leather glove, I settled my fingers at the base of her neck and felt for a pulse. Sure enough, it was there. She was alive, then. That was a good thing. I hoped Dr. Marlowe would get here soon, because I wanted some answers. Like who she was, for starters.

What the hell had she been thinking? I stared down at the woman, taking in every detail. She was pretty—gorgeous, actually—and I couldn't shake the feeling that I knew her somehow. Her skin was a pale ivory, and I ran my fingers over the contour of her jaw, taking in the heart shaped-face, the slightly pointed, stubborn little chin that jutted out mutinously, even as she slept.

A tiny scratch marred her cheek, and I stroked it with the pad of my thumb. Though her hair was pale gold, her brows were incongruously dark. Her features were striking, heart-stoppingly beautiful. I pulled my hand away as if I'd been burned, deeply uncomfortable with the realization.

I studied her long lashes, devoid of mascara, the way they rested gently on the curve of her pink-flushed cheeks. Anger raced through me. It was the goddamn middle of winter, and she was walking around in little more than a sweatshirt and a pair of dark pants, the thin fabric clinging to her lean legs. Clearly, she hadn't been thinking, since she'd chosen my house to break into. Aside from covering herself in black from head to toe, she hadn't tried to obscure her facial features. I wanted to see her eyes again. I was seriously tempted to peel open her lids and see those bright eyes in the light.

I picked up one limp hand and studied it. Her nails were short but well-manicured, and her hands showed no evidence of callouses. She was delicate, dainty. No scars that I could see. By outward appearances, she showed no signs of having ever experienced the harsher side of life. Who the hell was this woman?

My gaze strayed to her face again, up to the long pale blonde strands that floated around her face like a halo. I ran my fingers through them, inspecting the way the light played over her golden locks. There were too many different tones for it to not be natural. No wonder she'd had it covered up. It was such a distinct color; no one could forget that shade if they tried. But that only raised more questions.

The hairs on the back of my neck lifted again. I knew this girl—but how? We hadn't slept together; there's no way I would have forgotten a face like hers. Was she from Noir? Any given night there were several dozen women gracing the halls of the club I owned downtown. Most were regulars though, and I knew them by face if not by name. This woman… There was something distinct about her that I just couldn't put my finger on. Damn, it was going to drive me crazy.

I opened my palm and cradled her cheek, bracing myself for the barrage of images sure to come. Instead, I felt… nothing. There were no premonitions, no visions of any kind. Not even a stirring. Just her cool, pale skin beneath mine.

"Boss?"

"Yeah." I didn't bother to look away from the woman as Callum's voice floated over my shoulder.

"Dr. Marlowe is here to examine the girl."

I straightened away from her. "Send him in."

Less than thirty seconds later, a slight, older man strode into the room. "Fox."

"Doctor." I gestured toward the bed where the young woman lay, still unconscious. "Here she is."

His shrewd gaze landed on her then bounced back to me, his eyes impassive and probing at the same time. "Your man said she has a head wound."

I nodded. "She's got a decent sized gash behind her right ear."

His gaze swept over her again, lying deathly still. "Any preexisting issues I should be aware of, any allergies?"

"Not sure. I never met her before tonight."

He turned back to me. "What happened?"

"She hit her head." One white eyebrow lifted, and I smirked. "It's the truth. She scaled the fence, and I tackled her before I realized she was a woman. She hit a rock when she fell."

He grunted and set his leather bag on the edge of the bed. Once he'd arranged everything the way he wanted, he met my eyes, then tipped his head toward the door. "I'd like some privacy with the patient."

Instead of leaving, I moved to the opposite wall to give him some space to work. "I'll stay if you don't mind."

"It wasn't a request."

"It's not an option."

He made another little sound in the back of his throat but didn't argue. With efficient movements, he began to check her over. After taking her vitals, he looked at the back of her head.

He picked up the washcloth I'd left pressed to her wound. "I assumed you tried to stop the bleeding?"

"Yes."

"Good." He gently probed the wound, then returned her head to the pillow. "How long has she been out?"

I glanced at my watch. "Approximately half an hour."

He nodded, then did what I hadn't had the courage to do and peeled one eyelid open to check her pupils. Intensely curious, I drifted forward. My breath caught at the sight of misty dark green irises. They were gone a moment later as Dr. Marlowe drew her lid down and reached for his suture kit. "I'll need to clean her up and shave away the hair around—"

"No." I couldn't tell exactly why the word had flown out of my mouth, but my tone was terse and brooked no argument.

He sent me an exasperated look. "I have to. I can't risk anything getting in the wound."

"Just the bare minimum," I conceded after a moment. It was bad enough that she was going to wake up in a strange place. I couldn't figure out why the hell it bothered me so much, and the fact that I was worried annoyed me even more. I waved a hand. "Just do what you have to do."

Marlowe eyed me, his gaze searching, and I struggled to rein in my wayward emotions. "Help me clean her up."

I felt off kilter, though I couldn't tell precisely what had caused it. Maybe the adrenaline was wearing off, leaving me slightly delirious. That made more sense, and I nodded to myself. Relieved at the conclusion, I turned my focus to helping Marlowe with my prisoner.

Once we'd removed as much blood from her hair as possible and flushed the wound, Dr. Marlowe carefully cut away a section of hair, then began the process of suturing the wicked gash. With a hypodermic needle, he injected the site with a local anesthetic, even though she appeared to still be out cold. I could only imagine her waking up in the middle of the process.

I winced internally as I watched the thin, curved needle penetrate one ragged edge of skin, then the other, before pulling slightly together. He tied off the stitch and moved to the next. Fifteen minutes later, he was finished, and I let out a sigh of relief. I kept waiting for her to wake up, but she never did. Once she was sufficiently sutured and bandaged, I replaced the dirty pillow case with a clean, dry one and tucked a blanket around her.

"She'll be fine," Dr. Marlowe said, as if reading my thoughts. "Call me if she develops a fever or if she remains unconscious beyond the next twelve hours or so. Once she's healing up, I can come check on her, remove the stitches."

Long after the doctor had left, I stared at the young woman. "Who are you?"

One way or another, I was going to find out who she was and why she was here.

CHAPTER Three

EVA

I opened my eyes, then immediately closed them again against the glaringly bright overhead light. My head hurt like a bitch, and I grimaced as I shifted uncomfortably. What the hell had happened? I'd gone to sleep, and then...

My eyes popped open. No, that wasn't right. I'd gone to Fox's house and made it over the fence before the man had slipped up behind me. I still couldn't figure out where he'd come from, because everything had been deathly silent, not even a whisper of motion until he'd stepped right up behind me. He was silent as a specter and fast as lightning, and I hadn't had a chance to fight back before one arm wound around my waist, his other hand coming up to cover my mouth.

I remembered the way his hands had roved over me, the surprise in his tone evident when he realized I was a woman. Then... Then what? My mind was an empty void, as blank as the wall across from me.

From my vantage point where I lay on my right side, I surveyed the small room. Where the hell was I? The walls were plain white, and a single bright fluorescent light shone brightly overhead. The others were turned off, probably to keep from blinding someone in the stark room. A standard-issue toilet sat in the corner, and I stared at it for a moment. I would need to use it soon—once I figured out exactly where I was. The room was small, maybe only ten feet deep by ten feet wide, and it looked like…

Holy shit. My eyes widened as my brain caught up. Was I in jail? Damn it. I could only imagine my father's reaction when I called him to bail me out.

I levered to my elbow, then slowly pushed to a sitting position and dropped my feet to the floor. My head spun, and I clenched my eyes closed against the pain swimming behind them. Nausea roiled in my belly, and I curled my fingers around the edge of the thin mattress to keep from pitching forward. After a long minute it finally subsided, and I peeked through slitted lashes. Mentally, I checked my body. I was sore pretty much everywhere, but that was no surprise considering the way Fox had tackled me to the hard ground.

I thought back to that moment. I distinctly remembered the way his eyes had widened when he realized I was a woman. He'd released me, and I'd made a break for it, but… Then what had happened? No matter how hard I tried, I couldn't remember anything after that. I forced my muscles to work as I pushed to my feet and cocked my ears, listening, waiting for something—anything. There were no windows in the small room, only a door that appeared to be made of steel. I stared at it in dismay. Looked like I would have to wait for someone to come get me.

I tipped my head up and for the first time, I noticed the small camera in the corner of the room. I followed its position —right to the bed. A shiver rolled down my spine. Shit. They must really be worried about me if they had me under surveillance. How long had I been here? With no windows it was hard to determine any semblance of time.

Thinking back to the headache that had racked my brain when I'd woken up, I assumed I'd been out for awhile. Long enough for Fox to call the authorities, apparently, and transport me here. Again, I couldn't help but wonder exactly where *here* was. My nose scrunched up as I looked at the bed. It wasn't even a real bed, just a metal cot bolted to the floor with a thin mattress on it. At least the rumpled sheets appeared to be clean, and—

My gaze locked on the pillow case and the brownish stains there. Was that blood? My blood? I traced the maroon smudge on the fabric before feeling the back of my head.

"It's yours," a smooth voice spoke from behind me.

My head ached as I whirled around, and my vision blurred for a moment as I fought to bring the man into focus. I took in the least daunting details first—the impeccable suit and expensive black shoes. A white button-down shirt, open at the throat with no tie. Definitely not a guard. My eyes slowly rose to his face, and my heart skipped a beat in my chest.

Dark hair topped his head, matching the stubble on his swarthy cheeks. His nose was slightly crooked, and he had a tiny dimple in his chin that added to his character instead of detracting from it. His skin, light brown under the harsh lights, hinted at a dark exoticism. But what sent ice through my veins were those eyes.

Dark and cold, they were completely devoid of emotion—of life. Casually lounged back against the steel door, he stared at me, unblinking. Oh, God. It was Fox—the same man who'd snuck up on me last night.

The image of Fox I'd conjured in my mind hadn't done him justice. This man was model-gorgeous, absolutely breathtaking, and I fought to draw air into my lungs under his intense scrutiny. I steeled my shoulders and faced him head on.

"Where am I?"

He didn't even blink as he regarded me. "How are you feeling?"

So he wanted to answer a question with a question? I stepped forward, closing the distance between us. "What happened to my sister?"

His eyes were dark and intense, empty. "Depends who she is."

My heart spasmed with pain, but the anger welling up inside me quickly took over. For some reason, I fully expected him to own up to Elle's murder. Instead, he acted as though he had no idea who I was talking about. "You torture and kill so many women you can't even keep track?"

The only indication that he had heard me was given away by a slight tic in the corner of his left eye. For at least twenty seconds, we just stared at each other. Despite my unease under his scrutiny, I forced my spine straight. Finally, I could stand it no longer. I tried again. "Where am I?"

"Where do you think you are?"

I gritted my teeth. "If I knew, I wouldn't be asking, now would I?"

Something flashed in his eyes, like a spark of surprise. It was quickly contained as he gestured with his chin to the room we were in. "You're in my home."

So, at least I knew where I was. He'd captured me on his property but hadn't called the authorities to come take me away. "Why?"

"Is there somewhere I should have taken you instead?"

I felt a blush stain my cheeks as I considered the alternative. He hadn't yet explained why he'd kept me in his house instead of turning me in, and I couldn't decide how I felt about that. Part of me was glad I wasn't in jail. But the idea of being in a strange man's home was unsettling to say the least. "What the hell do you want from me?"

One eyebrow arched upward. "Shouldn't I be asking that

of you? You were sneaking around my yard. I want to know why."

Against my better judgment, my smart mouth moved before I could stop it. "Because I hate who you are and the things you've done."

"The things I've done." He repeated my words back to me, low and smooth. His gaze slid over me slowly from head to toe, then back up again. The sensation sent goosebumps down my arms and made the hair on the back of my neck stand up. Those dark eyes bore into mine. "That's quite a long list. You'll have to be more specific."

I knew I was in way over my head, but I refused to back down now. "My father will find out where I am. He'll come for me."

"Will he?" The infuriating man quirked a condescending smirk as he pushed off the door and took a step forward, closing the distance between us.

He loomed over me, making the room feel crowded, as if the walls had begun to close in around me. I forced my trembling muscles to still. "Yes," I snapped. "He will."

My father had already lost one daughter; he wasn't going to lose another. Growing up, I'd always been the impulsive, headstrong daughter. Daddy had admonished me for it more than once, telling me that it would get me in trouble one day. I didn't seek out trouble, but neither had I turned away from something I felt was wrong. I stood up for those in need, those who needed help. It was part of the reason I'd decided to pursue a career in criminal justice. Against my parents' wishes, I wanted to help people. I wanted to apprehend the guilty, put them away where they could never hurt anyone again.

Fox must have seen the determined look in my eyes, because he gave a tiny dip of his chin. "We shall see. Until then, make yourself comfortable, and I'll have food delivered."

"You're just wasting your time," I warned. "I won't eat it." I wouldn't touch anything he offered me, even if I were starving to death. I didn't trust this man at all.

"Shame." His impossibly dark gaze swept over mine once more.

Propelled by fury at his utter lack of concern, my body seemed to move of its own volition. I slashed upward with my hand, aiming for his nose. One step ahead of me, he wrapped one huge hand around my wrist to deflect the blow. I brought my knee upward but he twisted his hips away, and my knee glanced off his thigh.

Before I could blink, he whipped me around, yanking my arm behind me so I was completely at his mercy pinned up against the cold steel door. Warm breath washed over my cheek as he spoke. "This is your one warning, little one. Do not push me."

With that, he released me, and I immediately retreated to the opposite side of the room, putting as much distance between us as possible. He was bigger, stronger, faster. I didn't stand a chance against him physically.

He straightened his suit jacket, studying me as he did so. "Do we have an understanding?"

I wrapped my arms around my waist and dipped my head. The only understanding was that I would never bow to his wishes, whatever they might be. Men like Fox negotiated in terms of money, and that was one thing my family had. Fox would ransom me, and Daddy would pay whatever he had to in order to bring me home. I just had to bide my time and wait for that to happen.

From beneath my lowered lashes, I watched the corners of Fox's lips twitch in a semblance of mirth. "Enjoy your dinner. You'll want to keep up your strength."

With that last little taunting threat hanging in the air, Fox was gone. I had no idea how he opened the door, only that it slid to the side, allowing him to slip through before it closed behind him again.

Releasing a huge breath, I sank against the wall behind me and tried to calm my racing heart. The air still crackled with tension even though he'd departed the room, as if his presence still lingered, watching over me. Determination firmed my spine. Well, he could watch all he wanted. I refused to bend to his will, no matter what. I would stay strong and wait for my family to come for me. It wouldn't be long now.

CHAPTER
Four

FOX

I watched the camera, and an irrational sense of anger washed over me. On the blurry black and white screen, the young woman sat on the bed, her knees pulled up to her chest. She looked small and vulnerable, dejected. I didn't know why it pissed me off so much. This was exactly what I wanted. I wanted to push her until she broke, until I pulled every detail from her. I still didn't even know who the hell she was, let alone why she had been skulking around my yard in the middle of the night.

She'd asked about her sister—another woman whose identity I still hadn't determined. Was she pissed over an affair? I couldn't imagine, unless her sister's relationship had been ruined. I stayed the hell away from married women despite the fact that they threw themselves at me, too. They were some of the worst. Always up for a discreet, quick fuck while their husbands were away or too busy to pay attention to them. In my line of work, fucking the wrong woman was tantamount to suicide. I wasn't going to ruin my business relationships for a piece of pussy.

It was hard to find a woman to fuck as it was. I couldn't handle the skin-to-skin contact like a normal person. Each time I touched a woman, visions overwhelmed me, making it hard to concentrate. I saw whatever was deep in their heart, visions of both the past and present. Sometimes useful, other times not.

A reminder tickled at the back of my brain, something I hadn't been able to forget over the past few days since the woman had arrived at my house. When I touched her, I hadn't gotten the slightest glimpse inside her. No vision, no intuition of her character... Nothing. Could be that she was unconscious when I'd tried to read her, but I seriously doubted it. I'd never not been able to read someone, and I fucking hated feeling at a disadvantage with her. I needed to figure out who the hell she was and why she was here. I needed to get in there, get close to her again, see if I could get anything from her. Unfortunately, she wasn't going to make it easy.

She'd been ensconced in the panic room for four days, yet she hadn't touched a single morsel of food. Each tray I dropped off in the morning remained untouched when I entered and retrieved it each night. The only thing she had done was drink minimal amounts of water, and then, only from the small sink in the corner of the room. It seemed she trusted me as much as I trusted her... Not at all.

Three quick taps came on my office door, identifying my visitor before she even stepped foot inside. "Come in."

Tall and willowy with beautiful classic features and dark brown hair always pinned into place, my assistant, Miranda, commanded the space as she opened the door and strode into my office.

I threw a surprised look her way. "What are you doing here?" I could count on one hand the number of times I'd seen Miranda outside of the club. She rarely stopped by my house, and the fact that she'd done so didn't bode well. "Is something wrong?"

Lounged against the doorjamb, she lifted a shoulder. "Thought I'd stop by and see how your situation was progressing."

"It's fucking not." I waved her in. "How's everything going at the club?"

"Same shit, different day." She crossed the room and paused in front of my desk. "Has she said anything?"

As the manager of my club, Noir, I trusted Miranda implicitly. Incredibly skilled with computers, Miranda vetted each of my patrons personally, determining whether to authorize admission or not. In addition to Noir, she handled the bookings for my underground games that happened on Saturday and Sunday nights.

Miranda was the soul of discretion, and my right hand. She hadn't hesitated to throw herself into the project when I'd asked her to help me. My eyes darted back to the screen, but not surprisingly, the woman hadn't moved. "Not yet."

"I think I may have her identity." She stepped forward and extended a manila folder across the desk to me before making her way to the sideboard.

I flipped it open, and a driver's license photo of the beautiful woman in the room next door stared back at me. My eyes drifted lower to her name. Evangelina Maria Jennings. Familiar, but I couldn't place it. I kept reading, absorbing every detail of the young woman I'd taken captive.

"She's pretty," Miranda commented as she poured herself a drink then crossed to the couch.

"Hmm..." I hummed a noncommittal sound. She was gorgeous; it was one of the first things I'd noticed about her. All that long golden hair and pretty, misty green eyes. She looked like an angel—appropriate, given her name.

Born and raised in Chicago, Evangelina had attended private school until she'd graduated six years ago. She was now studying criminal justice at a local college. Something clicked in my brain, and I flicked back a page to double check I'd read it correctly. Her current address didn't match the one on her driver's license. I assumed that meant she had either moved recently or lived locally, though not with her parents. Interesting.

I turned to the page containing her family's information, and my eyes were immediately drawn to the mother's last name. Lillian Rhodes, mayor elect for our great city. Her father was William Jennings, one of the assholes who'd gotten in too deep in my gambling rings, borrowed too much.

Just to make sure, I continued reading. Sure enough, continued in the familial connections was the name I was looking for: Elenora Masterson. Elle had been the wife of slimy senator Spencer Masterson—and Eva's sister.

William Jennings was a weak little worm of a man who was just as bad at business as he was gambling. He'd gained influence through his wealthy in-laws, but his poor investments had cost him dearly. He'd lost a good sum of money over the past two years and had turned to gambling in my club in the hopes of overturning his financial ruin. It hadn't worked. He'd borrowed from me and lost, and I was still waiting to collect my debt.

But as much as I despised William, I hated Spencer Masterson more. Groomed to be a politician from the day he was born, he was entitled and arrogant, with an addictive personality to match. He abused every substance known to mankind, and I'd had him—as well as William—banned from my clubs as well as my games. A co-ed had charged Masterson with rape back in college, but his familial influences had gotten him off the hook. He hadn't been so lucky with me.

Now I knew—in part, at least—why Evangelina was here. The question was, had she shown up of her own accord, or had someone convinced her to approach me? William was stupid, but Spencer was conniving. Would one or both of them knowingly send her into the lion's den? It was always a possibility. Men like that were concerned only with themselves. Perhaps they thought I'd take it easy on her since she was a woman. If that was the case, they were bound to be disappointed.

I could feel Miranda's eyes on me, and I lifted my gaze. "I assume you verified this?" The look she threw my way could've frozen lava in place, and I chuckled. "Have to ask."

"Triple checked," she responded, leaning forward to set her glass on the table. "She's currently enrolled in one of the local colleges and resides with a roommate, Rose Winthrop."

"Interesting."

"Why do you think she's here?"

I lifted my gaze to Miranda's worried gaze. "Revenge."

She lifted a brow. "Does she have a death wish?"

I let out a half-laugh as I gestured toward the screen. "Doesn't look like she gives a fuck about anything."

Most women would have begged. Screamed. Pleaded. But not Evangelina. She'd uttered not a single word since our first encounter, had barely even moved. She was as stubborn as they came, and I respected it as much as I loathed it.

"What are you going to do?"

At Miranda's question, I stroked my thumb over my chin and dropped my gaze back to the paper in my hand. "I'll have to think about it."

There was no way I was ever going to tell Evangelina about her sister. "I'll take care of it," I finally said, gesturing to the file. "Please forward her name on to Dr. Marlowe and have him pull her medical records."

"Done."

She pushed to her feet. "Anything else?"

I hesitated for a brief moment, debating what I was about to do. "Are you up for some shopping?"

"You sure?"

"Yes." I nodded. "Put it on the company card, and get yourself something."

She dipped her head. "Thank you."

I knew I didn't have to tell her to keep this to herself; Miranda wouldn't breathe a word.

"Don't forget—" Miranda stop just in front of the door. "We've got a couple of whales tonight who will want to see you."

Right. I'd been so preoccupied that I'd almost forgotten. My high rollers deserved one-on-one attention. They spent a good deal of money, sometimes dropping upwards of a hundred grand a night at my games. "Make sure they're comfortable until I get there."

"Will do."

Miranda left the room, and my eyes moved back to the computer screen, to the woman who lay curled up in a ball on the thin mattress. I needed to decide what to do with her, and quick.

CHAPTER Five

EVA

I stared at the white wall across from me, my mind curiously blank. It seemed like that was all I did these days. Time no longer had any meaning. With no windows to give me any kind of indication whether it was day or night, it was impossible to tell exactly how long I'd been here. Fox hand-delivered fresh trays of food several hours apart, at what I assumed was morning and evening, but I couldn't be sure. I had touched none of them, except the tiny piece of bread when I could stand it no longer. My stomach ached from starvation, but pride refused to allow me to give in.

The lights overhead stayed on all the time. It was both reassuring and daunting. It meant that I could see Fox anytime he entered, yet it also meant that I was constantly on guard. For that reason, I drank as little as possible. I wasn't exactly sure why, but I was terrified that Fox would catch me on the toilet. I felt like I was barely hanging on by a thread.

I was certain that a good number of days had passed, but I hadn't heard a single word about being released. Each interaction with Fox so far had been utterly silent. He would enter the room, glance at the tray of uneaten food sitting on the table in the corner, send a glare my way, then drop off the new tray as he took the old one. Each time he entered, he looked increasingly agitated. I found a sort of grim satisfaction in that. If nothing else, it at least meant I was getting some sort of reaction from him. I still refused to trust him. I didn't think he would poison me if he was going so far as to keep me locked away to ransom back to my family, but I couldn't be sure.

I jumped as the door swung open, and Fox's large, dark form filled the space. Pushing awkwardly to a sitting position, I scrambled backward until my back was pressed to the wall. He had dropped off a tray for me not long ago, and judging from my body's internal clock, he shouldn't be back to deliver another until several hours from now. My heart skipped in my chest. Was he finally releasing me? I stared up at him filled with a mixture of excitement and fear.

Fox stepped inside and closed the door behind him, then leaned against it. For a long moment, he just watched me. I didn't dare say a word. A long minute later, he pushed off the door and crossed the room. I watched warily as he moved to the table, inspecting the tray of food he'd left for me earlier. He let out a soft sound and gave a little shake of his head as he turned and pinned me with his dark eyes.

"Still not eating, I see." He ventured closer, and I shifted away from him, curling my arms around my legs protectively as he took a seat on the edge of the bed.

My pulse kicked up as I watched him. Never before had he expressed any interest in me other than to bring me food. What had brought him here now? Fox wasn't a good man; he didn't do anything out of the goodness of his heart. No, there had to be another reason he was keeping me alive. Hopefully it wouldn't be much longer now until my family managed to track me down and bring me home. I had to have hope that it would happen; otherwise, I had nothing.

"Are you ready to be amenable yet?"

I eyed him, wondering just what the hell that meant.

At my silence, his face hardened a bit. "Care to explain what you were doing sneaking around my property?"

I seriously doubted he'd like the answer to that question, either. I bit down on my tongue to keep from spilling the truth under his intense scrutiny, and his lips pressed into a firm line of displeasure.

"It will only be worse if you don't speak."

His dark eyes glinted with the promise of retribution, and fear propelled me to tell him something. I decided that, with a man like Fox, it was best to go with the truth—or, at least, some variation of it. "I wanted to hurt you, to take something from you."

"You weren't planning to kill me?"

That would have been a futile effort anyway. I gave a tiny shake of my head, and he tipped his own dark-haired head to one side. "Why not?"

"I never would have made it to you," I admitted. "Your guards would have been on me before I even got close to you —or you would've killed me yourself."

He appraised me for a few seconds. "Not stupid, then. Just stubborn."

I stiffened at the implication.

"The doctor will be here in a moment." He must have noticed the surprised look on my face, because he continued. "I keep Dr. Marlowe on my payroll, so he's well accustomed to… situations like this."

Like keeping someone hostage, he meant. I swallowed down the bitter bile that had risen in my throat. "Then why bring him in at all?"

"Your stitches need to be removed. I'm sure you would prefer I not cut into your scalp."

"Definitely not."

With a single hard nod, he turned and slipped out the door again, leaving the room empty and silent. Curling my legs into me, I waited for what seemed like forever before the door cracked open again. An older man barely taller than myself stepped inside, and my gaze landed on his smiling face.

"Hello," he held out a hand as he approached, and I slipped my palm warily into his to shake. "Glad to see you awake. How are you feeling?"

"Fine." I shot a look at Fox hovering in the doorway, a dark expression on his handsome face. Turning my attention back to the doctor, I spun so my back was to him as he directed. I flinched when he removed the stitches.

"Looks good," he finally replied. "Any headaches? Issues with sight? Anything notable?"

If I lied, would it get me out of here? I darted a look Fox's way and immediately decided the answer was no. Whatever course of action he'd set, he refused to deviate from it. I could probably bleed out right here on this bed, and he would refuse to take me to a hospital. "No, sir."

"Glad to hear that. If that's all, I'll be on my way."

I desperately wanted to reach for him, call him back as he packed up his things, then moved toward the door.

Fox dipped his head at the doctor. "Callum will show you out."

With that, he closed the door, leaving us alone once more. He took a few steps toward the middle of the room and pointed once more to the dinner tray. "Now that your stitches have been taken care of, you need to eat."

"I'm not hungry."

"So goddamn stubborn. You think starving yourself is going to help?" He stared at me. "I have half a mind to—"

"That's awfully generous," I muttered.

He blinked, looking caught somewhere between baffled

and furious. For a moment, I was extremely proud of my snarky quip. Then he exploded. "What did you say?"

I shook my head. "I—It was nothing."

I forced my trembling muscles to still as he thrust his face so close to mine our noses almost touched. "Such a big mouth for such a little girl. Look around you," he snapped. "Do you think you're in any position to speak back to me?"

I glared up at him. "What do I have to lose?"

"Everything." He growled. "In case you haven't noticed, you're completely at my mercy. No one is coming for you."

"They will." My voice shook, belying my confidence.

"You're mine now," he said as he pushed off the bed. "Get used to it."

"Please!" I shifted to my knees, reaching out to stop him from leaving. I made one last effort to appeal to him. "My family has money. They'll—"

He barked out a mirthless laugh as he spun toward me. "What? I should ransom you?"

"Well…" Wasn't that what he wanted?

"Do I look stupid to you?"

I couldn't help but shake my head at the rhetorical question. He looked dangerous and huge and unyielding—but never stupid.

"I don't need money," he continued. "And with ransoms come the authorities. Rule number one for a man like me is to stay as far away from the authorities as possible."

I swallowed hard as that knowledge sank in. He would never contact them, even if I told him who I was—*especially* if I told him who my family was. If he learned I was the mayor's daughter, he'd probably kill me and dispose of my body the way he had with Elle. He wouldn't risk raining hell down on himself just for ransom money.

Satisfied that he'd made his point, Fox straightened and tugged his suit jacket back into place. "Eat. You'll need the energy."

With that, he departed the room, and I slumped back against the wall as tears stung my eyes. I was well and truly trapped, unless my family came to my rescue—and that prospect was looking less and less likely every day.

CHAPTER

Six

FOX

I lifted my head at the single, hard knock before the door swung open, revealing Callum. "Sir? Your guest is here."

"Thank you." I stood and buttoned my suit jacket as Callum stepped aside and gestured for the man to enter. I nodded to Callum, who closed the door behind him, ensuring our privacy. The dark-haired man crossed the room toward me, and I rounded my desk to meet him.

"Mr. Capaldi, good to see you again. How are you?"

"Fine, thank you."

I motioned for Matteo to make himself comfortable on the couch. "Care for a drink?"

"Scotch, if you have it."

I tipped my chin in acknowledgement, then crossed to the sideboard. I spoke as I poured both of us a drink. "How's business?"

"Same," he grunted. "Ever since the marriage contract fell through, the war with the Russians has become increasingly worse."

"So I've heard." His cousin had been set to marry Nikolai

—the future Bratva captain, and a particularly heinous human being. His previous wives had all mysteriously disappeared, but there was no question as to what had happened to them. I'd never forget the marks he left on wife number two. We'd moved in the same circles, though he didn't let her out much. She lasted only a few months in his care before he killed her. Death was surely the better option than dragging out the pain of living with him.

Rather than subjecting herself to the same fate, the Capaldi girl had fled town. I hoped she was far, far away. A furious Nikolai had taken another woman instead, a sister to one of the members of the Irish mafia who roamed the outskirts of town. The Russians and Irish were now banded together and putting pressure on the Capaldi family to concede.

I passed him the tumbler, then I settled myself in the chair across from him. "What's your plan?"

"That's why I'm here, actually. Massimo would like to arrange a meeting."

I lifted an eyebrow. "For what purpose?"

Matteo stared at me. "We need an ally. I would like that to be you."

"I'm not sure how that benefits me."

In truth, I had no desire to put myself in the middle of a feud between the Italians and Russians. They'd been going at it for years, fighting for control of a city the way they had been for generations. There was no progression, only the same shit they'd been doing every day for decades. In a situation like this, I preferred to remain impartial. This wasn't my war. They could kill each other for all I cared, but I wouldn't risk my business. It was a precarious balancing act to offer support while maintaining distance. One had to be incredibly selective of their partners so as to not be screwed over.

I carried out my own operations on the outskirts of the

city, controlling the flow of drugs coming down from the border as well as the gambling ring beneath the very club we sat in right now. Noir had been the perfect cover, built right on top of an underground city rife with tunnels. It made it ideal if we ever needed to vacate the premises in case of a raid. It had only happened once, but never again since I'd made friends with several members of the city council. I still wasn't quite sure why Matteo wanted my help. I didn't have nearly the manpower he did.

Matteo's response threw me for a loop. "I heard you're looking for something."

"Yeah? What's that?" I studied him as he stared at me.

"Information."

It was no secret that I'd put out feelers to try to track down a man I'd been looking for for decades. "And?"

"I may have something for you."

No amount of information was worth aligning myself with the Capaldis against the Russians. It could potentially sign my death warrant, and I wanted no part of it. "I don't believe it's worth it to me."

He held up a hand. "I'll tell you what I've heard. All I ask in exchange is that you agree to a sit down. You don't have to give me an answer now. Just consider it. We would make it worth your while."

"And what would you expect from me?"

"Allegiance. We'll supply you with whatever you need. All we ask in return is a 10% profit from your games."

I almost laughed out loud. Did he know how profitable those games were? "Unfortunately, that leans more heavily in your favor. That is something I cannot agree to."

Matteo leaned forward, resting his elbows on his knees. "We can discuss the details later. But I'm asking your help as a show of good faith."

I quirked a brow, curious. "For?"

"Things within the family are... changing," he said

hesitantly. "I'd like your assistance during our transition. It will be ugly for awhile, but I need to do some in-house cleanup."

I nodded slowly. "And the sit down?"

He leaned back in his seat. "I don't have everything in place yet. I'll have to let you know when I'm ready."

I thought it over. "I don't promise to agree to anything."

"Understood. So let's get to what you want to hear." His dark gaze speared me. "I've heard rumor of a shipment coming across the border."

There was no question in my mind what he was talking about. I was apprised of the drugs coming into the States from the north, but this was a different commodity entirely. "How reliable?"

"Extremely. This is the third shipment in the past six months."

Son of a bitch. The asshole—whoever the hell he was—was either incredibly brave or stupid, or both. I was certain he had extensive far-reaching contacts to make something like that possible. "Same product?"

His gaze darkened. "Unfortunately."

Anger simmered in my gut. "I appreciate your information. Any idea who might be responsible?"

He shook his head. "I've dropped questions in a couple people's ears but no one seems to know who's bringing them in." He paused for a second. "What will you do with the product?"

I met his gaze and held it for a minute. "I'll take care of it."

He pushed up from the couch and gave me a slight nod. "I'll be in touch. I appreciate your time and consideration."

"My pleasure."

I hadn't gotten a name, but I was one step closer. I needed to intercept the shipment. It was so close I could taste it. One of these days I was going to pull the thread that would lead me to the man who'd ruined my life—the man responsible for turning me into the monster I'd become.

I braced myself as I took Matteo's outstretched hand. The moment our palms touched, images flashed before my eyes. Matteo himself sat at a table across from another man—or, rather, what was left of him. The older man sat sprawled in his chair, head drooping listlessly to the side, the back of his head a gory mess. In my mind's eye, I saw his blood and brain matter splattered over the walls and ceiling. A young woman, her startling green eyes filled with fear and horror, knelt on the floor next to him. So this was the housecleaning he'd spoken of.

A handshake sealed the deal for me. People said it was the measure of a man; over the course of my thirty-eight years on this earth, I'd come to understand that it meant the difference between life and death—literally. My visions were imperative to my business and who I aligned myself with.

The visions had plagued me for years, yet it never got any easier. I hated to be touched, and I despised having to touch others. Sometimes, though, it couldn't be helped. And sometimes, like now, it was incredibly convenient. I recognized the man from Matteo's vision, so I knew it hadn't yet happened. Sometimes my visions showed things that had already happened. Other times, it foretold the future. It was difficult to tell sometimes how useful a particular vision would be, but more often than not, I was able to determine a person's true nature with a single touch.

I was still a child when I discovered how different I was. My first instance of this was growing up in the orphanage back home. A man had come to visit Sister Agnes. It was a moment that had changed the trajectory of my life irrevocably. He'd entered the office with Sister Agnes and had stayed there for what felt like forever. I remembered feeling impatient, because the nurse who typically oversaw us was busy, and I wanted to ask her to go outside and play. When they finally came out, I had grabbed her hand. The moment my palm connected with hers, images flashed in front of my eyes, things I was too young and naïve to understand at the time. Children chained. Caged. Bloodied. Sobbing.

When I asked Sister Agnes about the children, she'd immediately pulled me aside. A scared look entered her eyes as she questioned me. Like the babe I was, I told her everything I'd seen. She swore me to secrecy, told me never to reveal to anyone what I was capable of. She warned me not to speak of them to anyone, then told me that she would pray for me. She should have prayed for herself instead.

I'd learned to hide my affliction from others, but I'd never forgotten that moment. Sometimes the people we trusted the most were the ones who could hurt us the worst. Pushing away the dark memories plaguing me, I held the door for Matteo as he exited the office, and we made small talk as I showed him to the front door.

Once he was gone, I retreated to my office. Opting for the couch instead of my desk chair, I slouched against the plush cushions and closed my eyes, drawing the vision into my mind's eye and replaying it. The future was not looking good for the Capaldi family. Fucking Italians. They knew nothing of loyalty, always the first to roll under pressure. It had never been like that for me. Forced between life or death, there was no choice. You did as you were told, no questions asked. Fortunately for me, I was now the one giving orders instead of taking them.

Speaking of... I sat forward in my chair. It was time to see how my captive fared.

CHAPTER
Seven

EVA

The door flew open, but I didn't bother to look up. I didn't need to. The hard-edged voice announced my visitor before the steel door hit the wall with a resounding bang. "Get up."

Fox moved into my peripheral vision, dressed once again head to toe in black. Like a snake striking, one hand whipped out and grabbed my ankle, then tugged me toward him. I let out a soft cry as my atrophied muscles protested. He released me and swore under his breath when I pulled my legs in close to me again, curling my arms protectively around my shins.

"Enough of this," he snapped harshly. Without waiting, he slipped one hand under my knees, and his other arm wound behind my back. "I won't let you sit in here and starve yourself. If anyone is to be responsible for your death, it will be me."

I didn't dare look at him as he carried me through the doorway and into a spacious, dark-paneled office. Sunlight streamed in through the large windows along the wall to my right, and I squinted my eyes closed. Though the lights had remained on in the cell, they were dim compared to the bright light pouring into the room. Allowing my lids to drift shut, I let my head loll against his chest as we moved through the house. I knew I should be watching my surroundings, taking in every detail for later—when I escaped. But my mind and body were so exhausted I could barely keep my eyes open.

Initially, fear and hunger had kept me awake. For the first few days I'd hardly slept a wink, terrified that he would storm in when I least expected it and kill me. After his second visit—several days ago, by my calculation—my concern had faded away. I still didn't trust him, but he didn't terrify me the way he had when I'd first woken in that tiny room. After the dozens of horrific stories I'd heard, I fully expected him to torture me, draw out my death until it was slow and painful. Instead, he'd brought me food and water each day as if he were concerned for my well-being, had a doctor come to care for my wound.

I didn't know how much more I could take. I'd hardly moved from the bed, and my body ached from being confined to one position for so long. My stomach had stopped growling long ago. I couldn't remember the last time I'd eaten anything of substance. Days, maybe? I'd picked at the food here and there to keep from starving completely, but I would never give Fox the satisfaction of eating the full meals he had delivered. I knew it was stupid, but I couldn't help it. I should be eating and building my strength, but I continued to hope that Fox would enter the small cell and tell me that I was free to go home.

Ensconced in his arms, I felt the jarring motion as we moved up a set of steps, and my eyes flew open. On the second floor of the house, Fox stepped into a large bedroom, then crossed to the *en suite* bathroom. Stopping next to the large bathtub, he gently my feet to the floor. Dizzy from fatigue, I swayed, and he let out another soft curse. "Sit."

He lowered me to the edge of the tub, keeping one arm around my waist for support. With the other hand, he plugged the drain, then turned the handle on the large soaker tub. Soon, steam rose and curled into the air as it began to fill with warm water. Fox turned back to me, and I shivered under that intense, dark gaze. His fingers curled in the hem of my shirt and practically ripped it off. I could smell myself as I raised my arms over my head, and I somehow summoned the energy to blush. Fox's hands moved behind my back to unclip my bra and slide it down my arms. The second it hit the floor, I moved my hands to cover myself, but he batted them away.

"You're not the first naked woman I've seen, nor will you be my last," he said as he lifted me to my feet. Grasping the waistband, he worked my dark pants down my legs, taking my panties and socks with them.

When I was completely, embarrassingly bare, he rose to his full height and stared down at me. "Do you need to use the toilet first?"

My eyes darted to the side, and I gave a little nod. One huge hand grasped my chin and lifted my gaze to his.

"Are you going to do something stupid?"

I shook my head. Those dark eyes seared into mine for a long moment before he finally nodded. "You have two minutes. I'll be right outside."

Releasing me, he scooped up my discarded clothes, then strode out of the room, closing the door in his wake. I stood frozen for a moment before I pushed myself into action. I grimaced as I made my way across the room. My legs felt sluggish and sore, almost like they were asleep. I used the toilet, then moved back to the bathtub. The large mirror over the sink caught my attention, and my eyes widened at my reflection there.

Though I had done little in the way of physical activity in the cell, my face and body were streaked with dirt, and I could see the bones of my ribs clearly beneath my skin. I lifted one hand and ran my fingers over the hard ridges. I'd lost a lot of weight—at least ten pounds—more than I'd anticipated. I swallowed hard as my gaze lifted back to my face, to my gaunt cheekbones and dark circles underscoring my eyes.

Ashamed and angry—both at myself and at Fox—I tore myself away and climbed into the tub. A soft groan escaped my lips as I slipped into the water. It was almost too hot, but it felt so soothing that I wasn't going to complain. I tipped my head forward and straightened my legs, stretching my sore muscles. I ran my hands over my thighs and down my calves, the soft hairs tickling my palms.

The door swung open, and I automatically pulled my limbs in under Fox's scrutiny. "How does it feel?"

"Good."

His lips twitched. "Most women like their water hot enough to scald the skin right off their body, so I figured you were the same."

Was he trying to joke with me? I couldn't tell. Confused, I dropped my gaze back to the clear water swirling around my legs and watched from the corner of my eye as he approached and knelt next to the tub.

Grabbing a bottle of shampoo from the ledge, he poured some into his palm and began to attack my oily, stringy hair. His fingertips brushed the wound on the back of my head, and I winced. I wasn't sure how long it'd been, but it was still tender.

"Sorry." His apology seemed sincere, though his face remained expressionless. I appreciated it regardless.

"It's okay."

His gaze flicked to mine for a second before returning to my hair. "Lean back." I did as he instructed, and he gently rinsed the bubbles from the long strands until it ran clean. "Can you handle the rest?"

"Yes." I reached out to take the soap from him, but he tightened his hold on it as he studied me. One black eyebrow arched upward and after a moment he relented, pressing the bar of soap into my hand. I watched as he pushed away from the tub and headed toward the bedroom. "Fox?"

Halfway to the door, he halted midstep and glanced over his shoulder at me in silent question.

I swallowed hard. "Can I… have a razor?"

He seemed to ponder my request, then gave a brief nod. "I'll get one."

With that he exited the room, and I let out a sigh of relief. He was so intense, always keeping me on edge. Not wanting to waste another minute, I rubbed the bar of soap over my skin, working it into a thick, sudsy lather before rinsing, reveling in how good it felt to be clean again.

Fox reappeared and passed me a disposable razor. "I'll be right outside."

I couldn't tell if it was meant as a threat or a reassurance, but I nodded regardless. His dark form moved to the bedroom, and I could see part of him where he perched on the edge of the bed. My gaze dropped to the feminine pink razor in my hands. It still had the plastic protective case on it, so I knew that it had never been used. But why did he have it? It seemed strange for a man like Fox to have pink razors just lying around.

My breath caught as something occurred to me. Did he have a girlfriend? A wife? I'd never seen a woman around while I'd surveilled the house, but that didn't mean he didn't have a woman in his life. I couldn't be sure why, but my stomach clenched at the thought. Then again, would he have kept me here knowing another woman was in the house? He'd carried me through the house where anyone could see. I seriously doubted even he would do that.

Which left a second option. He'd purchased it for me. But why? A throat cleared from the region of the bedroom, jerking me from my thoughts. I shaved my legs and under my arms as quickly as I dared, then set the razor aside and pulled the stopper on the drain.

At the sound, Fox stood and moved toward me. "All done?"

I nodded, watching while the water made a tiny cyclone on its way down the drain before a large hand moved in front of my face. I slipped my palm into his, and he helped me to my feet, then wrapped a towel around me. He led me to the bedroom, and pressed gently on one shoulder, pushing me down onto the edge of the large mattress.

Water from my hair dripped down onto my shoulders and chest, and I used a corner of the towel to wipe the droplets away. I felt better, but now I had nothing else to wear. As if reading my mind, Fox spun on a heel and strode toward a set of wide double doors adjacent to the bathroom. He threw them open, revealing a large walk-in closet. From a drawer built into the wall, he pulled out a bra, followed by a pair of panties. Next came a T-shirt and a pair of soft-looking yoga pants.

Fox stalked toward me, depositing the articles in my lap.

"If it doesn't fit, just set it aside. You've lost weight since you've been here, so some things might be a bit large."

My gaze dropped to the clothes. The tags were still attached, and I couldn't help but wonder if he'd bought everything specifically for me. "Thank you," I managed.

With a dip of his chin, Fox moved away again, giving me a modicum of privacy while I changed into the clothes. The stretchy material of the pants clung to my curves, but the t-shirt hung limply off my frame. Still, it was better than nothing, and I felt more comfortable with the excess fabric hiding my body from his view. Not that he hadn't already seen me naked, but I still didn't know what he wanted from me or why I was here.

I shot a look his way. "How long have I been here?"

"Just over two weeks."

The knowledge hit me like a sucker punch to the gut. Why hadn't Daddy come for me? Surely they would still be looking for me. Unless... Memories of Elle's disappearance came back to me. Her body had never been found, but the authorities were adamant that she was gone. What if Fox had staged a similar scene, making it look like I had suffered a similar fate? With no one actively looking for me, he could keep me for his own nefarious purposes—whatever those might be.

My heart cracked open, and a shiver worked its way down my spine as my last remaining shred of hope dissipated into thin air.

CHAPTER
Eight

FOX

I watched from the corner of my eye as Eva pulled on her new clothes. Disgust rose in my throat, threatening to choke me. She was much too thin. I wanted to rail at her, to command she stop being so goddamn stubborn and eat, but I knew that if I demanded it, she would only balk and do the complete opposite out of spite.

Three quick taps came from the door, and I opened it, accepting the tray of food from Rodrigo with a quick dip of my chin. I locked up behind him, then carried the tray to the small nightstand next to the bed. Picking up the plates, I handed one to Eva, then settled myself on the edge of the mattress. She watched me warily but eventually picked up her fork and twirled it in the pile of noodles. I'd requested something packed with carbs that would replace some of the weight she'd lost. As she had every day for the past two weeks, my cook, Carmen, had obliged with a dirty look. She was just as tired of Eva's untouched food being sent back to the kitchen as I was. This time, though, Eva wouldn't have the choice to not eat. I'd sit here all goddamn afternoon until she ate every last piece of the homemade pasta.

Eva waited until I'd taken several bites before scooping up one of her own, apparently deciding that I wasn't trying to poison her. Silence descended over us as she dug into the food, her appetite voracious. When she was almost finished, I cleared my throat.

"So." I stared at the profile of her pretty face—the delicate sweep of her long lashes over her cheeks. The pert little nose that turned up slightly at the tip, a small dusting of freckles dotting the bridge. Those luscious, full lips that I wanted to taste—and that I wanted wrapped around my cock. "Tell me about yourself, angel."

Her eyes flew to mine. They widened slightly before narrowing in suspicion. I could practically hear the wheels turning, wondering if I'd used the endearment because it was so close to her name. She searched my eyes for a moment before turning back to the plate in front of her. "Such as?"

I held back a laugh. Besides what the fuck she'd been doing sneaking around my property in the dead of night? "Who are you?"

That vivid green gaze darted to mine, resentment flickering deep inside. "Like you don't already know."

Of course I did, but I wanted to hear it from her lips. "You know my name, but I'm at a disadvantage here. What's your name?"

Her lips rolled inward in thought before she spoke. "Eva."

The abbreviation of her given name pleased me. It was an admission of sorts, and I liked that she was too innocent to think of using an alias. Or perhaps it was as she said—she had a feeling I already knew everything about her and was testing her. "Beautiful. Very fitting."

Her eyes flicked to mine, filled with confusion. "Thanks… I think."

I chuckled. "It was a compliment. A lovely name for a

lovely woman." She hummed a noncommittal response, so I continued. "And what do you do, Eva?"

Annoyance flickered over her features. "I'm in school."

I turned slightly and made myself more comfortable so I could see her better. "What are you studying?"

"Why?" Her eyes were filled with suspicion, and I shrugged.

"Why not? You pique my curiosity."

She let out another beleaguered breath. "Criminal justice."

I fought the smile that tugged at the corners of my lips. "Why criminal justice?"

She rolled her eyes and returned them to her plate. "Like it would matter to you."

It did, actually. I was intensely curious as to why such a beautiful young woman had chosen such a long and difficult career. "Indulge me."

Her green eyes blazed. "Accountability. I see the crime run rampant in this city, yet the repeat offenders spend a short amount of time behind bars before they're back out, doing the same stupid thing all over again."

"You don't believe people will change?" She speared me with a hard look, and I bit back a laugh. She wasn't wrong. "Very noble of you." Naïve, but noble. "Isn't that a bit ironic, considering you were caught trespassing?"

Those arresting eyes moved to mine and held. "That's awfully rich, coming from you."

I lifted a brow. "What, exactly, are you implying?" Not that I didn't already know, but I was curious if she would have the balls to accuse me of what I suspected.

She half-laughed. "You accuse me of something so petty, yet you've done much worse."

She was so entertaining. I couldn't help but toy with her. "Have I?"

She turned more fully to face me. "I want to know the truth."

I didn't pretend to not understand what she was asking. "You said before that you believed I was involved with your sister. Even if I was responsible for her death, I would never tell you." I set my plate aside, then turned back to her. "Now—"

"What do you mean, you won't tell me?" She demanded. "She was my sister—I deserve to know what happened!"

I studied Eva, her eyes bright with anger and rightfully so. I would never tell her what had transpired. There was still an innocence to her, and I couldn't bear to sully that untouched, pure part of her soul. "You already know what happened."

"That you killed her?" Her eyes narrowed to slits, and fire crackled in her gaze. "I overheard that. But what I can't understand is why."

Inwardly, I seethed but managed to clamp down on my anger. I stared at her coldly. "I explain my reasons to no one, least of all you."

Tears shimmered in her eyes. "I hate you—I hate everything about you. I wanted revenge, I wanted to hurt you the way you—"

Her words cut off on a soft cry as I fisted one hand in her shirt and dragged her toward me. "I strongly suggest you curb that tongue of yours before it gets you in trouble, angel."

"I'll never give in to you. You're despicable—"

Anger burned over my flesh. "Have you ever been punished, Eva?" I allowed my gaze to stray slowly over her body, acute satisfaction filling me at the way she physically recoiled under my scrutiny. "Did anyone even care enough about you to discipline you the way you need? Or were your parents too busy for you? Did they make the nanny do it instead?"

Her cheeks blazed bright pink, and her chin dropped a fraction as my words hit their mark. "Let me tell you what I know about you." I took one of her hands in mine, tightening my fingers around hers when she tried to pull away. "You've never done a hard day's work in your life. You've been coddled and protected, and your choice of career is your way of biting back at society. You think you're helping people, but you're not. You're full of dreams, Eva. You're too young and naïve to understand the real world outside the doors of your ivory tower. Wandering onto my property was the worst mistake of your life. Because now you're going to see firsthand just how awful the real world can be."

"You can't keep me here forever," she snapped, trying to pull from my grasp. "Someone will come looking for me. They'll—"

"They'll what?"

She shot me a defiant look. "My father will be looking for me."

She still believed that? I cocked a brow as I studied her. "Does he even know you're here?" She opened her mouth to speak, but I cut her off. "Because I seriously doubt your father is aware that you tried to break onto my property for revenge. And if he does, he's not a very good father."

She shot daggers at me. "Don't insult my father!"

"Don't change the subject. Tell me—your father has no idea you're here, does he?"

She was silent so long I thought she wouldn't answer. Finally, her chest rose and fell before she let out a measured breath. "Regardless, he'll tear this town apart to find me and bring me home."

"He's welcome to look." I shrugged. "But he will never find you. And I will never give you over to him."

Her stricken face snapped to mine. "Why are you doing this?"

"Because I can, angel."

"Don't you understand?" Those giant green eyes pleaded up at me, and I felt a tiny twinge of something in my chest. "I'll do anything—please, just tell me what it is you want. If it's money, we can get it. My family already lost my sister. They can't go through that again—I won't let that happen."

Stunned at her passionate declaration, I stared at her for a long moment. "Let me make sure I understand. You're more concerned for their welfare than your own?"

"They're my family." Her voice was heartbreakingly soft. "They mean everything to me, and I love them. Haven't you ever loved someone so much that you would do anything for them?"

Every muscle in my body went rigid, my tone flat. "No."

"But—"

I leaned close. "Men like me aren't made for love, angel. We're made for war—for blood and death. We take what we want and use it until there's nothing left."

"Please—"

"You're not leaving, and that is final."

Moisture glittered in her eyes. "Why? Why are you doing this?"

"Why do I want to keep you?" I smirked. "Because you intrigue me. Because you owe me for breaking in. Instead of turning you over to the authorities, I'll exact my own punishment."

Her tone turned bitter. "By using me for sex?"

I lifted one shoulder. "Whatever I deem fit."

"I hate you—you—you—monster!"

"Oh, Eva." I let out a little laugh. "You have no idea the things I'm capable of. You'd better get comfortable, because you're not going anywhere."

She glared at me but didn't say a word. I released her and braced my hands on my legs as I started to stand. "Good. Now that that's settled—"

Her arm whipped forward in a blur, and the metal glinted in the sunlight spilling through the window as she slashed the fork downward. I jerked backward, and a ripping sound filled the air as the tines punctured the fabric of my suit and sank into my flesh. More stunned than anything, I stared at the fork, then slowly lifted my gaze to hers. She stared at the fork protruding from my arm, her expression a mixture of surprise and horror, as if she couldn't quite believe what she'd done. Luckily, with two layers of fabric, the wound didn't feel too deep.

Wrapping my fist around the handle, I yanked it free and tossed it onto my plate as I stood, towering over her. She jerked backward, just out of reach, sliding off the bed as she did so. She tumbled to the floor and struggled to her feet before making a mad dash toward the door. But she wasn't quite fast enough. I shot out with my arm and wrapped one hand around her throat, dragging her to me. She thrashed in my arms, and I pressed her against the wall, lifting her until her toes barely scraped the floor.

She grabbed at my wrist with both hands in a futile effort to get free, but I held fast. I leaned in, so close that our noses almost touched. "Pull something like that again, and I will spank your ass so hard you won't be able to sit for a week."

Heaving a deep breath, I set her down, keeping her pinned to the wall at her back. Anger and hatred ran rampant over her features, and I drank it in. The wound in my arm throbbed dully, and for almost a full minute we just stared at each other.

"You refuse to give up." I shook my head a little as I stared down at her. "You know what that makes you?"

Victory flashed over her features for a brief moment. "A fighter."

"Stupid." She flinched at my harsh tone as the single word doused her bravado. "The sooner you figure out that you belong to me, the better off we'll both be."

CHAPTER
Nine

EVA

Across the table, Fox studied me. "You've been quiet."

I offered a tight smile before dropping my gaze back to the plate in front of me. My attempt to ignore the conversation went unheeded, and Fox continued. "You don't have to stay holed up in your room all the time, you know."

"Oh?" I tipped my head in question. "So I'm not your captive?"

He blinked once, hard. "I said you weren't confined to your room—not that you were free to leave."

"Right." There was no hiding the bitterness in my tone. Of course not. I was free to wander the mammoth house, the cold, dead gardens, explore the books in the den. Anything my heart desired—except my freedom.

I'd yet to figure out exactly what he wanted from me. Aside from these awkward silence-filled dinners interspersed with stilted conversation, he hadn't demanded anything else of me. I kept up my surly attitude, as I had for the past several days, so he wouldn't suspect anything. I'd considered sidling up to him to win his trust and try to get him to lower his guard. Unfortunately, I had a feeling that with a man like Fox, that would have the opposite effect. It took every ounce of self-control to remain calm as I counted the moments until dusk fell so I could put my plan into motion.

"You don't have to be unhappy here," he said softly.

I stiffened, avoiding his gaze. Fox wasn't a stupid man. How could he expect me to be happy while I was being kept here against my will? "May I be excused?"

A loud sigh filtered through his nose. "Of course."

I stood, watching from the corner of my eye as he followed suit. I couldn't figure him out. His manners were impeccable, yet he was a tyrant of epic proportions. He was a complete contradiction in every way, and that threw me completely off balance. I'd accused him of being cruel, but the truth was… he wasn't. Not yet, anyway.

We'd discussed nothing of importance during these ridiculous dinners, instead speaking of trivial matters—general interests, movies and the like. This whole situation pissed me off, and I was still salty about our conversation the other night. He'd feigned innocence, ignoring every question I posed, but I had a feeling he knew exactly who I was. It wasn't a stretch for him to assume the things he had, but it hurt nonetheless. He wasn't far off the mark about the way I'd grown up, and to have him so callously remark on it still stung. He'd read me like a fucking book, and I hated it.

He was keeping me for some purpose—whatever he deemed fit, he'd said. What the hell did that mean? His room was next to mine, but the adjoining door had remained closed and locked for the past three nights. So if he didn't want me for sex, then what? I saw him only for dinner each night, where he was polite and cordial. Afterward, we parted ways, and I wouldn't see him until dinner the following night. It worried me immensely. He had to have some ulterior motive —but I'd be damned if I would stick around long enough to find out what it was.

"Eva?"

I paused midstride, every muscle tensing at the sound of his voice. I didn't turn to look at him—I couldn't.

"Sleep well."

I swallowed hard and gave a little nod, then fled from the room. Had he read the truth in my eyes? Did he know?

My heart threatened to beat out of my chest as I practically raced through the house and back to my room. Safely ensconced inside, I shut and locked the door behind me, then leaned against it for a long minute as I waited for my breathing to return to normal.

Briefly, I considered pushing my plans back. Almost as soon as the thought crossed my mind, I discarded it. I needed to get the hell out of here—now. Turning on the lamp by the bed, I kept to my usual nighttime routine and picked up a book, pretending to read. My mind wandered over the next hour, playing various scenarios through my mind.

Finally, I slid from the bed and headed into the bathroom. In case anyone was listening, I ran the water like I was washing and getting ready for bed. Once I was done, I turned off all the lights and climbed back onto the bed.

Everything around me was silent and still, but I couldn't stifle the sense of unease running through me. I was antsy and on edge, waiting for something to happen. What, I wasn't sure. When another hour passed with no interruptions, I finally breathed a sigh of relief. Maybe I was just worked up because of what I was about to do.

Slipping into the closet, I changed out of the clothes Fox had purchased for me and pulled on the dark pants and shirt I'd worn that first night when I'd been caught. Moving to the window, I peeked outside. The yard was dark and still, and my stomach tightened. For the past three days since I'd moved into this room, I'd watched Fox's estate, keeping note of who moved around and when. He had more men than I'd estimated. In my initial reconnaissance, I'd counted only a couple men who permanently stayed with Fox. Inside the house, there had to be nearly a dozen.

So far, there seemed to be no rhyme or reason to their rotations. Sometimes they went outside, other times they were secluded in the house. Though the temperature had dropped a bit over the past few days, I didn't think that stopped them from patrolling outside. There was no way that I could get past the guards inside the house, which left me with only one other option—go out the window. Peering outside, I took a deep breath. The ground from the second story seemed like an infinitely long way down.

My room was dark, and I'd been standing here long enough that my eyes had adjusted to the dim light outside, the yard lit by the crescent moon high above. Allowing my gaze to rove over the façade of the large brick mansion, I took in every tiny detail. A narrow decorative ledge jutted out of the brick about four feet below my window and wrapped around the entire house from what I could see. Though it only stuck out maybe five or six inches, it would at least be enough for me to balance on. To my left, near the corner of the house, climbing roses wound their way up a piece of lattice that extended nearly to the roof. Once I had worked my way across the ledge to the lattice, I could climb down, as long as it held my weight, then cut across the yard and over the fence.

I still wasn't exactly sure how Fox had found me that first night. I assumed the fence had some kind of alarm, though I hadn't heard sirens or lights. The more I had thought about it, the more I assumed there was an internal alarm only. Hopefully, by the time I got over the fence, it would be too late for them to catch me. There were so many variables and risks involved, not the least of which was scaling that damn ledge.

My heart rate kicked up in my chest as I stared down at it. I wasn't terrified of heights, but I was smart enough to know that a fall from this height could result in some serious injuries. I'd attended dance classes when I was younger, so I wasn't too worried about my balance or slipping off. The problem was that there seemed to be no good hand holds between my window and the lattice affixed to the corner of the house nearly forty feet away. It seemed so close, yet so far. I had even considered lowering myself until I hung from my fingers on the ledge. If I did that though, my body would potentially be visible through the downstairs windows as I shuffled my way across. Not only that, but I couldn't find a good way to get down that low safely without falling.

Though I still didn't like it, my best bet was to climb out onto the ledge, keep my body as close to the brick as much as possible and hope for the best. All I knew was that I had to get out of here. I refused to remain captive in this house one more day without fighting for my freedom.

Returning to my bed, I waited anxiously for another hour to pass. Once it was fully dark out, I hurried to the window. There were no monitors on it that I had seen or felt, and I quickly slid up the sash after peering out into the darkness to make sure the coast was clear. Even though I saw no movement, I remained still and cocked my ears, listening for anything out of the ordinary. The air was cool and damp on my face, sending a shiver down my spine. Steeling myself, I drew in a deep breath and threw one leg over the sill. I quickly followed with the second leg, then rolled to my stomach and wiggled until only my torso was braced against the windowsill. Blind to what was behind or below me, my toes scrabbled against the hard brick before finally coming into contact with the stone ledge. I breathed a soft sigh of relief as I lowered myself onto the balls of my feet and eased my hold on the window.

Turning my head, I focused on the lattice to my right, a soft white beacon in the dim moonlight. Slowly, cautiously, I released the window and stretched my arms out wide, plastering myself against the side of the house. Slowly, I began to shuffle my feet toward the lattice, my figures digging into the small crevices of mortar between the bricks. It seemed to take forever before I reached the lattice, and my heart gave a little thump in my chest when my fingers brushed the cool wood. I continued to slide my feet until my right hand was securely wrapped around the lattice. Grabbing on with all my might, I allowed myself to relax for a moment.

Glancing around, I studied my surroundings again, but all remained silent and still. I cautiously worked one foot into the diamond pattern of the lattice, wincing as the wood swayed a little bit under my weight. Sending up a prayer, I shifted all of my weight to my right foot and placed my left on the lattice. The wood sagged but didn't break so I slowly began to descend, one cautious step at a time. My heart threatened to beat out of my chest as my feet hit the ground. For a moment, I knelt down and touched the dewy grass, thankful I'd made it this far.

Drawing in a fortifying breath, I scanned the yard and prepared my shaky muscles to run. I exhaled, then pushed off as hard as I could. Dodging between the trees, I headed for the fence on the east side of the property. I didn't hear anything behind me, but I didn't dare turn around to look. The minute-long sprint felt as if it had taken an hour, my lungs heaving, frosty breath rising into the cold night air. I finally reached the huge wrought iron fence and launched myself at it. Adrenaline pumped through my body, and I scrambled to get my hands on the uppermost rail, bracing my feet against the narrow spindles. Finally, I managed to clamber up and over. With a surge of triumph, I dropped to the ground on the other side.

My gaze swept the yard, but it remained empty and dark. A smile split my face, and I lurched to my feet again, swaying as I darted toward the road. I cut at an angle away from Fox's mansion, taking the side road that led out and around town. I jogged down the white line on the side of the road, my elation growing with each step I put between myself and the house I'd just escaped.

My ears perked up, and my heart leaped in my chest as the sound of a car engine met my ears. Not from behind me—but rounding the curve a half mile or so in front of me. I pushed my leg muscles harder, faster, as I ran toward the approaching vehicle.

"Here!" I waved my arms frantically. "Help me!"

I shielded my eyes against the headlights as the car slowed to a crawl, then stopped several yards in front of me. Wavering on my feet, I took a shaky step forward. "Please, I—"

The back door swung open, and my heart hit the pavement as a tall figure unfolded from the rear of the car. Tension crackled between us in the dark, cold night air. Before the man's face came fully into view, I already knew. It was him.

CHAPTER
Ten

FOX

I met Eva's gaze in the glare of the bright lights, watching the myriad of emotions playing over her face. Hope. Confusion. Dread.

Her muscles tensed as she prepared to flee, and I flexed my hands at my sides. "Do it. Run, Eva. Give me the satisfaction of hunting you down and dragging you back to the house again."

Her eyes flared, but her shoulders hunched inward in defeat. Despite her posture, I wasn't about to write her off. She'd already proved her craftiness more than once. If I gave her an inch, she'd take a mile. She was far savvier than I'd pegged her for. The fact that she'd almost outsmarted me—the fact that she thought she could—pissed me off. Somehow, I managed to tamp down my fury and extended one hand toward the car. "Get in."

She approached warily, the toes of her shoes dragging across the pavement as she walked, head down. I took a step backward, giving her some space. Her eyes darted toward me beneath those long, dark lashes, and she quickly ducked into the car, sliding so far across the leather seat that she was pressed against the opposite door.

I slid in behind her, leaving a good foot of space between us. If I got too close, any hold I had on my temper would disappear into thin air. I was already perilously close to dragging her over my knee and paddling her ass so hard she wouldn't be able to sit down for a week. Though the idea held merit, I'd never been the type of man to lay a hand on a woman in anger, and I wasn't about to start now. Even though she most certainly deserved it.

I met Callum's eyes in the rearview mirror and gave a slight nod. From the corner of my eye, I watched Eva cower against the door to my left. Tension hung in the air as we drove back to the house, and I could practically hear the wheels in Eva's head turning. Maybe later I would tell her that the guards had been watching every move of the stupid stunt she'd pulled. By the time her feet hit the ground, we were already on the main road and on our way to intercept her. She was smart, so I knew she wouldn't take the route that ran directly in front of the house. We'd driven down and around a side road that cut across the back part of the property so we could come up on her from the opposite direction. Maybe I would tell her all of that one day. But not today.

My ire grew as she sat still as a statue next to me, her eyes facing forward out the windshield like she could teleport herself out of the car if she tried hard enough. Good luck with that. She was in my house now, and she wasn't fucking leaving. It was a lesson she was going to learn very soon.

Callum pulled to a stop, and Eva reached for the doorhandle, but I wrapped one hand around her bicep, stopping her. "Come."

I practically dragged her across the smooth leather and out of the vehicle, then marched her toward the front door. It swung open, and Rodrigo glared at her with no small amount of disdain as we paraded past. Keeping one hand on her back, I forced her up the stairs and into her room. Once there, I loosened the tie around my neck and motioned for her to turn. "Turn around, Eva."

Her eyes widened and she fell back a step. "But—"

"Now!"

She jumped as I barked out the command and turned away from me, her entire body trembling with fear.

"Hands behind your back."

She slowly moved them to the small of her back, and I quickly looped the silk over them, securing them together. Shoving her forward, I threw her facedown on the bed. "Don't fucking move."

I stomped out of the room, slamming the door in my wake. I could go to my room, but it was too close, and I was still too angry. Instead, I stormed downstairs to my office. Rodrigo met me on the way. "How would you like me to handle this, boss?"

"Don't worry about it." I waved one hand. "I'll take care of it."

"You sure?" His dark brows drew together. "I can—"

"No." I already knew what he was offering, but I wasn't having any part of it. "She's staying here. Even if I want to fucking kill her sometimes," I muttered under my breath as I strode toward the sideboard and poured myself a drink, then settled in my favorite chair in front of the fireplace. Flames danced and twisted, and I watched them, lost in thought.

I'd completely mistaken the look in Eva's eyes over the past few days. I'd believed her to be scared when, in truth, she was furious. Her hate and disappointment had driven her to escape. Each time she'd looked away from me, I assumed it was in deference. I assumed wrong.

The truth was, I actually admired the brazen little bitch. Most women would have begged, pleaded, sold their soul to the devil in exchange for freedom. Not Eva. She waited, plotted, a storm of retaliation and anger brewing behind those dark green eyes.

She was brave—so incredibly brave—but so fucking stupid. How could she ever think to stand up to me? She didn't seem to realize that I could kill her right now—that, or she didn't care. It pissed me off that she was so unconcerned for her wellbeing that she would willingly place herself in harm's way.

My anger began to abate little by little as I sipped at the whiskey. I wondered how Eva fared upstairs. Was she scared? Worried? I hoped so, after her acrobatic performance outside. I wanted her terrified of what would happen, and I wanted to draw out her discomfort as long as possible. The longer she was made to wait, the more she would begin to worry. Her thoughts and fears would begin to take over, and she'd be a trembling mess by the time I got up there. I admired her strong, feisty side, but I wanted to know if she could ever truly submit to me. I wanted her obedience. I needed to see that she understood every action carried a consequence—some of them dire.

Twenty minutes later, I headed back to Eva's room. But when I swung the door open, she wasn't on the bed where I'd left her. Fucking of course not. That would be too easy. I spied her near the windows—the very same one she'd escaped from a couple of hours ago—her back to me as she tried to loosen the binds restraining her wrists. She jumped when I slammed the door, then whirled toward me.

"I told you to stay put!"

Rage turned her eyes a dark green. "You left me here all alone for an hour! What the hell was I supposed to do?"

"Fucking listen," I said as I crossed the room, stopping just inches from her. "It would serve you well to try it sometime."

"Like it has so far?"

She cocked her head to the side, a challenging glint in her eyes, and I felt another surge of anger well up. Goddamn, she knew every button to push. Fortunately, I knew how to push back—twice as hard.

"I was going to give you a chance to explain yourself." I snatched her arms and dragged her toward the bed. "But you no longer deserve the opportunity."

"I—What are you doing? Hey!"

She let out a little shriek of outrage as I sat on the edge of the mattress, then dragged her over my lap, tipping her forward until her ass pointed upward. Her legs kicked wildly as she fought to get free, and I draped my right leg over them, stilling her movements. With my free hand, I worked the material of her leggings over her ass and down her legs until her upper thighs were bare.

"I warned you." I palmed the flesh of her ass roughly, squeezing hard, and I was rewarded when she let out a soft cry. A crack split the air as I brought my hand down hard enough to leave a red mark in the shape of five fingers on her pale flesh. She sucked in an outraged breath, but I didn't give her a chance to speak as I brought my hand down again in the exact same spot, harder this time.

"Did you for one second think about your safety?" She let out a stifled cry as I smacked the left cheek twice in quick succession. "You could have broken your damn fool neck with a stupid stunt like that."

"Pl—please d-don't!" Her voice cracked under the uneven breaths racking her chest. "I—"

"I don't want to hear your pitiful excuses. Never again," I warned as I returned to the right cheek, smacking her reddened flesh several times before returning to the opposite side. Over and over, I spanked her mercilessly until my hand burned and her body bucked under the force of her sobs.

I paused for a moment, watching her muscles clench in preparation for the next blow. I was tempted to tell her to relax, that tensing only made it worse, but she'd asked to be punished the moment she climbed out that window.

The thought caused my anger to spike all over again. The image of her clinging precariously to the brick two stories above the ground would forever be burned on my brain. Those several minutes had seemed like the longest of my life, watching her scale the wall, my heart slamming against my ribs. Rodrigo had suggested we intercept her, but I wouldn't risk surprising her and causing her to fall. Little idiot could have died. Or, maybe worse, ended up paralyzed. She was so intent on escaping me that she'd completely disregarded her safety. She'd recklessly put herself directly into danger, and I wouldn't stand for it.

Eva screamed as I landed one last hard swat just under the crease of her ass, already bright pink and sensitive. I pulled my tie from her wrists, releasing her hands, and they automatically moved to cover her face, as if she could hide from the humiliation and shame shrouding her.

"You will never disobey me again, Eva. Do you understand me?"

Soft sniffles filled the air as the tension drained from her body, the fight spanked out of her. Sprawled over my lap, her body jerked under the force of her silent sobs, submission practically emanating from her. I'd known she wouldn't be the type to blindly accept her punishment; she resisted every swat as if it was a personal injustice. It would take a strong man to earn her trust and respect—and that man was damn well going to be me.

I lifted Eva in my arms and shifted her so she sat sideways in my lap. "Do you have anything to say for yourself?"

She kept her chin tucked to her chest as tears slipped down her cheeks, and she swiped angrily at the offensive tears. Something in me stirred, but I pushed it down as I studied her, waiting for a response. She refused to look at me, and that served to piss me off even more.

"When I speak, I expect an answer."

Dark emerald eyes glared up at me, glistening with moisture. "Fuck you."

I clenched my molars together so hard I feared they would crack. "I swear to God... that mouth. Did you not learn your lesson?" She dropped her gaze when I glared at her. "Or do I need to add another twenty lashes with the belt this time?"

She shook her head, but I felt no pleasure in her acquiescence. She was so headstrong, so stubborn. I'd hoped the spanking would impress on her the importance of following my instructions, but her pride kept getting in the way. If this continued, she wouldn't learn anything from her punishment.

"I'll ask you once more, Eva. What did you learn from tonight's little excursion?"

She was silent for several long minutes, but I was determined to wait until she broke. Finally, she lifted her head and stared out the window, her face pale, her eyes bleak. "That I'm stuck here."

I swallowed down my annoyance as I studied her profile, just inches away. She still sat on my lap, rigid as a board. She kept her body perfectly straight, leaning slightly away to keep as much distance between us as possible. Deliberately, I shifted my thighs beneath her bruised and battered bottom, eliciting a wince from her. "Are you going to try to leave again?"

I knew the answer before I even asked, but I watched in fascination as her head slowly swiveled my way, her expressionless eyes colliding with mine. "I would if I could."

She was good, I would give her that. The words sounded innocuous enough, and from anyone else I would have believed it meant she'd come to terms with the reality of her situation. But coming from Eva, I knew she meant the words exactly as she said them. She'd practically admitted that she was going to try again—it was just a matter of time. There was no challenge in her voice, only the harsh truth, and it filled me with anticipation. I looked forward to it almost as much as I dreaded it, because it meant I was going to have to show her firsthand how different things could be. She thought being here in my house was bad? Evangelina was in for a rude fucking awakening, because she was in no way prepared to deal with the devil I truly was.

"Challenge accepted," I replied softly.

CHAPTER
Eleven

EVA

For the past week, I'd remained in my room, hiding away from Fox. For the most part, he'd left me alone. It was almost like being back in the cell, except that I had the privilege of seeing the sun rise and fall each day. After his parting words six nights ago, I'd been waiting for him to make good on his promise. So far, he'd avoided me as much as I'd avoided him. The dinners we'd shared were a thing of the past. I almost wished we could go back to those awkward evenings. They were infinitely better than living in almost constant fear of what would happen next.

I'd be lying if I said I hadn't considered escaping again, but my bottom and legs ached at the reminder of what had happened a week ago. There was no doubt in my mind that next time would be even worse. For now I would have to outwait him. I would follow his every direction, win his trust. Then, once he'd lowered his guard, I would make my move.

It would take careful planning, but I had nothing but time on my hands. If what he said was true, it'd been almost four weeks since I'd scaled Fox's fence and been taken captive. No one was coming for me; it was my harsh reality and a hard pill to swallow. It also only strengthened my resolve to save myself. I could withstand anything he threw at me—I just needed to be patient and stay strong.

As if my thoughts had conjured the man, the doorknob turned and the door swung open, revealing Fox. There was a harsh set to his face, a look in his eyes I'd never seen before, and it sent chills down my spine. I shrank back as he stepped into the room, pinning me with that intense, dark stare.

"You're coming with me."

I shook my head and strove for calm as I regarded him. "N-no, thank you."

"It wasn't a request." His tone was hard and cold, leaving no room for argument.

"Where are we going?" My voice shook, and I hated myself for it. I didn't want him to see my fear.

"We will be having dinner with some acquaintances."

I eyed him warily, then glanced down at my leggings and sweater. "I don't think I'm really dressed appropriately to—"

"Doesn't matter."

As strange as it was, I didn't want to disappoint him; I didn't want to give him a reason to punish me again. The tenderness in my bottom and legs had faded, but I could still feel the phantom sting of his hand on my flesh. A small shudder ran through me at the thought. No one had ever spanked me when I was young, and his punishment had been painful not only physically, but also emotionally. I felt like he'd taken part of my body, part of my soul away that day.

"Well, just tell me where we're going, and…" My words trailed off as he closed the distance between us, and I automatically took a step backward.

"Turn."

My pulse kicked up, my blood rushing in my ears as my gaze collided with his. "Why?"

"Now."

I couldn't control my flinch as the single word thundered out of his chest and echoed in the room. I hated giving him my back; I felt vulnerable as hell. I wanted to keep him in my sight at all times. Following his orders, I reluctantly turned to face the wall. Smooth, cold metal snapped first around my left wrist then, before I could react, around my right.

I whipped my head toward him. "What are you doing?"

"I'll be introducing you to a few of my acquaintances."

Grasping my shoulder, he turned me to face him again, then bent at the waist and lifted his pant leg. I sucked in a breath and stumbled a step backward as he yanked a knife from the sheath around his ankle. He didn't offer any explanation, and I flinched, barely holding back my cry of terror as the blade sank into the material of my shirt and swept upward. The tip of the blade brushed the base of my throat, and I swallowed hard, feeling the sharp blade against my flesh.

"Don't speak." I gave a tiny nod, and he pressed the blade more firmly against my neck. "Don't make eye contact. Don't even think. Understood?"

I closed my eyes against the tears gathering behind my lids as he methodically cut the sweater off of my body and dropped it to the floor. The leggings went next, and every muscle in my body went rigid as I felt his fingers slide under the thin straps of my bra. With two quick slashes of the knife, the material fell to the floor at my feet as well.

"Let's go."

My eyes flew open, and fear clogged my throat as I tried to form words. "I—I can't go like this!"

He fisted one hand around my hair in a rough ponytail, then jerked back until my head was tipped up to his. "You seem to have difficulty following directions, so let me explain to you how this will work. You will join us for dinner. You will carry out my every instruction to the letter, and you will remain silent as you do so."

"But—" My words were cut off as his hand moved to my breast and tweaked my nipple hard. I let out a keening cry and jerked backward, away from the pain. Hampered by his hold on my hair and the wall at my back, I couldn't move. I could only stare helplessly up at him.

Dark brown eyes held mine as he swept his thumb in a gentle circle around my aching flesh. "Do we understand each other?"

I bit my tongue and nodded against the tears that had formed in my eyes.

"Good." Grasping my bicep, he directed me out of the room and down the hall, marching me down the curving staircase and through the lower level of the house to the formal dining room on full display for anyone to see. The whole way, I stared at the ground in front of me, my shoulders hunched forward as if it would help to hide my nudity.

One of Fox's men held the door for us as we entered, and I could practically feel his gaze crawling over me like a thousand tiny spiders. The sensation made me want to claw the skin off my body. I felt like my flesh was bright red from humiliation by the time we reached the dining room table. Fox moved to the head of the table, then took a seat. "Kneel."

There was no question that he was talking to me, but I had no intention of obeying his orders like a fucking dog.

"Kneel." There was an edge of warning in his voice just before his hand landed on the back of my neck. His fingers dug into my nerves there, and a soft cry stuck in my throat as my knees buckled. I dropped inelegantly to the floor, just barely resisting the urge to glare at him.

A man seated to Fox's left, the one closest to me, let out a little chuckle. "Looks like you are having some trouble with your sub."

"She just needs a little work," came Fox's smooth reply. "She'll be fine as soon as she's broken in."

"I could take her off your hands, teach her a thing or two."

I fought the urge to recoil as I studied the man in my peripheral vision. Hell, no. I would rather die than go anywhere with that man. I hadn't known him for more than thirty seconds, but I knew instinctively that I would rather run the risk of staying here with Fox. Better the devil you know.

From the corner of my eye, I watched as Fox relaxed back in his chair. "Maybe I've been too lenient with her," he replied to the corpulent man. "What do you say, Nikolai? Are you in the market for a new wife?"

"Not just yet," the man replied with a soft chuckle. "But I never could resist the temptation of a pretty face with the figure of a goddess." Nikolai gestured toward me. "May I?"

Panicked, I lifted my head slightly, looking at Fox. His face remained impassive as he stared at the man to my left. Finally, he shrugged. "It's why we're here, after all."

Icy fear slid through my veins, and goosebumps rose over my body from head to toe. My breathing increased rapidly and my stomach clenched as the man's fleshy hand lifted toward me. Time seemed suspended as it came closer and closer before settling on my breast. I swallowed down the whimper that sprang to my lips and clenched my hands where they were bound behind my back. I pressed my lips together and slammed eyes closed as he pulled and tweaked my nipple. His movements were clumsy and rough, and I bit my tongue against the disgusting feel of him.

I wanted to scream, but I forced it down as bile rose up my throat. His hand swept down my stomach to the tiny scrap of underwear I wore. His huge fingers yanked the fabric aside and he pressed one digit against my folds. I gagged and recoiled, and he let out a little laugh at my reaction.

"Delicate little thing, isn't she? I think I'd like to have her."

His hand lifted to my face, and I opened my eyes just as his thumb dragged over my lip. A mixture of hatred and fury welled up and exploded outward. I opened my mouth and sank my teeth into his flesh. Nikolai let out a grunt of pain, and triumph surged through me. He yanked against me, and I finally released him. The taste of him filled my mouth, and I spat on the floor. Before I could blink, the back of his hand connected with the side of my face, knocking me off balance. Stars danced in front of my eyes, and unable to catch myself, I collapsed sideways, my head cracking hard against the marble floor.

A loud screech filled the air as Nikolai shoved his chair back, a string of coarse Russian epithets falling from his lips. I tried to scramble away, but Fox grabbed me and lifted me to my feet. "My apologies. She bites."

I swore I heard a trace mirth in his tone, but it was drowned out by the thrum of blood rushing in my ears as Nikolai advanced toward me, still swearing. I automatically took a step backward but stopped when I collided with Fox. He maneuvered me to the side and delivered a stinging slap to my bottom. "Go stand in the corner."

It literally hurt to obey his command as I forced my muscles to move. A thousand emotions flooded through me, humiliation and anger battling for supremacy. I couldn't decide whether I wanted to cry or scream until I had no air left in my lungs.

Behind me, seated once more at the long table, Nikolai spoke. "Whatever the cost, I'll take her. The little bitch needs to be taught a lesson."

"Perhaps," Fox conceded. "I will review your offers at the end of the night and let you know what I decide."

I'd almost forgotten about the second man, he'd been so quiet. I could feel his gaze on my back, but I didn't dare turn around to look. Tears glazed my eyes as I wallowed in my predicament. I should have listened to Fox; I should have kept my mouth shut no matter what. Fox wanted rid of me and would surely sell me to Nikolai. And if he did that, I would die. There was no question. I didn't know who the second man was, but if he was in the same league as Fox and Nikolai, he had to be just as bad. I had to find a way to stay here with Fox—I just had to. I would find a way to earn his trust, whatever the cost to my soul. I was a survivor, and I would do what I had to in order to prevail.

CHAPTER
Twelve

FOX

This fucking woman. I forced myself not to react as she followed my instructions and retreated into the far corner of the room. A pink mark in the shape of my palm bloomed over her ivory skin, turning my blood to fire.

Nikolai was correct; Eva was too goddamn defiant for her own good. But even thinking of him taking her home, breaking her in, made my stomach turn. I'd seen firsthand the things that had happened to some of the women he had before. Nikolai was particularly brutal, known for torturing the women before finally putting them out their misery. He hadn't even reacted to my slight earlier when I asked after his wife. I hoped for the poor woman's sake that she was already dead so she wouldn't have to endure his torture anymore.

There was no way Eva would last with a man like Nikolai. She had strength of spirit, but her body was delicate. I could only imagine what he would do to her. In my mind's eye, I saw the dark purple and black marks that he had left on his second wife, Arabella. Once, she had spit fire just like

Evangelina. In the span of just a few months, he had managed to extinguish her spark, leaving her praying for death.

I tried to defuse the situation. "Let's enjoy our dinner and discuss business afterward, shall we?"

I turned to the man on my right, a man who went by the name Johnson. Like me, he was an independent dealer. While a majority of my assets were legitimate business holdings, Johnson's were not. He peddled drugs, firearms—whatever the situation called for. If a client wanted it, he could get it.

Two hours later, I showed both men to the door with the promise of contacting each of them regarding my decision. I didn't mention I'd already made up my mind. Once they were gone, I strolled back into the dining room. Eva stood in the corner, fingers laced together just above her butt, legs spread wide, exactly the way I'd left her.

I leaned one hip on the table, then crossed my arms over my chest and regarded her. Even from here, I could see the faint quiver of her muscles. After her show of defiance with Nikolai, I should make her remain like that all night long. I picked up the steak knife that lay next to my plate and strode forward. It had been a test of sorts, leaving it out in the open like that, and a smirk jumped to my lips. It didn't matter that her hands were still bound behind her—I'd learned to underestimate nothing where Eva was concerned. If she'd wanted to go for the knife, she would have found a way to get it.

I moved behind her, pressing my chest against her back, pulling her bottom against my groin. Her breathing hitched as I lifted the blade and held it against the base of her throat. "You didn't go for the knife."

She started to shake her head, then froze as the edge of the blade scraped over her skin. "No."

"No, sir," I corrected.

"No, sir," she parroted through gritted teeth.

Twisting the knife so the blade lay flat, I drew it down her sternum. The metal left a faint pink line in its wake as it trailed over her pale, flawless skin. Her body curved slightly inward as she contracted her torso to put as much distance between her body and the knife as possible. I trailed the blade under one breast, then up to the nipple, brushing the flat edge over the tight, rose-colored tip.

Her chest jerked on a ragged breath as the cool metal connected with her sensitive skin. I smiled. "Why not? It was right there on the table. All you had to do was pick it up."

She swallowed but didn't answer, and I let out a growl. "Tell me, Eva," I prompted her. "Why didn't you grab the knife when you had the chance?"

"You told me not to move," she said in a low voice.

"And do you always do what I tell you, angel?"

"Yes, sir."

"Hmm..." I hummed a low sound in my throat. "Is that all?"

She gave her head another little half shake. "I knew I wouldn't stand a chance against you."

There it was—the truth. My smirk grew into a full-fledged grin. "Good girl. You can relax now."

I stepped away and watched as she shifted on her feet, letting out a little sigh of relief as she shook out her stiff muscles. I strode forward and set the knife on the table. "Get upstairs to your room. We need to talk."

"Fox, please—"

I knew what she was about to say, and I wasn't about to fucking discuss it where everyone could see. "Do you want me to take my belt to you here?"

Angry tears glimmered in her eyes before she dropped her gaze to the floor. I was impressed by her ability to listen, but I wasn't done with her yet. "I asked you a fucking question."

She gave a little shake of her head, and I drew in a breath, clamping down on my control. I spun her toward me and grabbed her face in one hand, directing her gaze to mine.

"When I ask you a question, you will answer me." I searched her dark green eyes, rife with bitter resentment. "Do you understand me?"

"Yes." It was barely more than a hiss of air escaping her teeth, and it made my vision bleed to red.

I squeezed her upper arms, tugging her up on her toes and pulling her so close my nose brushed against hers. "And? Should I punish you right here in front of my men? Take my belt to the same marks that have just begun to fade?"

A dozen emotions flitted across her expression before her eyes turned carefully blank. "No."

"No, sir."

She gritted her teeth. "No, sir."

Not perfect, but I had a feeling that was as close as I was going to get at the moment. "Let's go."

I wrapped one hand around her bicep and tugged her long, dragging her up the stairs and into her room. Once inside, I shut and locked the door behind me, then forced her toward the bed. I shoved her face down onto the comforter, then spun and made my way toward the closet. I felt her eyes on me as I pulled clothes from the racks and tossed them on the bed beside her.

"Fox…"

Storming toward the dresser, I ripped out the top drawer and carried it toward the bed. I met Eva's terrified gaze as I approached. She had rolled to her back and was struggling to sit up.

"W-what are you doing?"

I shifted my focus back to the panties as I dumped them on the bed. "What does it look like? I'm packing your things."

"Packing?"

"Yes." I crossed to the dresser and returned the drawer to its spot before reaching for the next one.

"You're sending me with them?"

There was no mistaking the fear in her voice this time, and

I slowly turned to meet her wide green gaze. I cocked my head to one side and lifted a shoulder. "Maybe Nikolai was correct. He can teach you—"

"No!"

Before I could blink, she was on her feet and staggering in front of me. "Please don't! I'll do anything." Her lungs rose and fell rapidly, her pupils huge as she pleaded with me. "Just... please don't make me go."

A shudder racked her body, and I studied her, my face impassive. "Why would I keep you? Both men made impressive offers to have you."

She swallowed hard and returned her gaze to mine, then licked her lips and gave her head a little shake. "They'll kill me."

"Probably." She flinched, and I shrugged. "How do you know I wouldn't do the same?"

Green eyes met mine. "You... you wanted me before. Please... I'll do anything if you'll just let me stay."

"Anything?" I tipped my head to the side, and she hesitated for a long moment before nodding. Interesting. Time to see how much she meant that. "On your knees."

She did as I asked, softly lowering herself to one knee, then the other. I watched as she remained stiff, staring straight ahead, and I pressed one hand to the top of her head. "Show some respect, angel. Bow your head."

Her chin dropped to her chest, and I bit back a smile at what it must have cost her to do so. She was so stubborn, so willful, that I couldn't help but toy with her. Pressing my lips into a firm line, I used the toe of my shoe to gently tap one knee. "Spread your legs. If you're going to stay here, if you're going to be mine, we need to discuss some rules. When I tell you to wait for me, I expect you to assume this position. Next time, you'll be completely bare so I can see that pretty pussy gleaming for me."

Her shoulders twitched, but she shifted slightly so her legs were in a wide vee, her butt resting on her heels as she stared at the floor in front of her. Warm satisfaction flowed through my veins, and I strolled behind her, watching her muscles tense as I leaned in close. "From here on out, you're mine, Eva. However and whenever I want you. Understand?"

She gave a tiny nod and, though I couldn't see her face, I could imagine the look in her expressive green eyes. In general, seeing a woman in this position did nothing for me. But the fact that it was Eva—seeing her bend to my will—accelerated my pulse and sent raw desire coursing through my veins.

The little schemer was too smart for her own good, and I'd be damned if I let her pull one over on me. If she thought she could win my good favor and make another attempt to escape, she was sorely mistaken. I was on to her now—and I wasn't about to let her slip away.

Pulling the small key from my pocket, I unlocked the shackles from one wrist, leaving the other in place. I rose to my feet, circling her until I stood in front of her again. "Are you ready to show me just how much you want to stay?"

Her gaze slowly rose, over my shoes and up my legs before snagging on my groin only inches from her face. One trembling hand lifted, and another shiver racked her slight frame as she brushed her fingers against the fly of my slacks. I could see the rigid tension of her body as she fought with herself, forcing herself to keep moving when everything inside her screamed to fight it.

Her clumsy fingers finally managed to grip my zipper and pull it down with a soft hiss. My cock swelled at the gentle touch, leaping toward her eagerly. A storm brewed in her eyes, loathing mixed with fear and resignation. It was a heady combination, but I grasped her wrist, stilling her movements.

Her eyes darted to mine. "But… I thought…"

I snorted a mirthless laugh. "You think I'd let that vicious little mouth of yours anywhere near my cock?"

She looked so adorably confused for a moment before embarrassment stained her cheeks bright red. Anticipation roared through me, and I held out my hand to guide her to her feet. "Come."

I led her to the bed, the cuffs around her left wrist clinking softly as she moved. Her thighs bumped the mattress, bringing her to a halt, and she tipped her face up to me. Her eyes were cloudy, conflicted with revulsion and acceptance.

I gestured with my chin. "Up."

She reluctantly climbed onto the bed, moving more slowly than someone three times her age. I slapped her ass, earning a soft yelp as she scrambled into the middle of the Queen-sized mattress. Once there, she threw a look my way. "Well?"

I bit my tongue, the look in her eyes curbing my urge to snap at her. I don't know why I hadn't seen it before; each time she defied me, a hint of fear flashed in her eyes. It was as if she knew she was supposed to stand up to me, but deep down, hated to do so.

"That mouth, angel. It's going to get you in trouble one of these days," I warned.

She lifted one shoulder. "We'll see."

There was that look again. The brave façade underscored by a wary watchfulness, just waiting for me to put her in her place. Dragging a deep breath into my lungs, I climbed onto the bed, watching those gorgeous green eyes widen further as I crawled between her legs, looming over her and pressing her back until she lay flat.

"We'll see," I repeated her words back to her. "We'll see you scream for me. We'll see you beg for my touch. We'll see just how much you need me to give you what you really want."

CHAPTER
Thirteen

EVA

His words sent a shiver of anticipation down my spine, but I forced it away. This was only a means to an end. I shouldn't be turned on, but completely bare as I was, I couldn't keep my body from responding. My nipples hardened painfully, and I could feel the slick wetness between my legs. It pissed me off that my body responded so readily to him when I knew what a terrible person he was.

I scoffed. "I'll never give you the satisfaction."

His eyes gleamed with challenge as he pushed himself further over me. I swallowed hard as his huge hand curled around my wrist and lifted it over my head. Pinned to the mattress as I was, I couldn't move—could barely even breathe. The cuff snapped into place with a soft snick as he secured it around the bed post, then turned his gaze back to me. "Let the games begin, angel."

Oh, shit. Now I'd done it.

I watched with no small amount of apprehension as he lifted himself off me, then retreated from the room. The moment he was off the bed, I snapped my legs together and tucked them in close to my body. Though I still wore the tiny excuse for underwear, they were little protection against a man like Fox. My pulse thudded almost painfully, blood rushing in my ears as I lay tethered to the bed, nearly naked. Was he coming back? Part of me hoped he would leave me alone for good. At the memory of his departing words, a chill settled over my body.

In the next room, I could hear him rummaging around, drawers opening and closing. What seemed like an interminable amount of time later, he returned. Fox paused for a moment, lounging against the doorjamb as he studied me, a tiny smirk decorating his face.

I stared back, unwilling to give him the satisfaction of seeing my fear and unease. I'd never been able to hide my true emotions well, and I fought now to keep my gaze clear and calm as I tempered my breathing.

Fox pushed off the door, and my heart leaped into my throat as my eyes dropped to the object he held partially concealed behind him. The pink vibrator was narrow, but its purpose was clear.

He stepped close to the bed, watching me watch him, then he set the vibrator on the edge of the mattress. He divested himself of his jacket and white dress shirt, and my pulse galloped as his toned skin was revealed with each garment shed. At the sight of his bulging biceps and tight abs, heat pooled low in my belly. I didn't want to be attracted to this man, but my body couldn't help it.

Still clad in his expensive dress slacks, he climbed onto the bed. "Open for me, angel."

His words stroked over me like a lover's caress, though I knew better. I clenched my muscles even tighter, drawing it out, but he only shook his head. "You told me you would do anything to stay. Were you lying to me?"

If I refused, it would mean my death sentence. And I would die before I gave myself over to someone like Nikolai.

Even if I didn't know or trust Fox, I'd rather be here with him. After all, it was my own fault that I'd ended up in this predicament. I would just have to endure whatever he demanded until I could formulate a plan to get out of here. Slowly, painfully, I dropped my knees open, turning my head away from him as I did so.

Above me, Fox chuckled. "Oh, Eva. I'm going to enjoy every minute of this."

Bitter bile swept up, burning the back of my throat. I forced it down again and closed my eyes at the feel of his fingers brushing over my stomach. Back and forth they caressed the waistband of my panties, his touch gentle but sure. It made me want to cry even more. I wanted him to get it over with. I wanted him to take what he wanted, then leave me the hell alone. If I had any prayer of getting through this, I had to close off my emotions. Drawing on every reserve I had, I let my body go completely slack and turned my mind to happier thoughts.

"Oh, no you don't, angel." Fox's voice penetrated my reverie. A soft slap landed on my left hip. "I want you here with me. Eyes on mine."

Against my will, I blinked my eyes open and met his cold gaze. He smiled, lethal and feral. "That's better."

I wanted to squirm under his scrutiny, but I forced myself to meet his eyes even when I felt his hands curled into the fabric of my panties and pulled them down my legs. He dropped them to the floor somewhere and shifted slightly so he was settled between my thighs. For a brief moment, his gaze released mine and dropped to my exposed center.

"Beautiful."

I flinched as he reached between us and gently ran a thumb through my folds. I drew in a sharp breath at the burst of exquisite pleasure that bloomed in my core. On the heels of that came revulsion. I could not want this—I would not.

Biting down on my tongue, I fought to keep my

expression neutral as he teased my clit for a moment, swirling his thumb around the sensitive bud. My heart raced, and a mixture of relief and disappointment shot through me when his hand swept upward, his pressure firm as he swept his hands over my hip bones and along the curve of my waist until he reached my breasts.

My nipples peaked and hardened as his fingers traced the undercurve of each breast. Plumping them in his palms, he brushed the pads of his thumbs over my nipples, and I couldn't help but arch into him. I wanted to close my eyes against the sensation, but he held my gaze captive, those dark eyes filled with desire drawing me in. His touch sent a flurry of fire burning beneath my skin, and I hated him for it—because I wanted more. His talented fingers pulled and tweaked my nipples until I writhed beneath him, moisture building between my legs.

One palm slid lower, to the base of my breastbone and he paused for a second before lifting his gaze to mine. "Your heart's racing," he observed in a low tone. "From fear? Or… lust?"

Oh, God, he was right. What was wrong with me? I bit my tongue, refusing to admit that his mere presence, the feel of his skin against mine, sent liquid fire pulsing through my veins, making every nerve ending tingle with need. As it had earlier when he'd pressed the blade of the knife to my flesh, my body ached for him. It was wrong—so, so wrong. But it felt so damn right.

Fox lifted a brow at my silence but didn't say another word. Bending at the waist, he finally broke my gaze and took one stiff peak in his mouth. I stifled a cry as he flicked his tongue over it before lightly biting down. Liquid heat pooled low in my core at the intense surge of pleasure-pain, and my hips jerked as my free hand moved to the back of his head. The short, spiky strands of his hair pricked my fingers, intensifying the myriad sensations streaming through my body. I'd planned to push him away. And I would—in just a second. But oh, God, it felt so good. His lips were soft as he licked and sucked and teased, and instead of pushing him away, my fingers curled into him, holding him close. The soft rasp of his tongue over my sensitive flesh had me nearly mindless with desire, and I let out a little whimper of need when he pulled away.

One hand coasted downward, and he let out a little sound as his fingers rubbed over my damp folds. He lifted his head. "You like that, angel?"

I couldn't answer him. I refused to admit out loud just how much his touch affected me. Pressing my lips into a firm line, I focused my gaze on the ceiling. Above me, Fox let out a little chuckle. "Have it your way."

The vibrator flared to life, and I gritted my teeth as he touched it to my clit. He slipped it deep inside me, plunging in and out, slowly fucking me with the wand. Heat swept over my body as tingles danced along my nerve endings. Pulling the vibrator free, he touched it to my clit again, and my hips bucked at the sensation.

Dipping forward, he took my other nipple between his lips and sucked hard. His teeth scraped over my flesh and I arched into him, dredging up every ounce of willpower to keep the mewl of pleasure from escaping. I resisted as long as I could until my body was on the edge. "Oh, God!"

Immediately, Fox pulled away with a low chuckle. My pussy felt empty, and I let out a little cry. Still slick from my arousal, he touched the tip of the vibrator to my nipple, drawing a small circle around the tight peak.

"Fox…"

"Yes, angel?"

I glared up at him. "I'm not your angel."

"Oh, but you are." His free hand moved to my other breast, and he tweaked and teased my nipple until I swore. "My beautiful, fallen angel."

I shifted, trying to ease the throbbing between my legs, but the motion only exacerbated the emptiness inside me. "Fox, please…"

I hated myself for begging, hated myself for wanting him. But my body ached for release, an unrequited desire coursing through me.

I watched as he rose up on his knees and worked his zipper down with one hand. I reached out to aid him with the hand not tethered to the bed, but he moved the vibrator back to my clit, and I sucked in a breath, grabbing onto the comforter for support as another bolt of ecstasy swept over me. "Fox!"

He pushed his pants down over his narrow hips, and a pair of dark boxers followed. I licked my lips at the sight of him springing free from the soft material. I could feel his eyes on my face, but I couldn't tear my eyes away from his swollen cock, a bead of moisture clinging to the tip.

I knew it was wrong; I was depraved for even thinking it. But the vibrator suddenly wasn't enough. I needed him inside me, filling me, taking me, stretching every inch of me. "Fox, please…" My voice broke on the words.

"Tell me, angel," he commanded as he fucked me with the vibrator. "Tell me how much you want me."

My words came breathlessly as he brought me to a feverish pitch. "I want you."

His hand stroked up and down his cock, his movements mirroring the vibrator sinking into me then retreating. My stomach muscles tightened with my impending release, and I thrust my hips upward, pushing myself toward the sensation of the vibrator's pulses.

Just when I was almost there, Fox changed tempo, and I let out a growl of frustration as my orgasm slipped away again. "Fox!"

He laughed, his hand moving up and down his length. "Oh, sweet angel. I don't think so."

"Please—I—"

"No." He gave a little shake of his head as he traced my outer lips with the wand. "You were very, very bad this evening. You deliberately disobeyed me, and for that, you need to be punished."

I was already shaking my head, readying to agree to nearly anything as long as he would continue to touch me. "I promise, I won't—"

"You're right, you won't," he parroted back to me. "You will never pull something like that again."

The vibrator moved back to my clit, and my mouth pulled into a grimace as I threw my head back at the exquisite pleasure shooting through me once more. It lasted only a few seconds, then it was gone again. Tears spilled over my cheeks, and I pleaded with him. "Please, Fox. I can't—I can't handle anymore… I need to come!"

He immediately pulled it away, and I wanted to howl as it left me suspended on the precipice of orgasm once more. Above me, Fox laughed. "You want to come, angel?"

I hated myself for begging, but my body buzzed with need like a live wire. "Please, Fox. Please, yes!"

"Too bad. You don't get to come tonight."

"What?" Stunned, I went completely still. Surely I hadn't heard correctly. My eyes jumped to his. "You can't—"

"I can do anything I like," he said with a smirk as he touched the wand to my clit again, making my hips buck in response. Just as quickly, he removed it. "You, however, may not."

Over and over he brought me to the edge, then left me there until I screamed in fury and unfulfillment. Fox worked himself with his hand until he finally came with a ragged groan, spilling his seed over my stomach. I couldn't bear to look at him as he climbed off the bed and left the room, leaving me sticky with his desire, naked and alone on the huge bed. The door to his adjoining room snapped closed with a soft click, and I knew he wasn't coming back.

I'd never felt this way in my entire life. Dirty. Used. I hated him, but I hated myself more for begging for my release. My body still pulsed with pleasure and need, and a sob ripped free from my throat. Tears soaked my pillow as I lay curled into a ball in the empty dark room, self-loathing curling around me and settling into my bones.

CHAPTER
Fourteen

FOX

Eva didn't come out of her room all day. Although I'd seen her first thing this morning when I released her from her bonds, she'd ignored me completely. Feigning sleep, she'd kept herself covered, head turned away from me. She'd stiffened when I pulled the cuffs away, so I knew she was awake. Feeling a little guilty myself, I'd stayed quiet and left her to deal with the emotions raging inside her.

A flush of embarrassment crept up my neck at the memory of last night. I couldn't believe I'd left her the way I had, still partially bound and covered in come. It was fucked up, even for me. I'd meant to punish her by withholding her pleasure, but I'd never meant to take it that far. The moment I'd seen her naked and begging for release as I brought her to the edge of bliss over and over, it'd pushed me beyond reason. The sexual tension between us was palpable, and I hadn't jerked off for days. At the time, overwhelmed by desire and need, it had seemed like a good idea. I'd regretted it almost the moment I climbed off the bed.

I'd retreated to my room, desperately needing space and

time to think. Though our rooms were connected by a single door, it was the longest trip I'd made in my life. I'd stopped and turned back a dozen times only to force myself to keep moving again. I'd had to fight the urge to go back to her, clean her up, take care of her. I fucking hated leaving her that way, but it was something I had to do.

It was clear she didn't truly understand what we were doing. She'd been raised to be polite and perfect, always reserved. She was too headstrong, too stubborn, and if I gave in too easily, she would never understand her body's true needs. There was nothing I wanted more than to help guide her through her conflicting emotions, but it was something Eva had to deal with on her own. No matter how much it hurt both of us, she had to learn her lesson. She would need more work—a lot more work. But damn, she would be worth it.

Thinking of breaking her in made me hard. I loved that look in her eyes when she ran that pretty mouth. I wanted to strip her down, take that sassy, feisty inner strength and mold her into the woman I knew she could be. I had a whole plan for her—no sex until she'd hit all of the milestones, proving she was adapting, that she wanted this as much as I did. She was going to have to beg for my cock.

Admittedly, things had gone a little too far last night. I'd meant to tease her a little, humiliate her. But the moment I saw her flawless skin on display, her wet pussy gleaming for me, I hadn't been able to control the heat that stole over me. Against my rules and better judgement, I'd almost taken her. I'd wanted to fuck her and never stop. Thank God I caught myself when I had. Me coming on her was a degradation, and a bonus punishment. I knew it was fucking with her head, but she deserved it.

It was dinnertime before I had a chance to seek her out. Without knocking, I threw open the door to Eva's room. She sat on the bed, nose buried in a book, and her head snapped my way, eyes wide. As soon as she realized it was me, she turned her face back to the pages in front of her. Irritation bubbled to the surface as I strode toward her.

I stopped only inches away, giving her no choice but to look at me. "Carmen told me you haven't eaten all day."

Those pretty green eyes lifted, reluctantly meeting mine. "Carmen?"

"My cook."

She nodded but didn't say a word, only redirected her gaze to the words on the page. Irritation turned to anger, and I ripped the book from her hands before tossing it on the nightstand with a flick of my wrist. "What the hell did I tell you about that?"

She quirked a brow. "I'm not allowed to read, either?"

Ah. And we were back to the cool aloofness she exuded so well. "Not the damn book." I glared down at her. "Stop fucking starving yourself. You need to eat."

"I'm not hungry."

"You're going to eat."

"No, thank you."

I reached out and grabbed her chin, turning her face to mine. "Food or my cock. Which is it going to be?"

Something flashed in her eyes but was gone just as quickly as it'd come. "Food. At least it won't leave me high and dry."

I swiped my tongue over my teeth, unsure whether I wanted to laugh at her insult or choke the life out of her. "You've been thinking about my cock?"

"Why would I do that?" Her eyes sparkled with challenge. "From what I've seen, it's not worth my time."

I gave my head a slow shake. "That mouth, angel, I swear to God. One of these days—"

My words were interrupted by a knock on the door, and I speared her with a hard look before moving away. I accepted the tray that Xavier passed through the doorway, then returned to the bed and took a seat next to Eva. A sense of déjà vu swept over me, and I held the plate in my lap. "You're going to eat every single bite."

She rolled her eyes. "Yes, master."

"Close. You can call me Fox. Or, since we're in the bedroom, you may want to practice calling me sir."

She huffed a little laugh. "Yeah, sure."

"I'm sorry." I cocked my head toward her. "Did you say 'yeah, sure' or 'yes, sir'? I couldn't quite tell."

She glared at me, her body practically trembling with rage. "I said—"

She opened her mouth wide to enunciate the word, and I shoved a piece of bread inside. "Do something useful with your mouth for once and put something in it."

Her expression morphed from furious to surprised then back to angry, but she chewed it anyway, shooting daggers my way all the while. I held up another bite of food, and she eyed it before raising a brow. "I can feed myself."

"Perhaps." I lifted a shoulder. "But I want to."

She looked as confused as I felt when the words came out, and she took a bite without arguing for once. Thank God. We continued that way for several long minutes until she shook her head. "I'm full."

I set the fork on the plate and moved it to the side. "You need to eat more."

She shrugged and threw a challenging look my way. "Being kept prisoner doesn't exactly fuel one's appetite."

"Well, you'd better get used to it, angel. You're mine until I say otherwise."

The look she sent me was so full of loathing I was surprised I didn't perish on the spot. "I'll never be yours."

I clenched my molars together. "You're already mine. One of these days I'm going to fuck that smart mouth of yours."

"You can go fuck yourself." Her cheeks blazed brightly with color, sparks shooting from her eyes. "You—"

The word trailed off in a gasp as I yanked her over my lap,

face down. She slapped her hands on the ground to keep herself from falling as I forced her forward until her ass was pointed to the ceiling. "I warned you, angel."

She let out a yelp as I landed a hard smack on the right cheek.

"Fox! I—"

I ripped another slap across the left cheek, and her body jolted under the force of it.

She let out a growl of fury and twisted so she could throw an angry glare my way. "Some man you are, abusing women and—"

"Don't make the mistake of confusing discipline for abuse," I cautioned. "If you break the rules, Eva, you must be prepared to deal with the consequences."

"What rules?" she spat. "The ones you seem to make up on a whim?"

Goddamn it, why did she have to be so difficult? "My house, my rules, angel."

The material of her leggings was thin, but I wanted to feel her flesh beneath mine, see the bright pink blooming over her skin. I slid my hand under the waistband of her pants and, despite her protests, worked the fabric down her thighs until her ass was bared to me. I kneaded the right cheek roughly before smacking it again, several times in quick succession.

Goddamn, her ass was so smackable. I fucking loved the way it bounced and colored under my touch, and I set about with a volley of sharp slaps that drew ragged breaths from her lungs as she writhed beneath me. My hand stung, but I kept it up until I'd counted to twenty.

Afterward, she lay limply over me, her body twitching occasionally as she fought to control her ragged breathing. One hand swiped at the tears coursing down her face, but she kept her gaze firmly forward, avoiding me completely as I maneuvered her to her feet. I had a distinct feeling that the tears weren't those of pain; no, Eva was ashamed—of her actions, of her reaction to me and the things we'd done. Though she detested the punishment, the idea of being spanked turned her on.

I was treading a fine line between trying to correct her actions while simultaneously awakening her to her body's needs. Push too much, and I would lose her; be too lenient, and she would walk all over me. As much as I despised punishing her, she needed a taste of what would happen if she continued to defy me. I liked her fiery and independent, but only one of us could call the shots, and it was damn well going to be me.

Hooking my fingers in the material of her pants, I shoved them down to her ankles. "Step out."

Avoiding my gaze completely, she lifted one leg, pointed her toes, and allowed me to slip the fabric over her foot. I repeated the action on the other leg, then slapped her ass one last time for good measure. "Go stand in the corner."

Chin to her chest, she moved gingerly across the room. Beneath the hem of her short-sleeved shirt, her bottom and upper thighs glowed bright red, and the sight shot a spark of heat straight to my groin. Goddamn. Everything about her turned me on.

Nose to the corner, she stood there, one hip cocked to the side. Clearly I hadn't spanked all of the attitude out of her. Time to fix that. "Spread those legs, angel. Hands on your head."

I bit back a smile as she slowly followed my directions, tension and defiance evident in every line of her posture. I could practically hear her unspoken words, silently screaming at me, calling me every name in the book. This was the worst for her—the shame, the humiliation. But she had to learn her place in my house. She pushed me further and harder than any woman I'd ever known.

I waited several minutes, until I thought she'd had enough, before calling to her. "Come here, angel."

Eyes pinned on the wall behind me, she strode forward, stopping a foot from me. I stared up at her pretty face, set in a mutinous expression. "Anything you would like to say?"

She shook her head, and I bit back a laugh. So stubborn. "Do you know why I punished you?"

Her eyes flashed as they finally met mine. "Because you're an arrogant, overbearing narcissist who—"

I shot one arm out, wrapping my fingers around her throat and dragging her closer, right between my knees. I moved the other hand to cup her pussy. Liquid seeped over my fingers, and I felt her flinch as I rubbed her folds. "Keep it up, and I will fuck you into next week."

She glared up at me. "You'd get off on hurting me, wouldn't you?"

I had her flat on her back before she could finish, and her words trailed off on a squeak of surprise as I pinned her wrists to the mattress next to her head. "What do you get off on, angel?"

She blinked as if she didn't understand the question, then lifted her chin. "Not alpha males who think they control everything and everyone around them."

A slow smile spread over my face. "You know what I think?" Her chest rose and fell, drawing my attention to her breasts. I dipped my head and kissed the swell of one. "I think you like it when I take control."

There was a long pause as she searched for words, then— "You can take your control and shove it—"

I crashed my lips to hers, stealing the remainder of her insult. For a moment, she was too stunned to react. Then, as if finally realizing I was kissing her, she flew into action. Her teeth snapped at my lips, and I bit her lower lip in turn.

She pulled her head back with a little whimper of pain, but I wasn't about to let her go that easily. I claimed her mouth again in a brutal kiss. I widened my mouth, forcing her lips to open beneath mine, and I swept my tongue over hers. A shudder racked her body, then, as if giving herself over to me, she threw herself into the kiss. Her tongue tangled with mine as she kissed me back fervently.

I transferred her wrists to one hand and trailed my fingers down her arm, over her chest until I cupped a full breast in my palm. I groped her roughly through the material of her shirt, but it wasn't enough. I yanked the hem up and delved under the cup of her bra, eliciting a tiny whimper of need from her. She arched into my touch as I took the tight bud of her nipple between my thumb and forefinger and rolled it until she tore her mouth from mine, gasping and breathless.

I lowered my head and took the peak in my mouth, loving the way her skin tasted as the flavor exploded over my tastebuds. I let go of her wrists completely, and her hands curled around the back of my head, holding me close to her chest. With my other hand, I worked the other breast free, then went to work teasing and tweaking that side as she let out little moans of pleasure.

I could feel the heat from her core through the material of my pants, and I lifted my body off hers just enough to work my hand between us. I cupped her hard, and her hips bucked under my touch. Eva struggled to sit up, and I pulled the shirt off over her head before shoving her back to the bed.

A quick flick of a button had my fly loose, and I shoved my pants down my thighs until I was free of the material. I loomed over her and took her mouth in another hard kiss. Her legs automatically wound around my hips, and fire swept over my skin as my cock brushed her hot folds. She wrapped her arms around my neck, but I grabbed her wrists and shoved her down again. Grabbing her hips, I flipped her onto her stomach and yanked her to her hands and knees so her pretty ass, still a soft pink from her punishment, was right in line with my hips.

I swept my fingers through her folds, and a feral smile broke over my face when I found her dripping wet, glistening with arousal. She clenched her thighs together as if to prevent me from exploring, and I used one knee to shove them apart again. I thrust my fingers deep inside her, listening to her wanton cries as I fucked her with my hand.

Her body moved with each plunge of my fingers, trying to force them deeper, topping from the bottom. That would never work. Gripping her hip with my free hand, I pulled my fingers free and delivered a stinging slap to her ass. She let out a little shriek, and I roughly massaged the blooming red spot.

"I'm in charge here, angel. You won't come until I'm good and ready for you to cream all over my cock." At my crude words, I delved my fingers back inside, coating them with her juices, then fisted my cock, using the lubricant to prepare myself. My cock leaped as I stroked over the swollen head, and I lined it up with her pretty pink slit.

A roll of my hips had me sinking an inch inside, and she breathed out a little gasp at the sensation. I knew I should put a condom on—but I didn't give a fuck. She'd been tested by Dr. Marlowe, and I knew she was on birth control... That was good enough for me. No longer able to resist the heat of her body, I shoved inside with one swift stroke.

She let out a high-pitched sound as her muscles squeezed around me, stretching to accommodate my sudden intrusion. Christ, she felt so good. I pulled out, then plunged back in, my cock bottoming out inside her.

Fuck, I loved the sight of her perfect, tight ass. I palmed the globes, digging my fingers into her flesh hard enough to leave bruises, holding her tightly in place as I pistoned in and out. Sex had never felt this good before. It was dirty and rough, and she let me take her exactly the way I wanted. I hadn't expected her to oblige so easily, and it threw me more than a little off balance. Everything about Eva was fucking with my head, from the sweet, musky scent of her arousal to the sexy little sounds she made as I fucked her harder and harder. My balls slapped against her pussy as I rammed into her over and over, wanting to punish her—punish myself.

Leaning forward, I grabbed her shoulders and lifted her so that her back was pressed to my chest and her butt rested on my thighs. From my vantage point, her breasts jiggled with every hard stroke, and I palmed them, kneading the soft flesh. Her head dropped back as I tugged on the stiff peaks, pulling panting breaths of ecstasy from her lips.

Her pussy clenched tightly around me, and I knew she was close. Abandoning one breast, I slipped a hand between her legs to her distended clitoris. She bucked wildly as I fingered the sensitive bundle of nerves, and a keening cry ripped from her throat as she hurtled toward the edge of orgasm. Gripping her hip in one hand, teasing her clit with the other, I thrust up into her, each stroke harder than the last. She shattered on a scream, her pussy flooding my cock with her juices, then pitched forward.

She caught herself by placing her hands on the bed, but I shoved her so her chest was pressed flat, arms spread out to the sides. Here, her ass was pointed straight up in the air, and I reveled in watching my cock slide in and out of those pretty pink folds. Her skin was so creamy, so white...

I picked up the pace, watching her fist her hands in the comforter to brace herself against my frantic pace. My muscles tensed and fire licked up my lower back. My mouth pulled into a grimace as my cock swelled with my release, and I pulled free, spreading my come over her pussy lips and the tight little rosebud of her ass. Beneath me, Eva shuddered, and I grasped her ass hard. I pressed the globes together, watching the sticky fluid slide between her cheeks. My essence slipped over her feminine folds, igniting a possessiveness within me I didn't understand. I swiped it up with my fingers and smeared it over her, inside her—and marked her as mine.

CHAPTER Fifteen

EVA

I could feel the heat of embarrassment rising up my neck and over my face as a primal, feral sound welled up and out of his throat. His hands moved all over my ass, over the curve of my hips and between my cheeks. I closed my eyes and buried my face in the mattress, hyperaware of every movement even though I couldn't see him.

His thick come slid over the curve of my ass, between my cheeks, and he swept his hand through it. Long, lean fingers slipped into my folds, and the sound of wet flesh filled the air as he shoved his fingers inside me and fucked my pussy with his come-covered fingers. I sank my teeth into my lower lip to keep from crying out. It was disgusting, filthy, dirty… and utterly perfect.

My skin prickled and my breath came faster as he worked my clit, sticky with our combined arousal. Oh, God. I wasn't ready to come again—I still hadn't recovered from the first one. My body still buzzed with a mixture of shame and ecstasy, and I felt trapped somewhere between Heaven and Hell as he pushed me closer and closer to the edge.

My hips jerked of their own volition, wanting—needing—more. I moved with his increasingly hard thrusts until the orgasm built to a raging inferno. With one strong arm around my waist, he kept me in place as the heat inside my body took over and finally erupted. I splintered into what felt like a thousand pieces, and I clenched my eyes closed, trying to hold onto the sensation as long as possible.

Through it all, Fox rubbed me tenderly, slowly letting me down and bringing me back to reality. Panting, I turned my head to the side and dragged in a deep breath. Sated and feeling almost boneless in the aftermath of intense pleasure, I allowed him to gently lower me until I was sprawled out on my stomach.

I felt his weight leave the mattress, but I couldn't make myself move to watch. Every muscle felt heavy, as if I'd run a hundred miles, even my eyelids, and I couldn't muster the energy to blink them open. I listened to the sound of his feet padding softly toward the bathroom, then across the tile floor. He was back less than a minute later, and I jerked in surprise as a warm cloth landed on my lower back.

Silence reigned as Fox cleaned the come from my back and bottom. His hands caressed my back in long, gentle sweeps, and he massaged my tender flesh with strong, yet gentle fingers. His breath washed over the back of my neck as he dropped a kiss at the base of my neck. "Sleep, angel."

He lifted himself away, taking his body heat with him, and a shiver rolled down my spine. The click of the door closing echoed in the silence as he left the room, and a dozen conflicting emotions swirled inside me. I felt abandoned, sad that he left, as if all of the light and energy departed the room in his wake. I was annoyed that I felt deflated, but part of me was relieved that he was gone, because I needed time and privacy to think.

I'd never experienced anything like that before. I'd had two serious boyfriends over the course of my life, and they were the only men I'd ever slept with. But sex with them was nothing like what had just happened with Fox. It was carnal. Animalistic. It was fucking in its most basic form, driven by mutual need and desire.

No man had ever been able to make me come during intercourse. I'd always had to finish myself off afterward, and after so many failed attempts at sex, I'd pretty much resigned myself to the fact that I wasn't capable of orgasming with a man. Fox had proved that wrong. Even now, minutes later, my body still buzzed with contentment, and my mind felt foggy and unable to focus. All I could think about was him.

I finally managed to muster up enough energy to drag myself up and crawl under the covers. Even the whisper-soft caress of the silky sheets across my butt and legs hurt, and I winced. I reached back to massage my poor, bruised flesh. It was still warm and tender and I could still feel Fox's hands on me, the way his touch had burned through me, igniting a fire deep in my core. I was ashamed to admit that the hard edge of pain had turned me on, sent a ripple of ecstasy through me like I'd never experienced. I'd offered no resistance when Fox had thrust deep inside in one swift stroke, my arousal easing the way for him. Even now, my cheeks—all of them—heated at the thought. He'd pounded into me, his upper thighs slamming against my tender bottom as he'd pumped in and out.

I'd been sensitive from the spankings, but the pain of his ramming into me from behind had taken my pleasure to a whole new level, and I'd come harder than ever before. I didn't understand it, and it left me incredibly unnerved. I pulled the comforter up to my chin as I curled into a tiny ball, staring vacantly at the ceiling. Without Fox, I felt... bereft. Empty.

It was strange. It was wrong. I knew it, but I couldn't help it. I'd barely known the man for a few weeks—during most of which I'd been relegated to the cell—but there was some kind of connection between us that I didn't understand.

I expected him to use me for sex. I hadn't expected to like it so much. He was harsh and controlling, yet strangely tender. I couldn't figure him out. Then again, I wasn't sure I wanted to. I was already feeling too much, and that terrified me. I didn't want to be one of *those* women—the ones who made excuses for their boyfriend or husband's bad behavior because they'd been conditioned to do so. I'd promised myself when I first arrived that I would never give him that kind of control over me, and my vow over the past few days had only strengthened.

Though he'd punished me after I'd broken out of my room, he hadn't laid a hand on me since. I couldn't explain why, but for some reason I trusted him not to snap and hit me for no reason. He was a killer, but he seemed to derive no pleasure from beating women just for the sake of doing so. He'd only reprimanded me when I was in the wrong.

Oh, God. I wanted to smack myself. It was already starting. I'd tried to escape from the man who kidnapped me, and here I was, justifying the punishment he'd doled out. Could I get any dumber? I scowled into the darkness, furious with myself for letting the man fuck with my head. He could have my body; I could even admit to enjoying the sex. But the man would never have access to my mind or my heart.

CHAPTER
Sixteen

FOX

I tapped the end of my pen against the desk, staring off into space as I contemplated the past few days. Things with Eva had gotten way out of hand. I'd meant to punish her, tease her a bit, teach her a lesson. But finding how aroused she'd been after her spanking had driven my need to new heights. She was so fucking perfect, and she didn't even realize it. She craved the discipline, craved my touch. The moment my fingers slid through her folds, every good intention had evaporated into thin air.

I hadn't been able to resist. The spanking, the humiliation, had turned her on, though I seriously doubted she even knew why. She probably still thought it was wrong, and she was too naïve to understand her own body's reaction. Undoubtedly, she'd never been introduced to anything like it. Despite movies and books, she probably never once imagined herself in that position. She was strong-willed, and in her mind, she probably thought she was exempt from those depraved, dark urges. But she was only as human as the rest of us, and deep down, she needed the harsher side of punishment to feel true pleasure.

I replayed the moment she came, her cunt squeezing me, a sound of pure female contentment leaving her throat. If that wasn't the best orgasm she'd ever had in her life, I would eat my fucking shoes. The sex between us was explosive, like nothing I'd ever experienced. I'd been completely swept up, out of my mind with desire for her. I couldn't figure it out. I hated feeling out of control, and that was exactly what had happened with Eva. I'd taken one look at her, felt her skin against mine, and threw every caution to the wind. And it had been… incredible. I wasn't sure sex had ever been so fulfilling. Maybe it was the novelty of being able to touch her, skin to skin. It was as exhilarating as it was unsettling.

I tried to push the strange emotion down, but it continued to plague me in the time since I'd walked out of her room. I couldn't figure out why I felt so… off kilter. I'd done things over the course of my life that were much worse than what I'd done to Eva, yet she'd somehow affected the rarely used portion of my soul reserved for good and bad. There was something about this woman that just made me lose my mind. I didn't want her, but I didn't want anyone else to have her, either. It was borderline obsessive, and I hated myself for the weakness.

I should have gotten rid of her—I still could. But I didn't want to. As I'd told her before, I was intrigued by her, drawn to her as I'd never been to another woman. Even though I knew the reasoning behind it, I couldn't turn it off. I resented her for making me feel anything at all, no matter how insignificant. I was always in control—always. Yet Eva threw me off balance, made me feel like I was floundering.

She was such an enigma, a confusing blend of strength and innocence, and it called to me. I wanted to break down every single wall, strip her of her high-born attitude and drag her down to the depths of hell with me. Eva was so beautiful, so perfect and pristine. She truly was an angel. She gave off a light that I couldn't resist—and I wanted to desecrate her, draw her purity into my dark, disease ridden soul.

She'd turned my entire fucking world upside down in just a few days. Seeing how turned on she was, how lost she had become in her pleasure, the way she'd responded to my kisses like she needed them to live... I had never wanted a woman so badly. I couldn't focus, couldn't get her off my mind. Even though it'd been nearly twenty-four hours since we'd fallen into bed, desperate for each other. I shouldn't want her again already—but I did. And that was something I just couldn't tolerate.

Sex with Eva had most definitely been a mistake. I couldn't show weakness, especially not to her. If she thought she could control me through sex, she was dead wrong. I needed to stay away from her for awhile until things returned to normal and this… *feeling*—whatever the hell it was—went away.

I'd managed to avoid her all day by sequestering myself in my office at home before coming to the club. Not that this was much better. All it did was remind me of her, of all the dirty things I wanted to do with her—to her.

I'd opened Noir over a decade ago, before sex clubs became fashionable. In the beginning, it had served as a venue for me to experiment and learn more about myself and to push myself out of my comfort zone. No one here judged the way people did in the real world. I couldn't stand to physically touch a woman, yet none of them had batted an eyelash when I wore gloves during our play. Though I'd learned that I wasn't truly a Dominant, it had helped me to learn about my own needs as well as those of my partners.

It had been an incredibly successful venture, and having the legal business made it significantly easier for me to dig up information I wouldn't have otherwise come across. People who came here tended to be private, but that didn't mean information couldn't be obtained for the right price.

A hard knock at my office door ripped me from my thoughts. "Yeah?" I barked.

It swung inward, and Xavier filled the space. "Hey, boss, there's a woman here who says she needs to speak with you."

"Who?"

"Narissa Stanhope."

I knew the name if not the face, but I couldn't figure out what business she might have with me. "Send her in."

With a curt nod, he closed the door. He reappeared less than two minutes later, a beautiful woman in tow. Her wide, dark eyes skated nervously over the walls of my office before landing on me. I offered a small smile to put her at ease. "Ms. Stanhope. What can I do for you?"

She glanced over her shoulder at Xavier before turning her attention back to me. "Could we... speak in private?"

"Unfortunately, it's my policy to always have security present when a client enters my office." I smiled to soften my words.

She nodded a bit, then licked her lips as she crossed her arms over her midsection. "I... I need to make a complaint."

I gestured to the seat across from me. "Take a seat, please, and we'll talk." She sat gingerly on the edge of the seat as if it physically pained her to be here. "Tell me what happened."

The woman's long, dark curls slipped over her shoulder as she hunched forward in her seat. "I don't want to cause any issues, but..."

Already on edge, plagued by thoughts of Eva, my temper began to fray. I grated my teeth and swallowed down the urge to rush her along. "Everyone here is held to the same standard," I assured her. "Whatever it is, I'd like to know."

Narissa gave a tiny nod, then drew in a deep breath before speaking. "I was doing a scene with a new Dom the other night, and things got a little... out of control."

"And by out of control, you mean…?" I prompted her.

"He ignored my safe word completely. At first, I thought he didn't hear me, since we were in the middle of a scene with a bull whip."

That word already had my hackles rising. I hated whips, and I especially despised people who didn't know how to wield them correctly. It was a powerful implement, and if anything, most people tend to be too gentle with them as they were afraid to hurt their partner. Others were ignorant or derived pleasure from the pain inflicted on the sub when used improperly.

"Who is the man in question?"

"Mark O'Brien."

I knew the name. He was a well-known real estate developer who was just as crass in his business dealings as he seemed to be with his subs. I lifted my gaze to Xavier. "Get me his information and add his name to the list. I'd like to speak with him if he comes in."

I looked back to Narissa. After two years at Noir, she was hardly a novice. I didn't take her as the type of woman who would abuse the use of her safe word, even with a newer Dom. "Is this the first time you've played together?"

Her curls bounced as she shook her head. "The second. He did the same thing the first time, but he was only using a flogger then."

"I know this is a rather delicate question, but I have to ask. Did he leave any evidence of physical assault?"

Her eyes dropped the ground, and her tongue started out to wet her lips.

"He won't know you're the one who came forward," I assured softly. "If he left marks on you, I would like to know."

Her eyes slowly lifted to mine, and she gave a barely perceptible nod.

"May I see?" I kept my tone low and even despite the fury

bubbling inside me. Bracing her hands on the arms of the chair, she pushed herself to a standing position and slowly gave me her back. I rounded the desk and paused beside her, my fingers just barely brushing the hem of her shirt. "May I?"

She nodded but didn't say a word, and I gently lifted the fabric up, exposing her back. She sucked in a breath as the fabric caressed the wounds lashed into her skin, and the sight of them turned the edges of my vision red with rage. I counted six deep slices from her shoulder blades down to the small of her back. I gently lowered her shirt back into place. "Do you want to press charges?"

Deep brown eyes met mine, wide with worry, and she shook her head. "I just… I just want to make sure he doesn't do this to another woman."

Part of me was disappointed that she had chosen not to file charges for assault. Regardless of the fact that this was a sex club, the marks he'd inflicted on her had been deliberate. "Rest assured," I said as I returned to my seat, "Mr. O'Brien will no longer be welcome in my club."

She dipped her chin. "Thank you."

"However," I continued, "you need to have those wounds taken care of. I assume you've not been to a hospital yet?"

The wry look she sent me needed no explanation. "Do we have your home address in the system?"

"Yes, sir."

I gave a brief nod. "I'll send a doctor to your place this evening if that works for you."

Her eyes widened in surprise. "Oh, that's not—"

I held up a hand. "Everything that happens in this club is my responsibility," I stated. "What time works best for you?"

Her eyes darted to the clock on the wall before meeting mine again. "Eight o'clock?"

I turned to Xavier. "Call Dr. Marlowe, please, and see if he is available to meet Ms. Stanhope at eight o'clock." I turned to her once more. "We'll confirm the appointment within the next ten minutes. Is there anything else?"

"No, sir. I... Thank you."

I forced a smile to my lips. "You're welcome."

Xavier escorted her from the office, and I sank into my chair, running my hands over my face. Sometimes I truly hated people. I threw myself into my work, and nearly three hours later, my phone rang.

"O'Brien is here. Would you like me to show him to your office?"

"Yes. Bring him here immediately," I responded. I had just printed off the paperwork for his termination when the door opened and Xavier stepped in, followed by a shorter man.

The man's beady eyes landed on me, and a false smile curled his lips. "Good afternoon, sir."

"Please, have a seat," I said smoothly. I was tempted to let him continue, to give him enough rope to hang himself, but I had no patience for small talk at the moment.

He did as I asked, all the while eyeing me curiously. "What can I do for you?"

"It has come to my attention that you've been particularly rough during some of your scenes."

"But—"

"Let me finish," I cut him off. He fell back into his seat, a mulish expression on his face. "From what I understand, you have blatantly disregarded your sub's hard limits and ignored the use of safe words."

His mouth opened to defend himself, but I spoke over him. "That kind of behavior is not tolerated in my club." I spun the paper around so that it was facing him. The understanding flickered in his eyes as his gaze landed on the termination paperwork, and his cheeks flushed an angry red.

He slapped one hand on the desk as he launched himself forward. "It was that bitch Narissa, wasn't it? That stupid slut doesn't know what the hell she's talking about. If she had just shut up and followed directions the way I told her to, she wouldn't have needed to be punished."

Typical abuser, I thought with fury. Never accepting any accountability for their own actions, they projected their shortcomings onto their victims. My gaze dropped to his right hand, still planted on my desk. Before he could think to pull it away, I snatched up the heavy paperweight on the edge of my desk and smashed it against his fingers. He let out a feral howl of pain and ripped himself from my grasp, cradling his broken hand to his chest.

Impassively, I extended a pen to him. A scowl twisted his lips. "You broke my fucking fingers! How the hell am I supposed to sign your damn paper now?"

"I'll accept the signature in blood as well," I said coolly. "Sign the fucking termination agreement."

With another glare at me, he took the pen in his left hand and hastily scribbled his name on the line. I nodded and swiped it off the desk with a nod to Xavier. "Please escort Mr. O'Brien from the premises."

"Yes, sir."

O'Brien yanked his arm away when Xavier reached for him. "Get your hands off me or I'll sue you!"

I laughed out loud. "Talk back to my men like that one more time and you'll be leaving here in someone's trunk."

The man threw one last disgruntled look over his shoulder before exiting the room, and I exhaled slowly through my nose. I was still antsy, on edge. I needed to either kill or fuck. Unfortunately, I wasn't prepared at the moment to do either. Watching the scenes here at Noir would only exacerbate my need, leaving me more unsatisfied than I already was.

Damn Eva for doing this to me. Letting out a growl of frustration, I prepared to head home—and another night of jerking off in the shower, Eva's image dancing before my eyes.

CHAPTER
Seventeen

EVA

I stared out the window, gazing out over the backyard. Cheery sunlight spilled in through the glass, a direct contradiction to my dismal mood. Shadows from the window panes fell over the plush carpet, over me, painting me in a gilded cage. They may as well have been bars in a cell. I would never be free as long as I remained here. One of these days I swore I would escape—even if it was the last thing I did.

The soft tread of shoes against carpet drew my attention. There was something about the way Fox carried himself, so steady and sure, that there was no mistaking him. I stiffened as his voice drifted over my shoulder.

"Thinking of running again?"

A cold chill washed over my skin. It was like he could read my mind. Pressing my lips into a firm line, I wiped all emotion from my face so he couldn't read my hate in the reflection. "Why bother? Your thugs would just bring me back anyway."

A chuckle met my waspish remark, and I tossed a look

over my shoulder at him. "Oh, no, angel. If anyone is to have the pleasure of dragging you back here and putting you in your place, it will be me."

"Lovely," I muttered, turning back to the window. "Something to look forward to."

Studying his reflection, I watched Fox stride to the table along the wall. Pulling down a small tumbler, he picked up a decanter of amber liquid and sloshed it into the glass. I turned, lifting an eyebrow as I met his dark gaze. "Starting early?" I taunted.

"I find myself drinking more now that you're here," he retorted.

For some unexplainable reason, his words stung more than they should have. "You could do us both a favor and just let me go. I wouldn't want to be the cause of liver failure."

"Now what would the fun be in that?" His lips tipped up in an infuriating smirk.

I tore my gaze away, unable to look at him for more than a few seconds at a time. I could still recall the taste of him, the way his hands felt as they glided over my skin. Heat raced through me, climbing up my neck into my cheeks. I was tempted to lean into the window, to absorb the delicious coolness from the glass.

For the past four days, we'd been able to mostly avoid each other. I assumed Fox had been working more than usual, because he hadn't insisted on any more awkward dinners. I was grateful for the reprieve. I still hadn't come to terms with my emotions from the other night, and I wanted to keep as much distance between us as possible.

"You need to eat more."

I whirled toward him. "What difference does it make to you?"

Another almost-smile teased the corners of his mouth. "You need to keep your strength up so you can continue to fight me."

I glared at him, trying to decipher the statement. As long as I lived, I would never understand the man. He'd killed my sister, held me captive, yet acted as though he cared for my well-being. "What the hell do you want?"

Any hint of mirth dropped from his face, and his eyes turned cold again. I regretted the words the moment I said them, but I couldn't afford to let myself feel anything for him, not even affability.

"I thought you might want to speak with someone, let them know you're okay."

I glanced at the black cell phone he held in his hand. My eyes darted back up to his. "You would let me speak to my family?"

"Not your family, no," he said, dashing my hopes. "However, I thought you would enjoy speaking with a friend."

"My roommate is probably wondering where I am, worried sick."

"Call her." He extended the phone to me, and I eyed him warily.

My teeth dug into my lower lip. Was this a trick? If I called Rose, was there any way I could let her know where I was so she could relay it to my parents? I racked my brain, trying to think of how I could drop a hint without Fox knowing.

He seemed to read my mind. "I will be right here the whole time, so don't try anything stupid."

With a roll of my eyes, I snatched the phone from his hand.

"Do you know her number?" One eyebrow ratcheted toward his hairline.

"Yes," I snapped. "I've always had a penchant for memorizing phone numbers. Those and license plates."

His head tipped slightly to one side as he inspected me. "That's an interesting talent to have."

I shrugged but didn't say a word as I stared at the blank

screen of the phone. "What's the catch?" I asked, meeting his eyes again. "If I do this, what do you expect from me?"

"Nothing." He shook his head. "I thought it might set you at ease to speak with a friend."

I nodded slowly. Silence fell for a long moment, then I started to dial. Rose's voice, full of curiosity, crackled through the line. "Hello?"

"Hey, Rose, it's me. Eva."

"Oh, my God! How are you? Where are you? Is everything okay?"

I let out a little laugh, turning away from Fox so he wouldn't see the tears gathering in my eyes at the sound of the familiar voice. "I'm fine. What about you?"

I meandered over to the plush sofa and curled into the corner as Rose began to speak. "Hectic as usual, you know how it is. But what about you? What have you been into?"

"Just… Hanging out. Nothing much," I responded.

Her voice was full of concern. "We were told you dropped out."

"I did… Yeah. I was just a little overwhelmed with everything this year and needed a break."

After everything that happened with my sister, it was partially the truth. I wondered who had told her that I'd dropped out though. It must've been the story that Fox had spun.

"They packed up your things a couple weeks ago," Rose continued, "but I found a couple shirts of yours in my closet."

"You can keep them," I replied. What did it matter anyway? For the foreseeable future, I was stuck here at Fox's mercy. Rose and I spoke for a few more minutes before I assured her once more that everything was fine.

"We'll have to meet up one of these days," Rose said.

A sad smile curved my lips. I knew it would never happen. "Sure. Sounds good."

We exchanged goodbyes, then hung up. Without meeting his gaze, I handed the phone back to Fox.

"Your plan must be working," I said, my tone dulled by misery. "Everyone bought the story that I dropped out. So now they just think I'm lazy."

He slipped the phone into his back pocket. "Better than the truth, angel."

I pulled my legs up, wrapping my arms around them as I turned my head away. My stomach felt tied up in knots, and I couldn't bear to look at him.

Finally, he broke the tense silence. "I won't be back until late. If you skip dinner again, I'll know about it."

I didn't bother to respond, and a few long seconds later, his feet carried him toward the door and out of the room. I dropped my forehead to my knees as despair washed over me. No one was coming for me. I was well and truly alone.

CHAPTER
Eighteen

FOX

Across the table from me Matteo stood, signaling that our meeting had come to an end. I stood and buttoned my jacket, my gaze catching on a bright red droplet of blood that had seeped into the fabric of my shirt. I slid a look at the body slumped over in the chair at the head of the table. Matteo gestured for his men to call for clean up, and I gritted my teeth as I took in the girl still kneeling next to the dead man.

She hadn't escaped unscathed, either. Her pretty features were twisted into an expression of shock and horror, maroon splatters evident on the curve of her cheek and temple. Her bright green eyes, so much like Eva's, met mine and held for a moment. I could almost see the thoughts racing through her mind. She'd likely never seen a dead body in person before, and she was still struggling to come to terms with it. I'd known this would happen, yet it still left me unsettled.

"Boss?"

I turned at the sound of Rodrigo's soft prompt and gave a slight nod. "We're done here."

My men flanked me as we made our way out the back

door of the small restaurant. Rodrigo moved toward the car, holding the rear door open, and I slid inside. My pulse pounded in my veins as he started the engine and put it in gear. I dropped my chin to my chest. Droplets of blood had splattered over my suit, and I absently fingered a tiny maroon splotch, lost in thought. Blood spatter was never perfectly round, each droplet different from the last, just like snowflakes.

Truth to tell, I was still a little unnerved by what had happened in the restaurant. I knew it was coming, but not being able to stop it sent a little trickle of guilt through me. I'd known the man would die; I'd seen it in my vision the day Matteo had visited my office. But watching it unfold, seeing the blank look in Matteo's eyes as he'd killed the older man was something entirely different. I'd taken lives, enjoyed it, even. But there was something darker inside Matteo, driving him. I'd met men like him before, and there was no mistaking that look. He killed because he enjoyed it. He would take whatever he wanted and destroy anything and anyone who stood in his way. I could feel the tension rolling off of him, the first sign that things were beginning to devolve. Having a man like Matteo in control was a mistake. The Capaldis would bear watching.

Wide green eyes flashed in my mind, and I couldn't help sneaking a glance out the window as we pulled away from the restaurant. Matteo led the girl to the car, and they ducked inside. From the corner of my eye, I watched until the girl was ensconced in the back of the black car. Would she be safe now? I seriously doubted it. I could practically feel the fear rolling off Giuliana, the distress carved into her pretty features. He'd turned down my offer to take her, and part of me wished I'd pushed harder. In my mind, her green eyes sparkled and darkened, turning into Eva's guileless gaze. All of a sudden, I had the overwhelming urge to get home and see her.

I'd been avoiding her for the past few days, ever since our last interaction in her bedroom. If I was being completely honest with myself, I could admit that I was still a little rattled from our previous encounter. It'd been fucking intense, and I found myself hoping over the past four days that she would fuck up again so I could punish her. Unfortunately, her behavior had been exemplary. I wasn't one to punish a woman without her needing it. But Eva... I craved her. She was so goddamn responsive. I lost all control with her, and I found myself wondering over the past few days why. More than twenty years ago, I promised myself I would never let anyone hold any kind of control over me again. But one night with Eva had everything unraveling. I loathed her as much as I desired her, and that was dangerous for both of us.

CHAPTER
Nineteen

EVA

It was late before I ventured out of my room again. After my run-in with Fox this afternoon, I'd watched him leave with a combination of relief and dread. I hated being here all alone. His guards skulked around the house, giving the illusion of protection. But I didn't feel safe. I felt like a specimen under a microscope, as if they were watching my every move, just waiting for me to slip up again.

More than once I'd caught the dark-haired man—Rodrigo, Fox had called him—watching me. There was something in his eyes that sent a chill down my spine, and I avoided him as much as possible. It wasn't hard to do, considering the size of the mansion.

Now, though, this late at night, it was mostly quiet. I peeked out into the hall, glancing both directions before leaving the sanctuary of my room. Quietly, I made my way to the stairs at the back of the house and descended to the main floor. They emptied close to Fox's office, but I preferred the relative privacy as opposed to the open, curving stairs at the front of the house.

Sneaking quietly past his office and down the hall, I made my way through the formal dining room and into the kitchen. The large room was lit by only the undercabinet lighting, and I slipped inside, using the soft golden light as a guide. Making my way to the fridge, I pulled open the doors and stared vacantly inside as my stomach rumbled ferociously. I'd turned down dinner again, and now I was starving.

It was stupid of me to continue to send food away. In doing so, I was only pissing off the cook and hurting myself. But part of me was mad at Fox, and he seemed to take it personally when I didn't eat. It was a small act of defiance, but it was the only thing within my control. Fox hadn't been around for dinner tonight, so I'd declined whatever Carmen had offered. I knew there would be leftovers in the fridge, but I was feeling rebellious enough to ignore them. After what I'd learned from Rose this afternoon, I wanted to needle him.

I was still furious that his ploy had worked. He'd paid people to pack up my things and tell some tale that I'd picked up and left, and they'd eaten it right out of his hand. I loathed him. I loathed myself for not saying otherwise to Rose when I spoke with her. I should have tried. I cursed myself for being a coward. What would he have done? Killed me? I discarded the idea. No, as much as I despised him, I didn't think he would kill me. Stupid, considering what had happened with my sister. More than likely, he would ship me off to Nikolai or someone equally horrible. I never wanted to see that man again. And if I pushed Fox too far, that was exactly where I would end up. I didn't want to be stuck here, but it was the lesser of two evils.

I was a little disappointed that he'd been ignoring me for the past few days, but part of me was also relieved. I needed to remember that I was his captive. Fox wasn't a good man. He'd killed my sister and threatened to sell me to the highest bidder—something I still couldn't figure that out. Looking back, it seemed like a test of sorts, though I'd been scared out of my mind at the time. I wondered if that was part of my punishment for trying to run away.

He seemed to know all along that he wasn't going to let me go. Though I was sure the other men had made Fox substantial offers to have me—something that still had the power to chill me to the bone—they were barely out of the front door before he'd taken me to bed.

And that was a whole other issue. I was still furious with myself for being so turned on, for enjoying it so much. Part of me wanted more. It was sick, but desire curled low in my belly when I thought back to that night when he'd spanked me, then taken me with an almost feral need. Despite the burning need I felt for him, I knew I couldn't sleep with him again. To do so would be to risk my conscience. I came here for revenge, and I was already wavering. I couldn't become complacent and let him use me as some fuck toy until he tired of me. I refused to let him undermine me and the reason I was here. Sex would only cloud the issue further, and I needed to keep my head clear so I could focus on escaping—for real this time. One of these days I would find a weak spot—either in his security or in Fox himself.

Resigned to my plan for the moment, I pulled out a jar of jelly, then raided the pantry for a loaf of bread and peanut butter. I smeared the gooey goodness over the bread, my stomach growling with anticipation. Fox's cook was talented, but sometimes nothing beat old-fashioned comfort food. Leaning against the island, I stared out the darkened windows, contemplating what my life had become over just a few short weeks. I was almost finished eating when a deep voice floated through the darkness.

"Stop skipping meals and you won't have to sneak around in the dark."

My pulse immediately kicked up, but I fought to keep myself in check as Fox ventured closer. "I wasn't hungry at dinnertime."

"Hmm..." He leaned against the counter next to me and idly played with the knife I'd used to cut the sandwich. Grasping the handle, he picked it up, and my breath caught in my throat, watching the blade glint in the light. Without another word, he reached across me, deliberately close, and set the knife in the sink before turning his attention back to me. "You could have asked someone to bring you something."

"I can take care of myself," I said primly.

"Obviously." A condescending smirk tipped the corners of his lips as he studied the jars of peanut butter and jelly still sitting on the counter. "You're doing a stellar job."

"What the hell's wrong with peanut butter and jelly?" I challenged.

"Nothing—if you're twelve," he returned in that low, amused tone.

My cheeks burned at the insult. "No one will let me do anything by myself," I snapped. "The cook refuses to let me make my own dinner, and your housekeeper won't even let me clean my own room."

"Good." He smiled. "I would have to fire them if they did."

I gritted my teeth. "I was responsible for all these things before I came here, you know."

"Well, now you're mine. I'll take care of you and anything you need."

"What if you can't give me what I need?" I threw at him.

His smile grew to a full-fledged grin. "Oh, Eva, I can give you exactly what you need. All you have to do is ask."

I glared at him. "You deliberately misunderstand me. You offer sex. And mediocre sex at that. All I need is freedom."

Laughed boomed out of his chest. "Mediocre sex? Don't lie to yourself, sweetheart. We both know better."

I crossed my arms over my chest. "From what I've seen, it's not all that great."

"Really?" He advanced toward me like a sleek jungle cat ready to pounce. "So, you didn't cream all over my dick the other night?"

"I—"

"Because I'm pretty sure your screams are still echoing through the hallway upstairs."

"You're vile," I spat.

"Facts are facts, Eva. Tell me—do I turn you on?"

My core tightened as the scent of his cologne reached my nostrils. "No."

"Come on, angel." A shiver rolled down my spine at his deep baritone that caressed my skin, and I clenched my legs together. "Admit it. Tell me you want me."

I lifted one shoulder, feigning indifference. "There's nothing to admit."

No matter what happened, I would never let him see my weakness. I would never let him see what was truly inside me—that I craved his touch. And I hated myself for it.

CHAPTER Twenty

FOX

Such a stubborn little thing.

I studied her stiff posture, the look in her eyes completely at odds with the words coming out of her mouth. "I don't believe you."

Her gaze skittered over my shoulder, unable to hold my stare. "It's the truth."

"Look at me."

She rolled her eyes, still looking at the wall behind me. "Why?"

"I want you to look me in the eyes when you lie to me." She dragged her gaze back to mine, eyes flashing with fire, and I held back a smirk. "What did I tell you about that? What happens to little liars?"

She licked her lips. "They get punished."

"If I bent you over this counter right now, would I find your pussy dripping wet for me?"

A tiny tremble rolled through her body, and I could see the tension in her muscles as she fought to repress it. "No."

I gritted my teeth, caught somewhere between frustration

and satisfaction. She was asking for it. Did she even realize? I couldn't tell. "You said it yourself—bad girls get punished," I reminded her.

I spun her around and slapped her hands on the cool counter. Her legs shifted, and I hooked my thumbs in the waistband of her pants, then dragged them downward. I didn't have to touch her to know that she was drenched. Her sweet essence filled the air, and I dragged it into my lungs. Cupping her bottom with one hand, I massaged her cheek. Reaching behind me, I snagged a plastic spatula from the canister next to the stove top.

She thrust her bottom at me, yearning for my touch. She had no idea what was coming. I brought the flat side down hard and fast, and she shrieked in surprise when it connected with her skin. Her body jerked, and I forced her down until her breasts were pressed flat, levering my weight against her. I spanked the other cheek, and she rose up on her toes, sucking in a breath as red bloomed over her skin. Alternating between cheeks I paddled her ass, keeping the swats light, almost teasing.

"Going to lie to me again?"

"N-no," she panted out between breaths. "Oh, God—I swear. I won't, I promise."

I tossed the spatula in the sink next to her. "Hmm… We'll see about that."

Her tits were pressed to the cool, hard surface of the granite, and her legs trembled as I swept my fingers up and over the back of her thighs. Her skin was hot to the touch, and I gently massaged her sore cheeks as I slipped my left hand around her hip and between her folds. She sucked in a little breath as my fingers encountered the sticky wetness there.

"Mmm… Eva, I think you love it when I punish you."

I couldn't see her face, turned away from me as she was, but I caught the slight rise of her back as her breathing hitched. Still lightly rubbing her bottom with one hand, I sank two fingers deep inside her. She stifled a little sound of pleasure, and I smiled. Without warning, I curled my fingers into the tender flesh of her right cheek. Eva sucked in a breath as she lifted up on her toes, her sheath contracting around me.

My smile grew, and I lifted my hand, giving her a moment's respite before delivering another stinging slap to her ass. She moaned, her pussy clenching around my fingers, her cream dripping down my hand. My angel definitely had a little masochist in her. "So fucking perfect."

I pulled my hand free and turned her in my arms, then lifted my fingers and touched them to her lips. Her tongue darted out, licking up her sweetness. The sight was erotic as hell, and I kissed her hard. Reaching between us, I worked my belt free.

At the sound of the buckle clinking, her head whipped back, and her wide eyes met mine. "Not here." I lifted my brows, and she shot a quick look around as if checking to make sure no one else was present. "Please. Not in the open, where—"

I shook my head, cutting her off. "No one would dare come in while I'm here." My eyes skimmed over her, legs trapped in place by the pants tangled around her ankles. Stepping on the fabric pooled between her feet, I held it in place. "Step out."

She did as I bade, and I shoved my pants down then lifted her, setting her on the counter. She gasped at the sensation—affected by either the coolness of the granite or the feel of her tender, freshly spanked bottom on the hard surface, I wasn't sure. Her hands wound around my shoulders, and I tensed. Grasping her hands, I pushed her so she lay flat on her back.

"Hold on tight." Lining myself up with her, I plunged deep, pulling her forward and onto my cock. I let out a growl as her heat surrounded me, and I sank in all the way to the hilt. Hanging half off the counter, her weight pulled her down, and I swore I could feel every inch of her. I curled my fingers into the flesh of her bottom, lifting and lowering her onto my cock. Her hands slapped downward, then curled around the edge of the granite in an effort to hold herself up, and I leaned into her, pounding harder and faster. The sound of utensils clattering together reached my ears, but the sound was drowned out by the rapid tempo of the blood pulsing through my ears, combined with Eva's cries of pleasure. She contracted around me and came hard, flooding my cock with her liquid heat. I plunged deeper, harder, spurred on by her arousal. Eva threw one arm up, knocking the jar of jelly off the counter as she slapped a palm over her mouth to stifle her scream.

The sound of glass shattering filled the air and echoed through the room, mingling with my muted roar as I came. Her pussy was soaked, saturated with both our arousal, and I felt it slip out of her as I slowed to a stop. My breath sawed in and out of my lungs, and my body vibrated with the remnants of pleasure. I wanted to close my eyes and remain right here, with her still wrapped around me. Shocked by my thoughts, I reared back, pulling free of her. I shifted, and glass crunched beneath my shoes.

"Fuck." I slipped my arms around her and lifted her to my chest. She clutched at my shoulders as I carried her away from the mess on the floor. I slipped out of my jacket and wrapped it around her. "Your pants may have glass on them. Use this to cover up." She nodded jerkily and escaped without a word. Once she'd disappeared from the room I leaned against the counter and tipped my head back, staring vacantly at the ceiling. What the fuck was I doing?

The need to have Eva was all-consuming, and I loved it as much as I despised it. It made me feel weak, as if my carefully cultivated control was slipping through my fingers. She drove me half-crazy with desire, like getting back inside her was the only thing that mattered. Never before had I ever been able to touch a woman the way I did Eva. For whatever reason, my visions didn't plague me when I was with her. I could run my hands all over her without worry of images crowding my brain. It was exhilarating. I felt almost… free. Even when Eva had wrapped her arms around me, it didn't bother me nearly as much as when other women had done so. I didn't dare examine the feeling too closely.

I was acutely aware of the scars covering the expanse of my back, and I showed them to no one. I never allowed women to touch me, never gave them the opportunity to question what had happened. But with Eva, I found I welcomed her touch, the way her hands skimmed over my skin. Considering she'd stabbed me once, it was more than ridiculous. Opening myself up to anyone, Eva included, was dangerous. I couldn't afford to let anyone in, let alone reveal the truth of my past. If she got too close, learned too much, it could destroy me.

My mind was completely fucked, and it was all her fault. Eva was a complete paradox to me. I couldn't read her, not through vision or touch. But she stirred something deep inside me, some emotion I wasn't even aware I possessed. I needed to take control once more, prove that it was just a fluke—it wasn't Eva herself that had this kind of hold over me, but the sex itself.

I hated her for making me feel anything, everything. No other woman had ever affected me the way Eva did, and I resented the hell out of her for it. I needed to distance myself from Eva—the sooner the better. And I knew precisely the way to do it.

CHAPTER
Twenty-One

EVA

Pulling the edges of the jacket more closely together, I sidled to the doorway and glanced around. The hallway was empty, and I breathed a sigh of relief as I scurried toward the stairs. Thank God no one had been around to hear us. My cheeks flamed at the thought of what I had just done.

Most of the staff was aware that Fox was practically keeping me as his personal mistress, but what we had just done in the kitchen was a whole new low. I didn't think I could face any of them again if they'd overheard or walked in on us just a few minutes prior.

I headed toward the stairs, intent on making it to my room without being spotted. I was brought up short when a door to my right flew open and Rodrigo stepped out into the hallway. I let out a startled cry and stumbled over my feet in an effort not to run into him. "I'm sorry."

He didn't say a word, just stared at me with those lifeless dark eyes. I shifted away, still facing him, unwilling to turn my back on him. Though he never spoke to me unless absolutely necessary, I got a horrible feeling from him. I could feel his eyes on me sometimes, watching me, judging me. It was as if he despised me and wanted me gone. At least in that regard, we could agree. I had no desire to be here any more than he wanted me here.

His cold gaze swept slowly over me from head to toe, taking in my bare legs and feet before making his way back up to my face. My cheeks burned with shame, but I refused to shift under the scrutiny. "Excuse me."

Rodrigo dipped his chin a fraction, an almost insulting smirk on his face, as if he knew exactly what had transpired and why I was dressed this way. I felt my neck and cheeks burn with embarrassment, but I bit my tongue and notched my chin up. This wasn't my house, but Fox had decided that I was staying. It wasn't as if I had any choice in the matter. For the time being, I belonged here just as much as Rodrigo did. Unfortunately, I didn't think he believed it.

He watched me like a hawk, looking like he would gladly gut me the first chance he got—and enjoy every second. A killer lurked behind those eyes; I could feel it. There was a malevolence to him that surpassed even Fox, and goosebumps rose over my arms and legs as I took a step backward, putting distance between us. I wanted to stay as far away from him as possible.

Rodrigo was doing exactly as his boss had commanded and was keeping an eye on me. I couldn't blame him for that. He was the kind of man who used fear to control people, to bend them to his will. To show him any sign of weakness would give him full control over me, and I refused to let him see that he'd unsettled me.

Keeping the hem of the jacket tucked firmly around my bottom, I held my head high and took the stairs as if I had all the time in the world. When I reached the curve, I threw a look downward. Rodrigo stood there, still as a statue, watching my every move. A chill raced down my spine, and I fought the urge to break into a run. My heart thudded heavily in my chest as I crested the landing and out of sight. I snuck a look over my shoulder as I made my way down the hall and began to pick up the pace. When I finally came to my room, I threw myself inside and slammed the door, then locked it.

Heart slamming against my ribs, unease causing my breath to come quickly and erratically, I glanced frantically around. Fox's room was off-limits to the staff, and that directive seemed to extend to mine as well, with the exception of the housekeeper. For some reason, I couldn't shake my unease. I pushed off the door, cautiously searching every nook and cranny, waiting for someone to jump out at me.

Once I was sure the room was clear, I leaned against the wall in the large bathroom and drew in a deep, calming breath. Anger replaced my earlier fear. Who the hell did he think he was? So far, he hadn't said a single word to me, only conveyed his intense displeasure with those cold eyes. I couldn't exactly run to Fox and complain; Rodrigo was only doing as he was asked. He would, however, bear watching. I couldn't afford to turn my back on a man like him—not unless I wanted a knife in it. Figuratively or literally, I wasn't sure. He seemed capable of anything.

Locking the bathroom door, I shed Fox's suit jacket and my shirt, then climbed into the shower. My inner thighs were sticky with our combined come, and heat burned my cheeks. I'd allowed him to take me right there in the kitchen where anyone could see. No matter that he would have killed them. The moment he slid inside me, I'd forgotten to care about anything else.

Fire roared to life in my belly at the memory of him filling me, his mouth and hands taking control of every inch of my body. It was depraved, and I should be humiliated at my actions. But I couldn't dredge up the energy. I was still riding high on pleasure. Although I knew it was wrong, I couldn't help it. I loved the way he made me feel, as if he'd brought a secret part of me to life.

He commanded my body and my mind, delivering pleasure in exchange for my submission to him. As sick as it was, I would gladly let him do it over and over if he would fuck me like that again. My hands skated over the tender flesh of my bottom, and I bit my lip as the hot water pelted down on it, reminding me of my spanking.

Even tonight he hadn't doled out a true punishment. Though he'd spanked me for talking back, it felt more like a test of sorts. I just wasn't sure I liked what it revealed. Because he was right—I loved the control he wielded over me. I reveled in the way he took me in hand and dominated me. Everyone else in my life had coddled me, handled me with kid gloves because of my parents. But not Fox. He stripped me bare both emotionally and physically to reveal my true desires.

There was no hiding how much I loved those moments, loved the pleasure-pain it brought. I wanted it again. I secretly loved mouthing off to him, watching that fire burn in his eyes, the way they darkened as he took control over me and commanded my body. It was heady, and the sensation was made even stronger by my anger. There was no amiability between us, only revenge and distrust. We fucked like we hated each other, but that hard edge had begun to slip away.

I couldn't wrap my mind around why he'd chosen to kidnap me. Or keep me. He'd caught me sneaking around his property, yes, but I hadn't done any damage. In his eyes, though, it was the intent behind my visit. He'd chosen to hold me captive instead of turn me into the authorities. He said it was to avoid any run-ins with them, but I had a feeling there was more to the story. He'd had the opportunity to sell me off to one of his acquaintances, yet he'd declined. Why? It made no sense. Fox was a shrewd man. Why keep me and risk the trouble?

Fox was such an enigma. I was his captive, yet he took

every opportunity to care for me. He constantly admonished me for not eating enough or not taking care of myself. After my time spent in the panic room, he'd bathed me, cared for me, made sure I was healthy and hale. It baffled the mind how he could vacillate so easily between the considerate caretaker and the dominant asshole. Like in the kitchen earlier. He'd carried me far away from the broken glass to ensure I wouldn't be hurt. I found myself wanting to know more about him, to learn everything I could.

What was I thinking? God, I was such an idiot. If I was hurt, he would have to call in Dr. Marlowe to take care of me again. It was an expense and an inconvenience I was sure he wouldn't welcome. Still, I couldn't shake the feeling that there was something deeper written in his actions, that there was far more to Fox than what lay on the surface. I needed to get a handle on my emotions, bury them deep where they would never see the light of day. Fox cared nothing for me except to use me for his own pleasure. Everything beyond that was secondary.

Feeling suddenly cold and miserable, I shut off the shower and toweled off before climbing into bed. He'd said he was intrigued, not that he cared about me. So I would be kept as a fuck toy until he tired of me, then released to my former life? I couldn't imagine. Already, I could feel how gray and empty my world would be without him. Sadness warred with anger.

One thing remained unchanged. I was still his captive. Though the sex was consensual—I would never deny that—I refused to open any part of my heart to him. I needed to stay on guard, keep my walls up. I wasn't an idiot. Sex like that changed people, made them read more into situations than was truly there. And I couldn't afford that. He would tire of me eventually, and then he would discard me as I'm sure he'd done with a number of women before me. There was no room for emotion here. I would stick to my original plan and wait him out, then escape as soon as the right time came.

CHAPTER
Twenty-Two

FOX

Eva hovered on the bottom step, one hand resting on the newel post as she regarded me warily. Studiously ignoring her, I focused my attention on Xavier. "Please have the car brought around. I'll be gone for the night."

With a concise nod, he moved away to do my bidding. Feeling Eva's gaze on me, I could put her off no longer. I turned toward her. "My men will be here to keep an eye on you, so I advise you not to try anything stupid."

Dark green eyes stared into mine. "Where are you going?"

"Haven't we discussed this?" I cocked a brow. "You are not privy to the details of my life."

Her eyes narrowed briefly on me, and her chest rose and fell on a sharp inhale. "Enjoy your night."

Without another word, she turned and stalked back up the stairs. I watched her until she was gone, cursing myself for wanting her the entire time. This was precisely why I needed to get the hell out of the house. She was already starting to affect me, fucking with my mind. Disgusted with myself, I stormed out the door. A minute later, Xavier pulled around the driveway. He stepped out of the car and moved to open the back door for me, but I shook my head.

"I've got it." I needed to be by myself, to clear my head. I slid into the driver seat and put the car in gear, flicking a surreptitious glance toward Eva's window. A shadow hovered just off to the edge, and I swore I could feel her gaze on me. Anger at her, at myself, rose up, and I punched the gas, peeling out of the drive. Fifteen miles per hour over the speed limit, I made the drive to Marcella's house in record time.

Parking the Mercedes in the underground parking garage, I texted her to let her know I was there. I drummed my fingers on the console as I waited, my impatience growing as the minutes continued to tick away. Finally the tell-tale tapping of heels against concrete met my ears, and I threw a disgruntled look her way as Marcella slid into the passenger seat.

"Love to keep me waiting, don't you?"

She smiled. "A woman must always look her best."

"Hmm..." I put the car in gear and backed out of my space, then headed toward the exit. I tossed a glance her way. "You may want to put your seatbelt on."

She waved away my suggestion. "I don't want to wrinkle my dress."

Rolling my eyes, I turned my attention back to the road in front of me as I pulled into traffic. I cursed the fact that we were in the city. What I wanted right now was a long, vacant stretch of road where I could open the engine and fly around the curves, letting the sound of gears turning, fluid pumping, fill my ears.

Not that it mattered. I glanced over at Marcella's beautiful profile. I'd work out my negative energy on her after dinner, and everything would go back to the way it was before. Even as I thought it, my stomach twisted, and Eva's face popped into my head. I quickly shoved her away and searched for something to say.

"How's Sebastian? Still not ready to settle down?"

She was too well-bred to roll her eyes, but I felt the gesture regardless. "Not yet."

Her boyfriend of nearly six years continued to string her along, yet I had a feeling he would never marry her. Marcella was a pretty trophy for him to keep on his arm, but he was a notorious playboy. Not that I was any better, but we both knew what this was. Marcella reached out to me when she needed the attention that Sebastian Moreau couldn't—or wouldn't—give her. He didn't seem to mind our arrangement, because I was certain he had no fewer than a dozen women at his beck and call.

"We planned to go to Spain last month, but he cancelled last minute. He's in Monte Carlo right now on business. I offered to go with him, but he declined."

Her tone was bitter but resigned, the sound of a woman who had learned to live with her boyfriend's indiscretions. Of course he wouldn't want her around. Why be saddled with a girlfriend when he could gamble and fuck as much as he wanted?

"You deserve better," I said.

"I know." Her voice was sad. "Part of me wonders if he'll ever commit."

I seriously doubted it. "If you're not happy, just end things. Any man would be lucky to have you."

"Except you." She tossed a smile my way, but her eyes were filled with pain.

This was a familiar song and dance. "You know I'm not that kind of man." I sighed. "I'm like Sebastian in that regard. I can't see myself ever settling down. Besides"—I let out a mirthless laugh—"what kind of woman would want to marry a man in my line of work?"

I knew some couples who made it work, but they were

few and far between. One of these days, I would breathe my last breath, and I had no desire to leave anyone behind who would mourn me. I'd learned long ago that I would never be normal. I could never have a family.

I knew Sebastian's reticence was what pushed Marcella into my arms. Deep down I think she hoped I would eventually give in and marry her, but I made her no promises. She'd hinted before that she was fine living in ignorance of my work and just wanted the physical side of things. But, much as I enjoyed Marcella, she could be needy and insecure —the exact opposite of Eva.

My cock leaped at the thought of her tight cunt, and I uttered a curse under my breath, shifting slightly in my seat in an effort to relieve the pressure building in my groin. No matter what I did, that infernal woman was always in the back of my mind. She was taking over every spare moment of my life, and it was time to put a stop to it.

"Everything okay?"

Marcella's concerned, honey-colored eyes studied me, and I forced a smile to my lips. "Looking forward to spending the evening with you, beautiful," I lied. "It's been much too long."

"You have no idea." She rested an elbow on the console and leaned toward me, her tone flirtatious. "I've been feeling very neglected."

"Can't have that." I threw her a tight smile before turning my gaze back to the road. "We're almost to the restaurant."

"Oh, good. I'm starving." Flipping down the visor, she checked her appearance, touching up her makeup and lipstick even though she'd just applied it mere minutes ago. It was just one more difference between her and Eva; Eva rarely wore makeup even though I'd purchased it for her. Truth to tell, I liked her even more without it. She lacked the flawless, airbrushed finish that Marcella sported, the dewy glow on her cheeks made possible by whatever combination of products were caked on her flesh. Eva was comfortable in her own skin, and it made her even more beautiful. She wasn't ashamed of the faint freckles dotting her nose or the tiny imperfections that, to me, made her all the more perfect. Next to Eva, Marcella seemed shallow and—

Goddamn it. Realizing that I was comparing the two women once again, I gritted my teeth and practically slammed to a stop at the valet stand.

"Honestly, Fox," Marcella admonished, one hand grasping the door handle. "In a hurry?"

I let out a low growl but didn't bother to respond as I threw open the door and climbed out. The slight breeze whipped my jacket open, and I buttoned it before rounding the car and holding out my elbow for Marcella to take. I had to find a way to get Eva off my mind. She was quickly becoming a distraction I couldn't afford. I prayed that tonight, once Marcella and I fell back into our familiar, comfortable routine, it would bring balance back to my life.

Admittedly, it'd been several months since I'd been with another woman. I was almost certain that was the root cause of my unease. The sex between us was good—but sex in general felt good, even when I couldn't touch the woman as I did with Eva. She was no better than any of the others; I just needed to continually remind myself of that fact.

I gave my name to the host at the stand, and he showed us to the table near the back of the restaurant that I'd requested. Situated far from the door and any windows, I sat with my back to the wall, giving myself a good view of the entire room. It was the only table where I could see the comings and goings from every direction, the least vulnerable spot in the entire place.

I ordered a whiskey while Marcella requested a dry red, and silence settled for a few moments as she glanced around, her eyes drinking in all of the other socialites and wealthy businessmen.

She clucked her tongue and leaned close. "Gus is with his mistress again."

I flicked a glance across the room to where Senator Augustus Marchand sat with a beautiful—and significantly younger—blonde woman. I nodded. "His assistant."

"That's what they all say." Marcella shook out her napkin with a snap and settled it over her lap to protect the expensive silk of her dress.

Darting a look her way, I caught the remnants of pain in her eyes. No doubt she was once more thinking of her piece of shit boyfriend. "I'm sorry."

The waitress delivered our drinks, took our orders, then disappeared again. Marcella took a long sip before answering. "Are all men like that?"

"In my opinion…" I trailed off as she stared up at me expectantly. People had spun fairy tales for centuries, and women in particular had fallen under their spell. Centuries ago, the tales had started out much darker, a warning for children to avoid the evils of the word. Today's fairy tales all had a happy ending—an optimistic outlook for young women to believe that their prince charming was out there, and that not all men were evil villains. I liked the original stories better—they were full of truth and wisdom. Women should be wary of men's intentions, but for some reason, I couldn't find it in me to tell Marcella that.

I cleared my throat. "I think the right man will love you the way you deserve."

Soft brown eyes stared into mine, and she nodded slowly. "I don't think I can handle much more."

Tearing my gaze away from her, I picked up my whiskey and took a sip. "He doesn't deserve you. Give yourself a chance to find a man worthy of you."

"Any suggestions?"

I wasn't stupid; I knew exactly what she was asking. Unfortunately, I would never be able to be with Marcella. As much as I liked her as a person, I had no desire to have her around all the time. It was precisely what made her the perfect hookup. She let me fuck her the way I wanted, then went back to her boyfriend. She was a font of information, and I'd gleaned more details about my associates through her than anyone else because she moved in the same circles. But she would never be a permanent fixture in my life.

I could feel her eyes on me, but I refused to rise to the bait. I gestured vaguely around the restaurant. "You know everyone and everything. You'd make the perfect politician's wife. What about Draven?"

A soft sigh escaped her lips, and she turned her gaze back to the room. "Maybe."

The remainder of our dinner was mostly silent with Marcella making the occasional observation about one of our acquaintances or telling me about some function held by the foundation where she worked. I listened with half an ear, perpetually on edge. I felt like I was going to splinter into a thousand pieces, sexual tension pulling me apart at the seams.

Finally, I could take it no longer. "Let's go."

I pulled out my wallet and tossed some cash on the table, then waited for Marcella to grab her things from the coat closet as we made our way to the door. My foot tapped an impatient rhythm on the sidewalk as I waited for the valet, and I didn't bother to hold the door for Marcella when it finally showed up.

I could tell she was miffed at me from her silence as we made our way back to her place, but I couldn't bring myself to speak. I didn't want to make small talk. I wanted to fuck her, fuck these feelings away.

We got to her building in record time, and I slid into the guest space in her underground parking garage. This time, I rounded the car and opened the door for her. I didn't lay a hand on her as we stepped into the elevator, but she expected nothing less. She knew the game; I touched her as little as possible, and she didn't dare lay a hand on me. The sex was always mutual and gratifying, but never intimate.

Inside the car of the elevator, I hit the button for her floor, and it jolted into motion. Ensconced in the private area with Marcella so near, I could hold back no longer. Closing the distance between us, I attacked her lips and mouth, pressing her to the wall of the elevator as it rose toward her apartment. Her displeasure melted away, replaced by lust as she kissed me back. Leaning into her, I ran one hand up her thigh and under the hem of her dress, determined to block out the images flashing at the periphery of my brain.

Her hands pressed flat against the reflective wall to brace herself, and I slanted my head, continuing my assault on her mouth. She tasted of red wine, and the earthy notes soured on my tongue. Ripping my mouth away from hers, I trailed kisses over her jaw and down her neck. At the base of her throat, her pulse thrummed wildly, and the heavy scent of perfume rolled off her skin. It was thick and overpowering, so unlike Eva's natural sweetness.

My eyes flew open, and I jerked away, almost stumbling under the force of the movement. Marcella stared at me, mouth open in surprise, her lipstick smeared from our kisses. Goddamn it.

"I can't do this." I raked one hand through my hair. "I'm sorry, Marcella. I… Tonight's not a good night."

"Okay." Her eyes held a trace of confusion and sadness, but she didn't fight it.

The elevator door opened with a ding, and I didn't move to stop her as she exited the car. Out in the hallway, she turned and threw a curious look my way. I offered her a small smile that I didn't feel, and watched her disappear through the slit in the doors as the elevator closed up once more and began its descent.

Back in my car, I fumed all the way home. Fucking Eva.

Why the hell couldn't I get her off my mind? It was as if she had some kind of hold over me, and I didn't like the feeling one bit. I parked in the garage, then made my way up to the second floor by way of the back staircase. Callum nodded at me as I passed but I barely spared him a glance. I had business to take care of.

Moving into my room I kicked off my shoes, then opened the adjoining door to Eva's room. It was dark and silent, but that was no surprise. Moving on silent feet, I stared at her, spread out in the huge bed, fast asleep. One small foot peeked out from beneath the blanket where it hung over the edge of the bed, and a seething fury swept over me, turning my vision red.

Damn her for doing this—for making me feel. I was going to fuck these emotions out of me if killed both of us.

CHAPTER
Twenty-Three

EVA

I was torn from a deep sleep when a huge hand wrapped around my ankle, and I let out a startled yelp as I was dragged toward the foot of the bed. Rolling onto my back, my gaze connected with Fox's. It took several seconds for my muddled mind to bring his gaze fully into focus as I came awake. His face was dark with fury, his jaw set in a firm line as he glared down at me. Automatically on guard, instinct bubbled to the surface, and I kicked out at him.

He let out a roar of anger but instead of releasing me, his fingers clenched more tightly around my ankle, and he ripped me from the bed. I landed hard on my back, a grunt escaping my lips as the wind was knocked out of me. My chest ached as I dragged in a breath, and rage consumed me as I forced my muscles to move. "Goddamn it, Fox! What the fuck are you doing?"

Not bothering to respond, Fox reached down and fisted one hand in my hair. I shrieked as pain exploded across my scalp. Forced into moving or risk having my hair ripped from its roots, I scrambled to my feet and stumbled along beside him as he guided me through the door connecting our rooms.

Gritting my teeth against the pain, I let out a relieved breath when he thrust me facedown on the bed and released me. I whipped around to look at him as he stripped out of his dark jacket and tossed it in the direction of the chair to his right. He didn't bother to look; his dark, piercing gaze remained fixed on me, his brows drawn slightly together in anger.

A combination of confusion and anger welled up, rendering me motionless. What the hell had happened over the past few hours? He'd been cold when he left this evening, but this was extreme, even for him.

"What the hell is wrong with you?"

Without a word, his hands moved to the hem of my shirt and ripped it over my head, leaving me in my panties. No fucking way was he going to drag me out of bed in the middle of the night, then try to fuck me without some kind of explanation.

I planted my palms on his chest and shoved as hard as I could, but it was like trying to move a brick wall. He snatched my wrists in his huge hands and shoved me away. The back of my legs collided with the bed, and I bounced when my butt hit the mattress. I fought his hold, glaring up at him, but he moved between my legs, forcing more of his weight over top of me. It was too much; he was too angry, too out of control. He liked it rough, but he wasn't himself right now. Tumultuous as our relationship was, I'd always been a consensual partner. Right now, though, his eyes were feral and wicked, and I couldn't bear the thought of being raped, whether he was aware of what he was doing or not.

My breath heaved in and out of my lungs as I wriggled my body backward on the bed, trying to put some distance between us. When that didn't work, I screamed as loud as I could, hoping to break the spell of angry silence.

He froze, his hands still curled around my wrists as he stared down at me.

"I asked you a question!" I glared up at him, trying to shake free of his hold. "You sent me to my room earlier, but now you're seeking me out when you want sex? Who the fuck do you think you are?"

"You want to know what's wrong with me?" His arm whipped forward, and his fingers curled around my throat as he forced me to my back on the mattress. "You. You're driving me out of my goddamn mind."

Me? My mouth dropped open, and I was momentarily stunned into silence. All things considered, I'd been relatively well-behaved recently. "What the hell did I do?"

Fox released me and immediately reached for the waistband of my panties. I grabbed for the material, kicking at his hands, but he tore the fragile fabric from my body, then delivered a stinging slap to my left ass cheek.

"You've ruined me, you little bitch."

That was the last thing I expected, and I halted my movements as he stared hungrily at my naked body. I couldn't tell if I was offended by him calling me a bitch or if I was surprised at his venom-filled words.

"I can't think about anything but you. The second I pull out of your tight little cunt, the only thing I want to do is slide back in. I can't even be with another woman without thinking of you."

For a brief moment, his words filled me with a deep satisfaction—knowing that he desired me as much as I wanted him. A fraction of a second later, cold washed over my skin as the rest of his sentence sank in.

"Other women?" I couldn't help the incredulousness that crept into my tone, and Fox glared at me.

"Where did you think I went tonight?"

Lying naked beneath him, a white hot fury rushed through me, radiating outward and setting my nerve endings on fire. He was out with another woman tonight? Oh, hell no. With a flurry of movement, I kicked and punched at him, screaming at the top of my lungs. "Are you fucking kidding me? You're coming to me after you were with someone else? I'm not your goddamn whore!"

If he thought he could go fuck some other woman, then come to me with his dick still dripping with her juices, he was sorely mistaken. I lifted my torso and sank my teeth into the hand binding my wrists. He abruptly released me with a sharp expletive and shook his hand as if to dispel the pain. Shooting to my feet, I slammed my hands against his chest. "You motherfucker! I hate you!"

"Shut the fuck up!" He growled low in his throat as he lunged forward and grabbed me around the waist.

Fox easily overpowered me, forcing me back onto the bed before straddling my hips. Wrestling my arms, he pinned them, one by one, down by my side. With Fox's muscular thighs squeezing me tight and pressing me into the mattress, I was completely at his mercy. My only remaining weapon was my raging anger. "I'm not some sex toy to use and discard at your convenience!"

He slapped one huge hand over my face, covering my nose and mouth, then leaned so close that I could feel the heat of his breath when he spoke. "You are more trouble than you're worth. I should've gotten rid of you when I had the chance." Dark eyes still glaring at me, his free hand moved to my breast, and I winced as he fondled it roughly, his fingers digging into my flesh.

"Now that I've had you, though... it's completely fucked with my head. I held her, but all I could feel were your curves beneath my hands. When I kissed her, all I could taste was you."

The thought of him with another woman was enough to make me sick, and bile rose up my throat. A pang of irrational hurt ricocheted through my chest, and tears welled in my eyes, burning across the bridge of my nose.

"I tried so goddamn hard. Tried to forget you. Tried to convince myself it was a fluke." He shook his head as he squeezed my face tighter. "I couldn't even get it up, for Christ's sake. And it's all your fault. I walk around with a hard-on half the goddamn time, just thinking about when I can sink into your sweet pussy. You're on my mind every fucking second of the day, and for some insane reason I only want you." He took a breath, his head shaking slightly as if he couldn't quite believe it himself. "I found myself comparing her to you—and falling short in every way."

During the time he'd spoken, I'd stopped moving completely, shocked into stillness at his words. Despite my fury that he'd gone out with the intention of finding another woman to take to bed, he'd come home instead. To me.

"I've never felt this way before, so crazy for a woman. Only you." Fox lifted his hand away from my face and allowed his fingers to coast over my throat, down my sternum. My nipples peaked into hard points as he reached the valley right between my breasts. With his large hands, he cupped the round globes, pushing them together, thumbing the taut pink tips until I was crying out. "You know what I've decided?"

Heat pooled in my core as I half-listened to him, mindless with pleasure. Whatever it was, I hoped it would end with him fucking me. I bucked my hips in response, and he chuckled, a dark sound.

"Oh, angel." He tweaked my nipples hard, and a scream ripped from my throat as my back arched at the sensation. He released me and leaned forward. "These feelings have to go away eventually. I'll just fuck you until they do."

Oh, God. Yes, please. I licked my lips as I stared up at him, vision hazy with lust. "Do it."

"Don't fucking tempt me, angel." He curled his fingers into my breasts, and my mouth contorted under the sharp bite of pain.

Instead of dampening my desire, fire erupted along my nerve endings, and I bucked my hips toward him. "You want me," I taunted. "Take me. You know you want to."

He took my mouth in a brutal kiss, our teeth clashing under the force of it. His tongue rolled over mine, stoking, sucking, and I pulled against the almost bruising grip he had on my wrists.

Without breaking the kiss, he shifted his legs wider, freeing my hands. Seemingly of their own volition, they immediately moved to the front of his shirt. I flicked the buttons from their holes, tearing a few off in my haste to get him undressed. As soon as the edges of his shirt gaped open, I slipped my hands over his shoulders, shoving the fabric down his arms. He struggled out of the shirt while I attacked his belt, pulling it free of its loops. I managed to get him fully unzipped by the time his shirt hit the floor. Fabric hanging around his hips, Fox slid off the bed and shoved his pants the rest of the way down, then left them in a puddle as he lunged for me again. My knees lifted, gripping his hips tightly as my arms wound around his neck, my fingers sinking into his hair.

"You're mine, Eva," he growled, palming my ass. "You'll never belong to anyone but me."

I gasped as he slapped my left cheek, then massaged it. It didn't hurt, but the stinging sensation was just forceful enough to turn me on, make me want more. That sharp little bite of pain always came before intense pleasure, and my body needed it like I needed air to breathe.

He spanked me again, in the very same spot, and I sank my teeth into my lower lip as I closed my eyes. I let out a little whimper as his erection rubbed right over the sensitive bundle of nerves at my entrance. I needed him inside me, needed him to fill me up.

"Fox." I cracked my eyes open and met his own dark irises, hot with feral need. Curling my fingers into his biceps, I pressed myself toward him. "Fuck me. Make me yours."

CHAPTER
Twenty-Four

FOX

Our mouths collided in another hot, needy kiss, and I ran my hands over every inch of her that I could reach. Touching her ignited a fire within me that only she could extinguish. My cock brushed through her hot, slick folds, and heat curled low in my belly, my arousal swelling at the feel of her.

I slipped one hand between our bodies, coasting down to her slick center. Parting her folds with my fingers, I dipped inside. "Fuck, angel, you're soaked."

Eva let out a sound somewhere between a sigh and a moan. "Fox…"

Pulling my hand free, I lined the head of my cock up with her entrance and grabbed onto her hip hard enough to leave bruises. She cried out as I plunged forward, thrusting deep inside with one smooth stroke. Her pussy clasped me tight, the muscles pulsing as they accommodated my intrusion. I held myself there for a brief moment, reveling in the rightness of it before withdrawing and slamming back inside her.

Feeling her contract around me was like watching a piece of a puzzle fall into place. It was absolute perfection, the way we fit together—hard to soft, darkness to light. She tossed her head back, hands clamping down on my arms as I fucked her hard and deep. She was already so close, I knew it wouldn't take much to push her over.

Sliding my arms under her legs, I arranged her so that her legs were spread wide, the underside of her knees settled in the crook of my elbows. Still deep inside her, I leaned forward, folding her almost in half. Her pussy tightened as the position forced her to take me deeper, and an expression of sheer bliss contorted her face. I withdrew slightly then plunged forward, filling every inch of her and eliciting a sharp cry.

In this position, I was pressed right up against her swollen clit, and I used it to my advantage. Rubbing against it as I moved in and out of her, I could feel the swell of her walls as she hurtled toward orgasm. She let out a keening moan as her pussy spasmed hard around me, the muscles of her sheath rippling as she came. Her muscles gripped me tightly, urging me to come, too, and I couldn't hold back a second longer.

Gritting my teeth, I slammed into her with as much force as I could, the tingling in my lower body spreading and shifting into sexual bliss as I emptied my seed inside her. For a long moment, I held myself there, wanting to suspend the moment. Pulling out of her was almost painful, and I did so slowly before collapsing to the bed.

Next to me, a tiny tremor ran through Eva's body—remnants of her pleasure, I guessed. My body was still humming as I lay there, waiting for my heart to calm and my breathing to return to normal. My eyes fixed on Eva, I watched as she yanked the comforter over herself and curled into a little ball just a few feet from me.

A strange sensation, like drunken butterflies battering my insides, took up residence, and my brows drew together as she snuggled into the pillow. "What are you doing, angel?"

"Going to sleep."

Her voice was already drowsy, but we'd never slept together before—I'd never slept with any woman before. And I had no idea how I felt about Eva lying next to me all night long.

"I'm not a cuddler," I said flatly, hoping she would take the hint and go to her own bed.

"Me, either," she replied on a yawn.

My eyes narrowed, and I waited for her to get up but she never did. About a minute later, her breathing changed, and I knew she was out. Motherfucker. I turned to stare at the darkened ceiling, wondering not for the first time what the fuck I was doing. How had everything spiraled so quickly? I had a feeling things were never going to be the same again.

I had two choices: I could either let her stay since she was already asleep, or I could carry her back to bed where she belonged. I was tempted to do the latter, but I was exhausted both mentally and physically and I didn't want to move. Or so I told myself. Closing my eyes, I tried to ignore the body of the woman next to me.

I dozed off and on all night long and awoke just before dawn. Rolling my head to the side, I threw a look at Eva. True to her word, she'd stayed on her side of the bed, an arm's length away. Why, then, was I tempted to reach out and draw her to me? My dick throbbed with need despite our intense bout of sex late last night, and I reached between the sheets to stroke it. My morning wood protested at the feel of my hand, aching to be buried deep inside of Eva instead. But I'd already crossed one boundary last night. If the lines became any more blurred, they would disappear altogether. I needed this last wall between us. If she wormed her way under my skin, there would be no getting rid of her then. To my horror, the thought didn't scare me as much as it should have.

I slipped from the bed, taking care to make sure Eva stayed covered up, and strode into the closet. I dressed quickly, wanting—needing—to avoid Eva at all costs.

Slipping out of the room, I made my way first to the kitchen where Carmen greeted me with a warm smile.

"Good morning, Mr. Fox."

"Morning." I headed straight for the coffee pot calling my name.

"You look tired," she observed from behind me.

I didn't typically welcome comments like that from my staff, but Carmen was different. "I didn't sleep well," I admitted.

"Out late?"

"No. Just tossed and turned." I hesitated for a minute as I stared out the windows that overlooked the back yard. "Can I ask you a question?"

"Of course." She set down the skillet she'd pulled out and met my gaze.

"I was wondering…" How did I go about asking this—and why the hell did I even want to? I framed it up in the most generic way possible. "What would you do if you knew something was bad for you, but you wanted it anyway?"

A knowing light entered her eyes as she stared at me, reading between the lines. "Some things in life we're drawn to because they tempt us. They're forbidden, and we like the chase. Those things often lead down a dark and dangerous path. Other times"—she folded her hands on top of each other and rested them on the counter—"we are drawn to things that we truly desire. These are the hardest to reconcile because we feel we don't deserve them."

I gave a tight little nod. "Thank you, Carmen."

From her spot near the stove, she studied me. "Remember, Mr. Fox—there is nothing you're not worthy of."

I didn't know what to say to that, couldn't even begin to process something so wise—and untrue. I most certainly wasn't worthy of Eva. Would that ever change? I seriously doubted it. Escaping Carmen's searching eyes, I headed to the back of the house and into the sanctuary of my office. Rodrigo was just coming around the corner as I ducked inside, and he followed me in.

"Sir, I have news."

"What is it?" I sank into my chair and took a long drink of coffee, waiting for the jolt of alertness to hit my bloodstream.

"I believe I know when the shipment will be arriving."

"Show me what you found."

Rodrigo picked up a few documents I assumed he'd placed on my desk last night while I was gone. He directed my attention to a printout of an online conversation between four participants. "They're using code words, but it matches up to previous conversations we were able to find. They reference a 'little phoebe' in each of these."

My vision went red at the name. "Is that a person?"

"I thought so at first, but then I checked the dates again." He picked up a new folder and flipped it open, then handed it to me. He pointed to the timestamps printed along the left side of the paper. "These are dated October thirteenth. And these"—he flipped to a new page—"are from late August. I thought it was strange that they would reference the same woman in all three conversations, so I did some digging. A 'little phoebe' is listed as the sum of four and one."

I lifted a brow. "So, five. But five what?"

"Days, I think." He spread the sheets out. "Since we've always been alerted of the shipment after the fact, I went back and tried to pinpoint exact dates. It's difficult to tell for sure, but I believe that they're referring to the fifth day of the month."

I glanced at the calendar. The fifth of next month was just over a week away. "So you think we have just a few days until the next shipment comes in?"

"That's my best guess, yes."

I shook my head. "We need something more substantial. This is too big to gamble and hope it's correct. See if you can get anything more definitive."

He gave a single, concise nod. "Also, from some of the other words in the conversations, I think I've determined where those came across. It's been different each time, so we need to figure out where the point of entry will be this time."

I rubbed my temples. Easier said than done. This was the Canadian border we were talking about. There were more than five thousand miles to examine—not only land, but water access as well—and if we missed it, we were fucked. "All right. Bring Callum and Xavier in here, and let's check all points with easy access."

Which was to say, pretty much all of it. Fuck.

We spent the rest of the day trying to determine where the shipment would be coming through. There were hundreds of possible routes, and by the time darkness fell, I was frustrated and burnt out.

"One last thing," I said as I rose from my paper-cluttered desk. "Marcella says Sebastian is in Monte Carlo at the moment. Xavier, you still have a contact over there, right?"

He dipped his head in a nod. "Yes, sir."

"Have him check in on Mr. Moreau. And see that he encounters a streak of bad luck, or whatever else his creative mind can conjure up."

The corners of his mouth twitched. "Consider it done."

I couldn't change the fact that Sebastian was a cheating bastard, but I could hit the asshole where it hurt. I made my way upstairs to my room, vaguely surprised and disappointed when I found it empty.

Crossing to the connected door, I opened it and looked into Eva's room. She was just coming out of the bathroom, and she froze when her eyes landed on me.

"Come to bed."

She threw me a glance rife with confusion. "I'm getting ready right now."

A strange feeling swelled in my chest as I considered what

I was about to say. Meeting her gaze head on, I tipped my head toward my room. "My bed."

Eva blinked, but if she was surprised by my request, she didn't say anything. She turned off the light, then moved toward me, bringing with her the delicate scent of flowers and sweet woman. My hands automatically moved to her hips as she met me in the doorway, and I fastened my mouth to hers. Maneuvering us toward the bed, I grabbed the hem of her silky nightie and broke the kiss long enough to rip it over her head.

As I moved to the middle of the bed, I told myself it was easier this way—that with her next to me, I could keep a closer eye on her. But we both knew the truth. I wanted her, needed to feel her skin pressed to mine. In the next breath, she was moving into my arms when I reached for her and rolled her beneath me. Grabbing the waistband of her panties, I stripped them down her legs and tossed them to the floor. Dipping my mouth back to hers, I breathed her in, letting her heady scent fill my nostrils as I ran my hands over every inch of her warm flesh. Helpless to control my rampant desire, I gave myself over to the pleasure of being inside her.

CHAPTER
Twenty-Five

EVA

Twigs crunched beneath my feet as I crept through the darkened woods. A cool breeze whipped through the trees, and I wrapped my arms around myself. Overhead, the moon shone brightly, guiding my way. To where? I glanced around, feeling confused but drawn forward by some unseen force. Something waited for me deep in the woods, and trepidation filled me as I put one foot in front of the other, each step bringing me closer.

A familiar laugh cut through the air, and my ears perked up at the sound. "Elle?"

It came again, from farther ahead this time, and I picked up my pace. "Elle? Ellie!"

All around me tree limbs scraped against each other as they wavered in the wind, and the sound sent a chill down my spine. The breeze picked up, pushing me onward, deeper into the forest. I struggled against it, but my feet continued to move. Suddenly, the wind died and I stumbled to a spot in the middle of a large clearing.

My heart raced in my chest, and I spun in a circle, frantically looking for my sister. "Ellie!"

My name floated toward me on the breeze, and I whipped

around, the trees blurring before my eyes as I called out to her. "Elle!"

"Eva..."

My name floated toward me, and tears clouded my vision. "Where are you? I can't see you!"

Above me the trees parted, allowing a bright shaft of moonlight to illuminate the ground at my feet. My eyes scanned the disrupted leaves, saturated with a dark substance. Blood. *Fear stole over my body, rendering me motionless as I watched the ground shift and change. The brittle, dry leaves fell away and a huge, gaping hole split the earth at my feet. It morphed and elongated into a large rectangle, and goosebumps rose over my arms at the sight of the open grave.*

A shadow fell over the ground, growing until it obscured the trees and the moon, and I spun toward it.

"Eva..."

Ice slid through my veins as the shadow took on a hulking human-like form looming over me. Suddenly, it lunged forward, and I instinctively took a step back as fear took over. I sucked in a breath as I stumbled backward, away from the apparition. My heel slipped over the edge of the giant hole behind me, and I windmilled my arms as I fought to regain my balance. A scream caught in my throat as the soft earth gave way, and I tipped backward into the empty grave. A sense of weightlessness sieged me as I fell down, down, down, and darkness wrapped around me, pulling me under.

I lurched upward, gasping for breath, my body flashing hot and cold.

"Eva!"

A huge set of hands landed on my shoulders, and I screamed, throwing myself into motion. I fought off my attacker, kicking and flailing, until he pinned me down and a familiar voice penetrated my brain.

"EVA! It's me—Fox. Wake up, angel."

It took several seconds for the room to come into focus, and Fox moved to the side, giving me some space. My lungs still heaved erratically as the dream bled away, leaving me in my equally dismal reality. My heart felt heavy, and I fought the tears gathering along my lashes as I pushed myself to a sitting position and leaned against the headboard.

"Bad dream?"

I nodded, pulling my knees up to my chest and holding on tightly.

"Want to talk about it?"

For a whole minute, I sat there quietly, processing every emotion running through me. "I miss her."

"Your sister?"

"Her name was Elle." I swallowed hard. "But I think you already know that."

Beside me, Fox stiffened but remained silent. The fact that he didn't deny it sent a sharp pang of hurt slicing through my chest. I turned my head away so he wouldn't see the tears slipping from the corners of my eyes.

Fox exhaled, then shifted so he was sitting beside me, his shoulder brushing mine. "Tell me about your dream."

I couldn't speak over the tears clogging my throat. Instead, I shook my head, hoping he would just let it go.

"Sometimes talking about it helps."

Swallowing down the excruciating pain, I turned to face him. "Do you talk about the things you've done?"

Even in the near-dark, I could see his jaw set in a hard line. "That's different."

The dream was so real, the pain so sharp, that it felt like an anvil was sitting on my chest. My lungs ached as I drew in a breath. "Maybe I'm just as bad as you."

"Don't do that."

"What?" I couldn't help the bitterness saturating my

voice. "I'm sure it's pure coincidence that I crawled into bed with the man who killed—"

"Stop!" He grabbed me roughly by the shoulders, trying to make me face him. But I couldn't bear to look at him anymore. I fought against his hold, arms flailing until he pinned me to the headboard, my wrists in his huge hands pressed to the wall next to my head. "I want you to listen when I say this, because it's the absolute truth."

What the hell was wrong with me? I shouldn't want him, and yet I fell into bed with him every chance I got. Guilt ate at my soul, and I kept my head turned, my eyes clenched closed against the tears that escaped and slipped down my cheeks. "Eva. Look at me."

Dredging up every ounce of willpower, I finally met his gaze. He dipped his chin to look me in the eyes, and for several seconds he was absolutely silent, just staring at me. He gently lowered my hands to my lap, then cupped my face, wiping away the moisture tracking down my cheeks with his thumbs. "I know you're hurting, but you need to know—I never laid a hand on your sister."

I stared at him for a moment. I shouldn't trust him, yet I did. Maybe because I wanted to, or maybe it was because I wanted to believe that, deep down, he wasn't as bad as either of us thought. I didn't want to believe that I'd willingly crawled into bed with a cold-blooded killer. I studied his features in the dim light, searching his fathomless black eyes. "But you know what happened."

He sighed. "Yes."

I dropped my chin as tears burned the backs of my lids once more. There were so many questions I wanted to ask but couldn't bring myself to do so. Maybe one day I would be strong enough to hear the answer. Right now wasn't it.

"It was nighttime. Cold." He didn't pretend to misunderstand what I was talking about, just settled against the headboard next to me, his comforting strength washing over me. "I was walking through the woods when I heard her laugh. I don't know how I knew it was her, I just... did." Tears threatened once more at the memory, but I blinked them back. "I saw it. Where she was killed."

"Christ." His tone was low and hard. "I'm sorry—" I jerked away when he reached for me, and his hand dropped to his lap. "How do you know?"

"Pictures." God only knew how many times I'd looked at the photos of the crime scene the officers and techs had taken. Studying. Analyzing. Absorbing every detail, trying to decipher the truth. I could feel her in my heart—but my mind knew she was gone.

"I feel like she was trying to show me something."

"It was just a dream—"

"You don't understand," I snapped. "You might be able to take a life without a second thought, but I'll never be like that. She wasn't just my sister. She was my best friend. I feel like half of me is missing without her. Part of me wishes I'd died with her."

"Stop it." I gasped as Fox seized my face and turned me to him. He dipped his chin. "Don't ever say that."

"It's true," I whispered.

"No." Despite my protest, he looped an arm around my shoulders and pulled me close, tucking my head into the crook of his neck. "You're still here. You have so much life left to live. She'd want you to move on—I know she would."

How could I move on when I felt like I wasn't even whole? "Tell me something."

"If I can." His tone was guarded, and I closed my eyes, bracing myself for his response.

"Was it quick?"

He deliberated before speaking. "There was no pain."

I didn't know what to think of that. I wanted to be happy that she hadn't suffered, but my heart ached that she was truly gone. I pulled away, curling onto my side and burying my head in the pillow.

"Angel..."

"I can't." My voice broke. "Not... not right now."

This time, he let me go.

CHAPTER
Twenty-Six

FOX

Each night brought her closer to me. The morning following her nightmare, I'd awoken to find her cheek pressed to my bicep. The second morning, she'd been curled against my side as if seeking me out for comfort. By the third, I awoke to find her head on my chest, one leg thrown over mine. We hadn't revisited the subject of her sister or the nightmare she'd had, but I knew it was still looming in the back of her mind. I could see the remnants of shadows in her eyes occasionally, but something had shifted between us.

For the past four nights, we'd retreated to my room after dinner. We exhausted ourselves physically, then moved to our respective sides of the bed. But in the middle of the night, Eva would reach for me, and I would pull her into my arms. She slept with her head nestled right over my black heart, and I clung to her like a lifeline.

I slept longer. Better. Just having her near was as soothing as it was troubling. She made me feel weak, needy, out of control. At the same time, I felt more content, more well rested, more sated than I ever had in my entire life. I didn't like the power she wielded over me, even if only in sleep. Especially in sleep. That was when I felt most vulnerable, and a huge part of me resented her for making me need her. I'd thought it would fade. I thought once we'd worked this insane attraction out of our systems, that everything would go back to normal. But my desire for her had only increased.

Eva hadn't spent a single night in her bed since I'd turned down Marcella's offer. Though I rarely saw her during the day, Eva and I made love each night, as if it was the only time we could truly be open with each other. It was more passionate, more intense every time we came together. We were like fire and ice, ravaging everything in our wake, yet somehow making each of us stronger. Better. I'd seen a confidence in Eva I'd hadn't noticed before. Though she remained obedient and submissive in the bedroom, she held herself taller, straighter. She exuded a healthy glow, and her eyes were brighter.

I'd told her the truth. Although I knew every detail of what happened to Elle Masterson, I'd never laid a hand on her. I was grateful that Eva trusted me, believed me. I knew it didn't make the situation any easier, because she was still hurting, and I hated that. I should have lied and told her I was responsible for Elle's death. Maybe then Eva would have done the smart thing and retreated. But she hadn't. She was everything I'd ever wanted, and it scared the fuck out of me. I wanted so desperately to keep her, but I knew I shouldn't. The longer she remained with me, the more likely she was to be hurt.

I drummed my fingers on my thigh impatiently as I watched out the windshield of the truck, concealed between the trees along the side of the road. The soft white-yellow glow of headlights swept along the powerlines, sending adrenaline pumping through my veins as the large box truck came around the curve.

"Time to move."

Half a mile ahead, one of my SUVs pulled onto the road, forcing the box truck to slow down. Rodrigo pressed down on the gas pedal and pulled onto the road behind him. The truck was older, covered in dust and dirt, and I desperately hoped this was the transport we were looking for. In the first SUV, Xavier hit the brakes hard, and the driver of the box truck did the same, sliding to a screeching halt in the middle of the dark road.

"Let's see if this is our guy."

I threw open my door, ready to question the driver. Just as my feet hit the pavement, bright flashes of light came from up ahead, and the loud report of gunshots pierced the air. Guess that answered my question. The window next to me shattered, the sound of tinkling glass mingling with the soft whiz of a bullet as it zipped past my head. I dropped to a crouch behind the open door, returning fire blindly as bullets rained down around us, the sound of lead piercing steel filling the night air.

"Watch your aim!" I called out. The last thing we needed was for dozens of rounds to penetrate the back of the truck and jeopardize the cargo inside. I risked a peek around the edge of the door and jerked back as a round pierced the metal in front of me with a solid *thunk*. Stretching over the door panel, I let loose with another volley of shots and was rewarded by a guttural cry as one of my bullets hit its mark.

"One down," I said into the communications system in my ear.

"Two," came Xavier's response. "Driver is down with a chest wound."

Around us, everything fell completely, utterly silent, but I didn't trust it for a second. I had no idea how many men were inside the vehicle, but I was betting on at least two more.

"I want one of them alive." Pistol raised, I carefully approached the back of the box truck.

A flash from the muzzle of the man lying on the ground

exploded, and heat flared along my side, followed by an intense burning sensation. I let out a growl and popped off two more rounds, and the sound of metal hitting the pavement met my ears.

Gritting my teeth, I pushed down the pain exploding along my side and focused on the task at hand. My warm breath curled upward as it left my mouth, then dissipated into the cool night air as I scanned our surroundings. The driver of the truck lay facedown on the asphalt, a dark pool of blood spreading beneath his body. Xavier stepped over him, pistol trained on the cab of the truck while Rodrigo did the same on the passenger side. I watched as a man appeared in the opening, hands raised. "Don't shoot."

In response, Rodrigo grabbed the man and yanked him out of the cab, forcing him to his knees. The man's eyes were wide and filled with fear as he stared up at me. Over his shoulder, I flicked a glance at my men. "Is that all?"

They did a quick sweep of the cab, and Rodrigo nodded. "Affirmative."

I studied the man at my feet. "Who contracted the shipment?"

"I don't know shit!" The man panted out.

"Who do you work for?"

He shook his head. "I don't know his name."

"How do you get this job?"

"Through a friend."

"That's not good enough. I need answers." Dropping my pistol a few inches, I pulled the trigger, and the man let out a low howl as the bullet tore through the fleshy part of his thigh. He dropped to the ground, writhing and groaning as he clutched his wound. "What's your friend's name?"

It took him several seconds to form the word. "Lundy."

"Lundy have a first name?"

"Ask… him…" He grimaced. "He was driving."

I glanced at Xavier, who shook his head. Turning back to

the man on the ground, I leaned down and pressed the muzzle of the gun to his leg, eliciting a sharp cry from him. "He won't be telling us anything, so I'm going to need you to think a little harder for me."

He shook his head. "I don't... Fuck!" He clutched at his leg, a dark stain now saturating the material of his pants. "I need help!"

"And I need a name."

"I don't know!" he crowed. "He goes by Lundy. Never asked his first name."

"Not much of a friend, then, is he?" I lifted a brow, my gaze still fixed on the man writhing in front of me. "You always let your friends talk you into stupid stuff like this?"

"Needed... the money."

"Don't we all?" I slapped his leg and he let out another strangled sound as he twisted away from me. "Time's running out. I'm gonna need something else. Anyone Lundy was working with?"

"I don't know."

I sighed. "If that's how you feel." I lifted the pistol, and the man's hands flew up.

"Wait, wait!"

I lifted a brow. "Remember something?"

"I... I think heard him mention the name Grigori."

I studied the man. "Last name?"

"Don't... don't know."

"Here's what's going to happen." The man's glassy eyes fixed on mine. "You have three days to find this Grigori and deliver him to me. Understood?"

"Y-yes." His eyes closed, but his head bobbed.

Drawing in a deep breath, I pushed to my feet and turned to Xavier. "Deliver him to Marlowe and get him fixed up."

"Yes, sir."

I nodded. "Let's get this mess cleaned up before someone else comes along."

Xavier and Callum zip-tied the man, then lifted him to his feet and carried him to their SUV.

The dull throbbing in my side drew my attention, and I winced as my fingers slid along my waist, coming away wet with dark blood. "Ah, fuck."

"Good, boss?" Rodrigo's eyes were filled with concern.

"Fine. Have you checked the cargo yet?" He shook his head, and I moved to the back of the box truck, then lifted the latch. The door swung open with a groan, and the dark interior was slowly illuminated by the headlights of the SUV. Two dozen pairs of terrified eyes in small, dirt-streaked faces stared back at me. Gritting my teeth together, I directed my next words at Rodrigo. "Take care of it."

Less than ten minutes later, bodies loaded and weapons retrieved, we were headed home.

CHAPTER
Twenty-Seven

EVA

The sound of heavy footsteps in the hallway drew my attention to the door, and my eyes widened as Fox stumbled inside, a grimace on his face. He looked disheveled, his suit rumpled and his hair sticking up in places.

I slid off the bed and was halfway to him when the sight of the blood on his hands and face drew me up short. "Jesus! What happened?"

He held up a hand. "Nothing to make a big deal out of."

"Seriously." I gestured at his cheek, a maroon smear across his swarthy flesh. What the hell happened?"

Following my gaze, he grimaced again and gingerly touched his side. "Need you to clean me up."

"What?" My gaze drifted lower, to the parted fabric of his suit jacket, and my eyes widened at the sight of dark stains smeared over his blue dress shirt. "Oh, my God, you're hurt! We need to get you to the hospital!"

He waved off my concern. "I'll be fine."

I started to rush forward, then stopped myself. My emotions ping-ponged all over the place. My initial fear that he was mortally wounded disappeared, and I glared at him. "Where the hell is Dr. Marlowe? Call him."

Fox shook his head. "He's tied up taking care of someone else right now."

One of his men? Never mind. I told myself I didn't care as I shook my head. "If it's no big deal, then you can take care of the damn thing. You got yourself into this mess."

Whatever he'd done, the idiot had probably deserved it. I wasn't stupid enough to ask, and he didn't offer any details. His eyes darkened as he approached and gingerly took a seat on the edge of the mattress. "It's just a flesh wound."

Vacillating between worry and anger, I allowed the anger to take over. "Just a flesh wound? Really? I'm sure if you just slap a Band-Aid over it, it'll go away all on its own."

He scowled at me. "Don't be dramatic."

"Dramatic? You haven't begun to see dramatic." I crossed my arms over my chest, appalled by his stubbornness. I was annoyed that I was actually concerned over this man. I should be glad he was hurt; he'd brought this on himself. But the sight of the dark blood staining his shirt… I swallowed down my concern and gestured toward his wound. "I'm not touching that thing. Do it yourself."

"I would, but I can't reach it."

"Well, that's too bad, because—"

"Eva!" I jumped as he barked out my name, his dark eyes pinning me with a glare.

I forced the words out, my throat thick. "I can't."

"Do you not like the sight of blood?"

"It's not that. I just…" *Don't like the sight of blood on you.*

"Come here, angel."

Despite me shaking my head at his request, my feet drew me forward of their own volition. Fox took my hand in his. "I need you to do this for me, Eva. I can't do it on my own."

"You need a doctor—"

"No." He shook his head, his fingers tightening on mine. "No doctors, Eva. Just you and me."

"What about one of your men?" I asked desperately, trying to pull my hand away. "I'll go get Rodrigo or—"

"I want you." Dark eyes stared up at me. "I need you. Please."

My resolved shattered at the sound of that word slipping off his tongue. My hands shook, but I slid them inside his suit jacket, then carefully pushed it over his shoulders and stripped his arms free of the sleeves. His dress shirt was saturated with blood along his right side, and I carefully unbuttoned it and peeled it away so I could see better.

That was a mistake. The fabric of the shirt stuck to the wound, and several fibers were lodged in the torn flesh. The sight made me sick, and I shook my head as bile rose into my throat. "Oh, God." I shook my head again. "No way. I can't—I'm not—"

"You can do this."

"You need a doctor!" I heard the hysteria in my voice, but I couldn't control it.

"Eva." His tone was commanding yet gently. "Get the medical kit from under the sink."

"But I don't know what I'm doing! I can't—"

"Eva." He grabbed my chin and directed my gaze to his. "I'm fine. And you can do this."

I swallowed hard. "I don't want to hurt you." My admission came out on a whisper.

"Never." He shook his head. "I promise, angel. It's not as bad as it looks. Once you get it cleaned up, you'll see."

I seriously doubted that. Our gazes met and held for several seconds before I finally nodded reluctantly. "Okay."

I hurried to the bathroom and dug out the medical kit stored under the cabinet. By the time I got back to the bedroom, Fox was struggling to get the shirt off. His face was pulled into a grimace, and I hurried forward.

I set one hand on his shoulder. "Don't do that. I'll cut it off."

Digging through the kit, I found a pair of bandage scissors and sliced quickly through the fabric, allowing it to fall to the floor at our feet. With a trembling hand, I gently touched the skin near the wound. It was red and angry, definitely worse than anything I'd ever seen. The ragged edges of skin and tissue swam before my eyes, and I swayed on my feet.

"Eva." I lifted my gaze to Fox and found him watching me. He steadied me with his hands on my hips. "I trust you. You can do this."

I drew in a deep breath, trying to gather myself. He trusted me to do this for him. I had to do it. Finally, I gave a little nod. "Tell me what to do."

He gestured to the wound. "I need you to flush it, try to get the fibers out if you can."

I nodded slowly and licked my lips. "Maybe we should move into the bathroom so we won't make such a mess."

Fox stood and headed into the bathroom, then settled on the edge of the tub. He controlled his reactions, holding back any grunts of pain as I carefully cleaned and disinfected his wound. His knuckles were white where they gripped the bathtub, and I knew it had to hurt like a bitch. "I'm sorry."

"Don't be sorry," he said, his voice rough. "You're doing great."

"What's next?"

"Can you sew?"

My eyes widened, flying to his. "Is that a joke?"

"Never mind. There are some steri-strips in there. I need you to try to pull the edges of the wound as close together as you can."

I applied antibiotic ointment, then found the tiny fabric tape strips and placed them over the gaping flesh to close it up. Once I was done, I pressed a bandage over top to keep anything else from getting inside. I pulled one last strip of tape from the roll and laid it over the edge of the gauze square to keep it in place. My hands still shook as I replaced it in the kit.

"All done." I turned my attention to the medical kit and began to put everything away. "You can go now."

"Eva?"

"Yeah?" I kept my head down, unable to look at him just yet. Everything was still too fresh, my emotions too jumbled.

"You know, you're even mouthier when you're worried."

Despite myself, I let out a startled laugh. One huge hand moved to my face, turning me so I had no choice but to face him. Fox studied me, his thumb sliding over my bottom lip. "Thank you."

I met his dark eyes and nodded. "You're welcome."

He leaned in and kissed me lightly. "I'm beginning to think you really are my guardian angel."

CHAPTER
Twenty-Eight

FOX

"Boss?"

I lifted my head at the sound of Xavier's voice and leaned back in the chair. "Yes?"

"I had my friend in France check into Sebastian."

Ah, this should be good. "And what did he have to say? I hope the fucker lost a portion of that trust fund he's been living off of."

"Actually, there's no record that he was ever in France."

I lifted a brow. I wasn't surprised that he'd lied to Marcella, but why lie about going to Monte Carlo? It wasn't like she would have argued with him regardless. "And what was our good friend up to?"

"I'm not sure, exactly." Xavier gave a little shake of his head. "I checked with the pilot at the airfield where he normally flies from. According to the flight logs, Sebastian hasn't been logged as a passenger for the past six weeks."

Interesting. "I want eyes on him. Let me know what you find out."

"Yes, sir." He nodded. "Your guest is ready and waiting in the back room."

A wry smile curved my face as I rose from my chair. "Thank you. I suppose I shouldn't keep my *guest* waiting."

Leaving Xavier to track down Sebastian's whereabouts and recent activity, I headed out of my office. Soft notes of music filled the hall as I made my way into Noir's back room, a place reserved for friends—and the occasional enemy. My eyes landed on the man bound to the chair as soon as I stepped inside and closed the door behind me. Hopefully, my visitor would be able to shed some light on who was behind the shipment we'd intercepted last week.

I nodded to Rodrigo, who pulled the hood from the man's face. Clear blue eyes stared up at me, full of hate. A thin rivulet of blood ran from his split eyebrow into his eye, crusting the dark lashes. I took a step forward, closing the distance between us and forcing him to look up at me.

"You must be Grigori." His eyes narrowed but he remained silent. "I'll take that as a yes. I met an acquaintance of yours recently. Paul Holdren. Ring any bells?"

Something flickered in the depths of his eyes, but he lifted a shoulder in a show of indifference. "Dunno. I know lots of people."

"I'll bet you do." I smirked. "You were expecting a shipment a couple days ago, weren't you?"

Grigori blinked rapidly, belying his calm façade. "Maybe."

"I believe you know exactly what I'm talking about." I leaned close to him. "I'm curious, though. Why would a low level associate of the Bratva do this? It wasn't sanctioned by Nikolai. So why risk it?"

The man glared up at me, and his left eye twitched. "I have my reasons."

"I'm sure," I said smoothly. "Money? Blackmail?"

"Does it matter?"

"Depends on who you ask. Do you suppose it mattered to the children stolen from their families and transported halfway across the world to be sold off to the highest bidder?"

Grigori flinched, but I continued. "You know what happens to children like that, don't you? Do you enjoy using them, too? Do you like—"

"No!" The word burst through his lips. "I was just responsible for arranging transport. I don't know anything about what was inside."

I gauged his response. "Who were the men you hired?"

He shrugged. "Just a few street thugs willing to work for easy money."

"Mhmm... And who contracted this out?"

"I don't know."

"I'm afraid that won't work for me."

I stepped back and allowed Rodrigo to take over. Those lifeless eyes of his terrified people, and I knew I wouldn't have to wait long. Rodrigo landed a hard right hook before Grigori had a chance to blink. His head snapped back, and Rodrigo followed with a jab upward. The sound of his teeth gnashing together echoed in the small room, and blood trickled from the corner of his mouth. Rodrigo bent and pulled a K-Bar from his boot then, with a quick, precise, movement, sliced across the man's forearm. Blood welled and dripped to the floor in thick, heavy drops.

"Stop! Stop! Jesus!" Grigori made a choking sound and spat a dark splatter of blood to the floor. "I don't know! I swear!"

"I need a name," I said, infusing my voice with regret. "Otherwise..."

"I don't have a name—"

"Well, then—"

"Wait!" His chest heaved. "I did a little bit of digging before I took the job. I came across a specific word a few times, that's all I know."

"A word?" I lifted a brow. "And how the hell is that supposed to help me?"

His eyes bored into mine. "Could be a name or a place. Something. I don't have the resources to check and whatever it is, it's heavily guarded."

"And what is this word?"

"Araña."

I blinked. "What the fuck is an araña?"

"Spider." Rodrigo's voice floated over my shoulder, and I threw him a questioning glance. "It means spider in Spanish."

Like a spider weaving his web, trapping a bevy of unfortunate souls within. How fucking appropriate.

"Now we're getting somewhere," I murmured as I turned back to Grigori. "Sounds like a person. You've never been in contact with this... Araña? You know nothing about him?"

Grigori shook his head. "No. And no one else I know has, either."

"You've been asking about him?" Fucking moron. "That's an easy way to get killed."

He lifted one shoulder. "Honor among thieves and all that."

Better him than me. "I want you to find out everything you can, including where these last two shipments were transported."

He knew better than to argue. Grigori gave a solemn nod, and I gestured for Rodrigo to release him. Eva was waiting for me at home, and I had other—much better—things to do tonight.

CHAPTER
Twenty-Nine

EVA

Fox slipped from the bed, gently extricating his arm from where it was tucked beneath my pillow. He was always an early riser, and as I blinked my eyes open, I realized the sun was barely over the horizon, only the dimmest rays of light filtering through the windows.

I yawned and rolled to my back as I listened to the faucet turn on in the bathroom. For a brief moment, I considered trying to go back to sleep, but it was useless. Instead I lay there, the sheets still warm from his body heat.

I had a feeling that Fox was still uncomfortable sharing the bed with someone, so I was always cautious to give him plenty of space each night as we fell asleep. His presence calmed me, reassured me, and I was oddly reluctant to go back to my own room. Although we began each night on our own sides of the bed, somehow we both ended up gravitating toward the other. I wasn't sure who moved first, only that by early morning we were entwined together like two vines.

I loved the feel of him next to me, the way his arm draped heavily over my waist. I stirred every time he touched me, acutely attuned to his movements. It was as if I didn't want to miss a single moment with him. How much longer would this last? Just the thought made my heart clench as I threw the covers aside and rolled from the bed.

Stooping to pick up the long-sleeved button-up shirt that Fox had discarded last night before falling into bed, I shrugged it on, then padded toward the bathroom. Fox stood at the vanity shaving, and I met his eyes in the mirror as I entered.

"Sleep well, angel?"

I bobbed my head sleepily, covering my yawn with one hand as I moved behind him and took a seat on the edge of the large soaker tub.

A smile flitted across his face before he turned his attention back to his reflection. I watched as he meticulously shaved away the growth of whiskers from the day before. My gaze roved over his back, clad in a pristine white undershirt. I could just barely make out the outline of the bandage adorning his side through the tight material. Just over twenty-four hours ago, I'd stood in this very spot, piecing him back together.

Before I even thought about what I was doing, I was on my feet and moving toward him. His brows lifted as I leaned one hip against the vanity and studied him in the mirror. "How are you feeling?"

Unwilling to break our gaze, I heard the soft click of the razor as he set it on the marble countertop, then turned to face me. "Fine."

I nodded, not really believing him. He had to be in an incredible amount of pain. "Do you need painkillers or anything?"

A tiny smile, almost condescending, touched his mouth as he stared down at me. "It's nothing I can't handle."

Stubborn man. Frustrated but unable to walk away just yet, my eyes swept over his face. White foam still clung to his jaw, and my fingers itched to touch him. "You missed a spot."

"Are you offering to shave me?"

I lifted one shoulder even as my heart raced at the thought of carrying out the intimate act.

The corner of his mouth kicked up. "You think I'll let you near my throat with a razor?"

After everything that had happened recently, the words stung. I was good enough to fuck, good enough to patch him up when he needed help, but he would never truly accept my presence. Forcing down the emotion, I rolled my eyes and started to turn away.

A warm hand caught my arm, stopping me. "Eva."

Silently, I turned my head just enough to meet his gaze in the mirror. I watched as he picked up the razor and extended it to me. My eyes dropped to the implement before meeting his intense stare again. Finally, I slipped it from his grasp, butterflies kicking up in my chest as I moved in front of him. His hands moved to my hips, pulling me close, and I cautiously lifted the razor and cut away the remaining whiskers. When I was done, I set it on the sink and lifted my gaze to his.

"Thank you."

"You're welcome."

His eyes dropped to my mouth, and I found myself stretching up on my toes to meet him halfway as he dipped his head and kissed me. He tasted of mint, and the sensual scent of the shaving cream still clung to his skin, filling my nostrils. One hand moved to my face, slipping into the unruly tresses of my hair and tipping me slightly to the side.

I melted against him, momentarily allowing my insecurities to fade into the background as the world narrowed to just him and me. His arm tightened around my waist as if he never wanted to let me go, and I slid my hands upward, curving my arms around his neck, holding him close. He stiffened briefly, then immediately relaxed into my embrace.

After a minute, he pulled back and leaned his forehead against mine. "I'll be late again," he said apologetically.

I tried to hide my disappointment behind a forced smile. "That's fine."

"If you ever want or need anything, angel, don't hesitate to ask."

I nodded in agreement, and he kissed me once more before pulling away. I watched him finish his morning routine, a strange ache in my chest. I'd hated this man upon first coming here. So why was it that I only wanted him more with every day that passed?

I hardly remembered my old life at all. It all seemed so… pale compared to Fox. He'd opened my eyes to a need deep inside myself I never knew existed. He was nothing like I imagined, and I found myself wondering how I would ever go on without him—or why I would ever want to.

The remainder of the day passed slowly, and by late that evening I found myself in front of the fireplace in the den, watching the flames dance and writhe behind the grate. The soft scuffle of shoes against carpet made my ears perk up, and I felt Fox before he rounded the couch.

"I'm surprised you're still awake."

I lifted one shoulder as I stared up at him. "I couldn't sleep."

He gave a little half nod, looking lost in thought. "Not tired?"

"Not really." I watched as he turned toward the fireplace, his gaze faraway.

He was so damn handsome. Dark and mysterious, compelling beyond reason, he was everything I never knew I wanted. The sound of his voice startled me when he spoke.

"Do you play chess?"

It took my mind a moment to catch up. "I've never tried."

Those dark eyes met mine. "Would you like to?"

I felt like it was a test of sorts, though I wasn't sure why. "Sure."

Something flickered across his expression then was gone a moment later as he pushed to his feet and held out a hand. Slipping my palm into his, I allowed him to pull me to my feet and guide me to a small table in the corner. I'd seen the chess set before but had no particular interest in it before this moment.

I took a seat in one chair as Fox began to arrange the carved pieces on the board, naming each as he went and explaining their moves.

"The object of the game, as you're probably aware, is to capture your opponent's king," he said as he placed the king in the middle of the back row then picked up the remaining figure. "But the queen is the most valuable, powerful piece on the board. She can move any number of spaces in any direction."

"Okay." I watched intently, memorizing each game piece's capabilities. Fox started off, and the first few moves were uneventful as Fox talked through different scenarios. As I began to grow a little more confident, he became more aggressive. Half an hour later, we were each down several pieces—as Fox, I was sure, had allowed me to win some of his —and I was currently preoccupied with chasing his king around the board.

Suddenly, his bishop came from the side and captured my queen that I'd left unguarded. "Damn!"

Fox smiled. "You were so focused on trying to get to my king that you missed my last two moves."

I sat back in my seat, disgruntled. "I'm new to this. You're supposed to take it easy on me."

The look he threw my way was full of some unnamed emotion. "How will you ever get better if you're not pushed?" Before I could even begin to come up with a response to that, he continued. "Besides, angel, I've seen that devious mind of yours. I know better than to underestimate you."

Flattered by his backhanded compliment and not really paying attention, I moved my remaining bishop forward.

Fox tsked and shook his head as his rook moved into alignment with my knight. "Check. You left yourself wide open for that."

I couldn't even begin to care. Being with him like this had stirred something deep inside, something that refused to be quieted, and I grew more and more anxious as the seconds ticked by. A few moves later, he tipped over my king. "Checkmate, angel."

"Finally." Fox's arms came around me as I pushed from my seat and clambered onto his lap, careful to avoid his injured side.

His lips brushed over mine. "Is this my reward for winning?"

Not bothering to respond, I fell headlong into the kiss, forgetting everyone and everything but him.

CHAPTER
Thirty

FOX

My men crowded my desk, poring over a map and several pages of correspondence that we'd been able to obtain. The sun had descended hours ago, and though it was pitch black outside we continued to toil away to disentangle the convoluted riddles. Even so, I found my thoughts drifting to Eva, wondering what she was doing this very minute.

Over the past week, she'd begun to open up more and more, seeking me out during the day, joining me for lunch or taking up residence in the sitting room near my office in what I hoped was a gesture designed to be closer to me. We'd played chess several times since the other night as well, and each day her strategies became stronger, more complex. I smiled at the memory of the game of strip chess I'd challenged to her to, but had gone unfinished as lust took over and the game was forgotten. My side still bothered me, but the twinge of pain was nothing compared to the sheer bliss I felt when I was with Eva.

As if my thoughts had conjured her, a soft knock came from my office door. "Come in."

The door swung open, and Eva peeked inside. As soon as she saw my men clustered around me, her cheeks pinkened, and she began to retreat. "I'm sorry, I—"

I waved away her apology. "Did you need something?"

She shook her head. "No, I... I just thought you might want to break for dinner."

I flicked a glance at the clock over the mantle, which showed it was now after nine o'clock. As if the word dinner had triggered the reaction within my body, my stomach growled. I stood and gestured to my men. "We'll pick this up tomorrow."

Rodrigo met my gaze and held it for a moment before setting down the paper in his hands. I knew he was concerned about Eva reading the information, and I gave a slight shake of my head. My office was locked anytime I wasn't physically inside, so there was nothing to worry about. His lips pressed into a thin line, but he dipped his head and made his way out of the room. Eva moved aside as he left, keeping a healthy distance between them. Her eyes followed him cautiously, like she expected him to lunge at her. It wasn't the first time I'd noticed her discomfort around him, but she had nothing to worry about. She was no longer under scrutiny from my men; she was just as much a part of this household as they were.

I maneuvered around my desk and approached her. "Have you eaten?"

"Not yet." Her pale locks slipped over her shoulder as she shook her head. "I thought I'd wait for you. If you want company," she added hastily.

"Of course." I placed one hand on her lower back and steered her out of my office, then locked up behind me before guiding her to the kitchen.

"Carmen made lasagna earlier," she said. "I put it in the oven to heat up, so it should be just about ready."

"Sounds good." I gathered plates and utensils while she checked the pasta and pulled a steaming tray from the oven.

While I served the lasagna, Eva cut thick slices of Italian bread from a fresh loaf and slathered them with butter. I carried the plates to the smaller table situated in the breakfast nook, and she followed, carrying a glass of ice water for herself and an IPA for me.

"Thank you." I accepted the bottle as she held it out to me, then cracked the top and took a long drink. It'd been a hell of a day, and a migraine pulsed just behind my eyes from staring at the unintelligible code-riddled messages.

Eva slid into the seat across from me, and I found my gaze drawn to her as she picked up her fork and dug into her food. Every move she made seemed utterly fascinating, from the way she sat in her seat, spine perfectly straight, to the way she slipped the tines of the fork into her mouth and delicately transferred the food onto her tongue. Though she'd been with me for nearly a month and a half, I realized I hadn't learned much about her. Even more surprising than that was the fact that I actually wanted to.

"Tell me something, Eva." She lifted her brows as if waiting for me to continue, and I smiled a little. "Tell me anything."

Confusion was written plainly on her face as she spoke. "Like what?"

"I don't know." I rested my elbow on the table as I studied her. "What do you like? What do you dislike?"

Instead of easing, her expression became even more turbulent. "Why?"

Why, indeed? "I know nothing about you, Eva. A background check can only tell me so much about a person. I know everything about you—except who you are."

She gave a tentative nod, her teeth sinking into her lower lip. "I like to read."

I knew that, of course. She spent a majority of her day

reading in one of the sitting rooms or walking the garden when the sun was out. "What else?"

"I love music—it doesn't matter what it is, I'll listen to it. I like the way it makes me feel." I smiled as she continued. "But I hate to dance. My mother insisted we both be trained when we were young. I resisted, but Elle…" She stumbled over her sister's name but quickly recovered. "Elle always did what my parents demanded, no questions asked. She was an amazing dancer."

Her eyes had taken on a sad quality when she'd spoken of her sister, and I found myself wanting to lift that expression from her face. "I'm not much of a dancer either, not if you want to end the night with your feet intact."

She smiled a little at that, and I pressed further. "What else?"

"I…" She searched for something else. "I prefer to read, but I do love a good movie occasionally."

"What genre?"

"Thriller. Suspense."

I should have guessed. My angel had a quick and agile mind; of course she would prefer a complex plot that kept her guessing and analyzing. "We could watch a movie later, if you'd like."

Her gaze snapped to mine. "I—That sounds nice."

After we finished our meals, I slipped my arm around her waist and showed her to the media room at the opposite end of the house. She looked around curiously, and I smiled as I picked up a remote from a cabinet built into the wall. "Have you been in here before?"

"I've seen it, but I've never really spent much time in here," she said as her gaze swept over the dark walls and stadium seating arranged over the sloped floor, identical to a movie theater.

Most everything was concealed, from the speakers in the ceiling to the screen that began to lower as I pressed a button on the remote. Her eyes widened. "That thing is huge!"

I laughed. "If we're going to watch a movie, we're going to do it properly."

I allowed Eva to choose a movie to stream, and we settled into the soft leather recliners side by side. Slipping one arm around her shoulders, I pulled her close and rested my chin on the top of her head as she snuggled into my uninjured side.

Throughout the movie, I found myself focusing more and more on the woman in my arms. In and out of bed, I wanted more of Eva—a lot more.

CHAPTER
Thirty-One

EVA

My heart thundered in my chest, and I drew in a sharp breath as I peeked around the corner. For once, Fox's men weren't hanging around outside his office, and I darted across the hall before opening the heavy wooden door and slipping inside.

I'd never sought him out like this before, and I wasn't sure how he would react. It'd been twelve days since he'd shown up with that wound, and he seemed more and more on edge with each passing day.

Fox's head snapped up, and his hard expression melted away as soon as his eyes met mine. He pushed his chair backward as I rounded the desk. Eyes locked in his, I slid backward onto the hard surface and spread my knees wide. His eyes darkened with desire as they dropped to my exposed pussy, revealed by the dress I inched up my thighs.

"Thought you could use a break. You seem tense."

"Angel, you have no idea."

He stood and moved between my legs, swiping his fingers through my drenched slit. I leaned forward, then yanked his shirt from his pants. I froze when he let out a little hiss. I tipped my face up to him just in time to see the flash of pain in his eyes, and I immediately released him. "What's wrong?"

"It's nothing." He reached for me, but I evaded his grasping fingers, and my gaze dropped to his midsection.

"Is it your side? Is it still bothering you?" I reached for the buttons of his shirt, but he brushed my hands away.

"I'm just sore. Nothing a couple painkillers won't fix."

I tried to pull my hands free of his, but he held tight. "Let me see," I snapped as I shook him off. With a resigned sigh, he allowed me to pull his shirt free and unfasten the buttons. The fabric parted, revealing swarthy dark skin stretched over tight abs, and I sucked in a breath as his wound came into view. It was an angry purplish-red, swollen and inflamed. "Oh my God! This looks terrible."

"It'll be fine," he replied, a trace of irritation in his tone.

"It's not fine! It looks infected." He growled as I gently probed around the wound, and I slid off the desk to get a better look at him, my expression concerned. "You need to have someone look at this. We should take you to the hospital."

"No." He gave a single, firm shake of his head.

"You have to do something," I snapped. "Have you seen how bad that looks?"

He let out a little grunt. "It'll be fine. I've had worse."

"Quit being stubborn." I wanted to stomp my foot but somehow managed to resist. "If you let that go much longer, it's going to make you sick."

He waved his hand dismissively. "It always looks worse before it gets better."

"Are you kidding me right now?" I stared up at him. "It's been nearly two weeks. If it hasn't started to heal yet, it's not going to."

He reached for me. "Angel—"

"No!" I backed away, holding my hands in front of me.

"Don't. I'm not touching you again until you get that taken care of."

His face darkened, and his hands fell to his sides. "Don't push me, Eva."

"Don't be stupid," I retorted. "You know very well what could happen if you keep ignoring the problem."

After a long minute of tense silence, he finally relented. "Fine. I'll have Dr. Marlowe come look at it. Will that make you feel better?"

"Yes," I said, relieved. It physically hurt me to see him in pain. I didn't want to admit that I was actually worried about him, because that dredged up all kinds of feelings I wasn't ready to address.

"Good," he replied. "Now that that's taken care of—"

"You haven't taken care of anything," I cut him off. "Go call the doctor."

He muttered something in another language, and I glared at him. "What was that? I couldn't understand you."

"I said you're a pain in my ass," he replied, his eyes snapping with fire.

"Yeah, well, I'm the pain in the ass who's going to make sure you don't drop dead from sepsis if that wound gets any worse."

The corner of his mouth kicked up in a tiny smirk. "Worried about me?"

"No," I scoffed. "I just don't understand why you have to be so damn stubborn all the time."

"You're worrying over nothing. Silly woman."

I whirled toward him with a low growl. "I swear, sometimes I just want to smack you."

"You would never lift a hand to me," he replied haughtily.

It was true, but that didn't mean I wasn't damn tempted. "Only because your skull is too damn thick to beat any sense into it."

He grinned. "Have I told you how much I enjoy it when

you get all fired up? Makes me want to take a belt to that pretty ass then fuck you till you can't think straight."

The thought of him taking me exactly as he said sent little tingles of anticipation through my body. "Yeah, well... You'll be denied that particular satisfaction until after you talk to the doctor."

"Oh, I'll speak with him all right. But you can be sure that I'll remember this once I'm all healed up."

I cocked my head as I stared up at him. "I guess we'll just have to see."

A smile flirted with the corners of his mouth. "That mouth, angel."

"I seem to recall you being quite fond of my mouth," I shot back challengingly.

"That I am." He stepped forward, closing the distance between us, and cupped my chin in one large hand. His thumb swept over my lower lip, and I parted my mouth when he pushed against the seam of my lips. His free hand moved to my hip, his strong fingers curling into my bottom and pulling me closer, careful to avoid his wound. His hardness pressed against my lower stomach, and I sucked his thumb into my mouth, curling my tongue around it before lightly biting down.

Fox growled. "I can't fucking wait to have you again."

I lifted my hands and settled them on his chest. "Doctor first," I reminded him. "You're no use to me broken."

His hand moved from my chin, slipping into my hair and grasping the back of my head. He squeezed my bottom so hard it almost hurt. "You better rest up and enjoy the next couple days, because as soon as I'm better, you won't be leaving our bed for a week."

Our bed? I smiled at how much things had changed over the past month. Fox wouldn't appreciate me bringing it up, and I wasn't about to lose the ground I'd gained with him, so I kept the thought to myself. "Promises, promises."

He shifted to pull me closer but he sucked in a breath through his teeth when his side bumped my arm. I gently pushed him away. "No more putting it off. Make the call."

I crossed the room, and Fox threw me a disgruntled look as he dialed. "Just because I can't fuck you doesn't mean blow jobs are out of the question," he reminded me.

I laughed at his hopeful expression. "Be good for the doctor and I'll see what I can do."

CHAPTER
Thirty-Two

FOX

Marlowe stepped into the office and speared me with a look. "Three visits in the past couple of months?"

"It was actually my request to bring you here."

Marlowe's head swiveled at the sound of Eva's voice. His face relaxed when he saw her sitting in the corner, and a genuine smile graced his face as he turned toward her. "Ms. Jennings. How are you feeling?"

"Fine, thank you." She stood and smiled as she crossed the room to stand next to us.

Dr. Marlowe studied her. "Anything bothering you? If the painkillers aren't working, I can write a script for something else."

"Oh, no." She waved away his offer. "Nothing for me this time. I was hoping you could take a look at him."

Marlowe's brow rose, amusement twinkling in his eyes as he turned toward me. "Is that so?"

I stifled the urge to slap that look off his face. No doubt he was baffled by the way Eva was speaking up for me—and, even more so, why I let her. "An old wound is bothering me,"

I said by way of reply. "I'm sure it's nothing, but she insisted you take a look."

Beside me, Eva glared at me before turning to Dr. Marlowe again. "It looks bad. I cleaned it initially, but I'm afraid I did something wrong. It's all red, and it's been bothering him."

"How long?"

"Excuse me," I said, irritation evident in my tone. "I'm right here."

"I just noticed today," Eva said as if I hadn't spoken, "but the wound was from approximately two weeks ago. Right?"

She turned to me, and I blinked at her. "Am I allowed to speak now?"

"Only if you cooperate," she quipped before turning back to the doctor. "I would feel better if you took a look."

"Of course," Dr. Marlowe said. He slid a look my way and gestured for me to remove my shirt. "Would you mind?"

"Of course I mind," I muttered under my breath. "But it seems I don't have a choice."

"No, you don't," Eva replied smugly.

I caught her eyes as I unbuttoned my dress shirt, then peeled it over my shoulders and down my arms. My movements were slow, deliberate, and the look I shot her was full of retribution. She would get her way this time. Later, I would get exactly what I wanted—her.

Dr. Marlowe set his bag on the desk and was busy pulling on a pair of gloves as I peeled the edges of my shirt back to expose the wound. His gaze automatically followed my movements to the angry slash along my side before jumping up to meet my eyes. I held his stare for a long moment, communicating that he was to keep quiet. Finally, he gave a slight nod and returned to his tools.

"Is it infected?" Eva's face was twisted into an anxious expression of dismay, and my chest tightened at the sight.

Marlowe offered a reassuring smile. "Nothing we can't

fix," he said. "If you don't mind, however, I need a moment alone with Fox."

"Why?" Her green eyes darkened with worry. "Is... Is everything okay?"

"Of course," Marlowe said, his voice low and soothing. "Standard procedure. I'll only need him for a minute. You can wait right outside until we're ready for you to come back in."

His words seemed to reassure her, but she darted a look my way, and I nodded. "Give us two minutes, angel."

She nodded and began to retreat, throwing one last look over her shoulder at us before disappearing into the hall and closing the door behind her.

Once she was gone, Marlowe looked over at me. "You should have called me as soon as this happened."

"Didn't want to bother you. Besides, you were already busy with—" I grimaced as he pressed his fingers to the skin around the wound. "Fuck, that hurt."

"You have a massive infection," he said baldly. "It's really in your best interest to go to the hospital. We'll need to check for sepsis and—"

"No hospitals, you know that."

"We need to make sure the infection hasn't entered your blood stream."

"Then do it," I said. "But no hospitals."

"We need to get this wound opened back up and properly cleaned." He leaned closer, inspecting the red, swollen flesh.

"Just fix it," I said through gritted teeth. "But don't say a fucking word to Eva."

He eyed me, then nodded knowingly. "I understand. I'll need you to get comfortable." He stepped away and withdrew a hypodermic needle from his bag, along with a vial of local anesthesia. "I'll numb the area now and let it start to work. Then we'll reconvene to one of the bedrooms."

I turned my attention out the window while Dr. Marlowe set to work. Several minutes had elapsed, and I imagined Eva pacing the hallway outside. The thought brought a small smile to my face. Deep beneath that tough, prickly exterior of hers was a giant, soft heart. Just as quickly, my smile slipped away. That would be her downfall. She shouldn't be with a man like me; she was too good.

As if reading my mind, Dr. Marlowe spoke up. "She cares about you."

I cleared my throat. "She's worried the wound is infected."

"It is," Marlowe said succinctly. "But we both know that's not what I meant."

Still staring out the window, I didn't say a word. She was attracted to me, and I to her. But feelings beyond that? I had no idea. She had no reason to care for me. I was responsible for her sister's disappearance, and she'd been my captive for the past two months. She was dealing the best she could, adapting to the situation. It was nothing more than a case of Stockholm syndrome, as much as I detested it. I wanted her to be here because she wanted to be with me.

If we'd met on the street, would she have looked at me twice? I seriously doubted it. From the moment she'd woken up she'd been at my mercy. I'd stripped her of control, molded her into what I desired. She was my angel—but she would never truly belong to me. And I fucking hated it.

"Take care of her."

I turned to Marlowe and met his hazy blue eyes. "Always."

He gave a perfunctory nod and tipped his head toward the door. "Let's go before she storms in to make sure you're not dead."

I smiled. Seemed the good doctor had a pretty good feel for my angel after all. "I wouldn't put it past her."

"Good women like that are hard to find and even harder to hold on to."

He had no idea. I stood and preceded him from the office.

Eva stood across the hallway, one arm wrapped around her middle, the other hand resting at the base of her throat like she was nervous. The moment the door swung open, she pushed away from her spot on the wall.

"Are you okay? How is it?"

"Just fine," Marlowe assured her for what felt like the dozenth time. "We'll need to move to a bedroom where I can have a little more room to work."

Eva's gaze jumped to mine, and I easily read the wariness there. To head her off, I explained, "I reopened the wound, so Dr. Marlowe has to clean it up again, then stitch me back up."

She stared at me like she didn't believe me, but I refused to say anything more. It was my choice to have her take care of the wound; I wouldn't let her feel guilty for the job she'd done. Finally, she nodded and fell into step next to us as I led the way up the stairs and down the hall. Eva shot me a glance from the corners of her eyes, and I gave a tiny shake of my head as we passed my room. No one entered my room except myself—and now Eva. That was our domain, meant for no one else.

I held the door and allowed Eva, then Marlowe, to precede me inside. The doctor moved immediately to the bed and began to arrange his tools while Eva moved to the far wall and leaned against it, arms crossed under her breasts, a tense expression on her face. Following Marlowe's directions to get comfortable, I settled on the bed and stretched out.

I hated that look on her face, that mixture of concern and guilt. "Come here, angel."

I held out my hand, feeling Marlowe's gaze on me the whole time. Eva reluctantly pushed off the wall and approached, moving to the side of the bed. She took my hand, and I gave a gentle tug. "Sit."

Gingerly, she sat on the edge of the mattress as far from me as possible. I quirked a brow. "Why so far away?"

Her brows drew together. "I don't want to hurt you or get in the way."

"Never," I said firmly. "Your place is next to me."

I turned to the doctor and caught a tiny smile gracing his lips as he listened to my exchange with Eva. "Ready?"

He held up a scalpel. "Whenever you are."

"Go for it."

I turned my eyes to the ceiling as he made his first incision into the layer of flesh that had grown over the wound, closing it up and trapping the infection inside. I couldn't feel a thing, but I heard Eva's soft gasp from beside me, and I squeezed her hand as I turned to face her. "Eyes on mine, angel. Don't look if you don't want to."

Her gaze darted to the wound before meeting my eyes again, and she squeezed my hand in return. I kept my eyes on her as Marlowe worked. After what felt like forever, his voice floated over my shoulder.

"All done." He set a bottle of antibiotics on the nightstand. "You need to take two of these every day—until they're gone," he clarified. "Not until you feel better. If you stop taking them, the infe—" He cut off immediately at my hard glare and amended his words. "They won't be as effective."

"Understood." I grimaced a little as I pushed to a sitting position, and Eva was immediately at my back, supporting me as I rebuttoned my shirt.

"Why don't you just lie down for awhile and rest?" One hand still resting on my shoulder, she looked at Dr. Marlowe. "Shouldn't he be resting?"

"He should be," the doctor acknowledged with a small smile. "Maybe you'll have better luck getting him to listen."

"He," I said as I pushed to my feet, "is right here. And there's no rest for the wicked."

Marlowe ignored me and turned to Eva. "Take care of him, Ms. Jennings."

"Call me Eva," she said. "And I'll make sure he's doing what he's supposed to."

I lifted a brow her way. "How do you plan to accomplish that?"

A secretive smile tipped her lips but she didn't say a word. "Thank you for coming," she said instead to Dr. Marlowe. "I'll show you to the door."

Looping an arm around her waist, I kept Eva glued to my side as we headed down the stairs toward the front door. Marlowe departed with a nod and a promise to check in with me next week, and I closed up behind him.

"So," I said, cupping Eva's chin in my hand and lifting her face to mine. "Feel better knowing I've been taken care of?"

Her eyes softened, and she leaned into me. "Very."

"Good." I dropped a kiss on her lips, then turned, tugging her along behind me. "Now come with me."

CHAPTER
Thirty-Three

EVA

I followed along as Fox propelled me down the hall, then practically dragged me into the living room. He closed the door behind us, then moved to the couch. I started to sit next to him, trying to give him space, but he grabbed my hand before I had the chance. My eyes widened as he pulled me down so I was draped over his lap.

"Fox!" I hissed. "What if your guys see?"

"So?"

I knew his men weren't ignorant of the situation, but we usually tried to keep any antics within our bedroom. Any show of affection or emotion could be viewed as a weakness, and I refused to be the cause of it. I squirmed, trying to climb to my feet, but he held fast.

"You know what," I said, my voice low.

"What I do is none of their business."

I dug my teeth into my lower lip. "But—"

"You're mine to do with as I please." A surge of anger shot through me at his harsh words, a constant reminder of exactly why I was here. So much for hoping he'd begun to see me differently. Despite our time spent together each night, the subtle shift in his demeanor, he was still the same man he was months ago when I'd first arrived.

I leaned away with the intention of leaving for good this time, but he pulled me back, dropping his mouth close to my ear. "And what I want is to have you here… just like this."

I froze as his low-spoken words caressed my ear, a warmth seeping into my bones as I turned to look at him. I didn't say a word, just stared at him, and he stared right back. Finally, he lifted one hand and cupped my face, drawing me to him. My eyes closed as his lips swept over mine, gentle and sweet. It lasted only a moment before he broke the connection.

A warm glow surrounded my heart, and a contentment settled over me. Things had changed so much over the past several weeks. He'd held me captive, yet here I was willingly giving myself to him. As unconventional as our situation was, I wouldn't trade it. There was more to him than met the eye, I was sure of it. What I didn't know was whether he would ever truly let me in enough to find out who he was deep inside. I wanted Fox—and I wanted him to want me in return.

I swallowed hard, terrified he'd read every emotion on my face. "How are those stitches feeling?"

He coasted his fingers over my knee and up my thigh. "Good enough."

I shifted in his lap, trying to evade his questing fingers, but he took advantage of my position and he moved upward to the apex of my thighs. One long finger dipped low, brushing my folds, and I slammed my legs together.

"Seriously." I laid one hand on his chest and tried to steer him back to the conversation at hand. "That wound looked bad. Are you still in pain?"

He laughed a little. "Between the antibiotics and the anesthetic, Marlowe gave me so much medicine I won't feel anything for days."

I rolled my eyes. "That's an improvement, at least."

"Mhmm…"

The finger between my legs moved, still searching for my center. I bit my lip and arched a little as he pressed on the bundle of nerves. Unable to stand it any longer, I reached between my legs and pulled his hand away.

Fox grinned, well aware that he'd gotten to me. "Didn't we have a deal of sorts? I agree to see Marlowe and you provide a… service for me?"

He lifted his eyebrows, and I fought to hold back my smile. "I don't recall a specific timeframe for said service."

He growled a little and shifted me in his lap. His erection pressed up into my bottom, a hard ridge pressing against the fly of his slacks. "No time like the present."

"Perhaps." I lifted one shoulder and slid from his lap, evading his clasping hands. "When you're done, come upstairs. I have a surprise for you."

"You know I don't like surprises, angel."

His tone was playful, and I smiled. "Maybe it's time to change that. Ten minutes."

His dark eyes smoldered with heat, and I couldn't help looking back at him as I left the room. My breath caught at the intense look he sent my way. The lust crackling in the air was tangible. I turned and hurried around the corner, taking the stairs at the back of the house up to the second floor.

Ducking into my room, I closed and locked the door behind me, then darted into the bathroom. I ran a brush through my hair and quickly fluffed it before brushing my teeth and spritzing on some of the perfume Fox had purchased for me.

Stripping out of my clothes, I dropped them into the hamper on my way by, then slipped through the door that connected Fox's room to my own. It smelled like him, and I stopped in my tracks, breathing deeply. It never got old. Even though I slept here every night, I never tired of feeling him around me. His presence permeated the space, and I reveled in it for a moment before forcing myself forward.

The door to the hallway remained closed, and I placed myself between it and the bed, dropping to my knees in the center of the floor so I would be the first thing he saw when he stepped inside. I'd shaved this morning so I was completely bare, open for his perusal. Spreading my knees wide, I carefully arranged my hair, allowing it to cascade down my back, leaving the view of my breasts unimpeded.

I hoped he would see it for exactly what it was. I'd fought him in the beginning, but somewhere along the line I'd begun to care for him. It scared the hell out of me, but I felt that, in his own way, he cared for me, too. I wanted to be with him, just not as his captive. I would gladly stay with him if he would only ask. My submission was my way of showing him, meeting him halfway.

Turning my palms upward, I dipped my head at the soft tread of footsteps moving in front of the door. A smile curved my mouth as the door swung inward. Part of me wished I could see his face, but the sudden stillness that fell over the room told me everything I needed to know.

I felt confident. Strong. It was strange. Although the position was submissive, it filled me with power. I loved the way Fox reacted to it, the weight of his gaze a firm caress over my bare flesh. With barely a look he ignited a fire within me, but I knew I did the same for him.

Even out of the bedroom I felt less timid. Never before would I have propositioned him in the middle of the day. It wasn't merely that I was growing more comfortable with him each day. It was… I couldn't quite describe it. It was as if, by giving myself up to him this way, I'd been conditioned to take exactly what I wanted. And all I wanted was him.

CHAPTER
Thirty-Four

FOX

I watched Eva go, a strange sensation tightening my chest. Several seconds later, Rodrigo appeared in the doorway, as if he'd been hovering just outside. He cleared his throat, and I threw a look his way. "Any updates on who contracted the shipment yet?"

"No, sir." He shook his head. "We've flushed out the warehouse Grigori told us about, but they weren't able to tell us anything of value."

Past tense. Glad they'd been disposed of, I nodded and slowly pushed to my feet. "Any update on the children?"

"Miranda's been able to track down parents of three of them so far." In addition to her work at Noir, the halfway house had been Miranda's responsibility for the past six years. A rescue herself, she'd taken it upon herself to save other victims of human trafficking.

We'd opened a house where they could be properly cared for until they were returned to their homes, and she used her computer skills to track down the children's parents and reunite them. In the cases of orphans, they were schooled and given new identities, giving them a new lease on life. One where they would be free and safe from harm.

Most of the children came from orphanages and had no family to speak of. Miranda worked tirelessly to find families for them here in the States, vetting each one personally and checking in periodically to ensure they were taken care of. In all the years we'd been doing this, we'd only had one instance where a child needed to be removed from the adoptive family. Miranda had taken care of it personally, and I was damned proud of her for being the survivor that she was and helping others. She knew what it was like to be in their position; while I did the dirty work of tracking down the transporters and handlers, watching over the children was her way of giving back. She was like a guardian angel to them.

Eva reminded me of Miranda. I wondered how she would react if I told her the truth behind my actions. One of these days soon I would tell her everything—when the time was right.

"Thank you."

"Sure thing, boss."

I felt like he wanted to say more, but I had other things to focus on at the moment. Pushing from the couch, I slapped a hand to Rodrigo's shoulder as I passed. "Thanks."

She'd asked for ten minutes, but I couldn't be away from her one more second. Still, I took the long way, winding my way through the lower floor of the house and ascending the main staircase to give her an extra moment to herself. I felt like some indefinable feeling was pulling me toward my destiny, and my heart raced at the thought. More and more, I'd begun to see Eva as my future. I wanted her around every moment of the day, wanted to listen to her speak about everything and nothing.

I paused for a moment, my hand resting on the doorknob to my room. A little thrill of anticipation zinged through my veins as I turned the handle and stepped inside. I froze midstep, my heart banging against my ribs as I took in the sight before me.

Eva knelt on the floor at the foot of the bed. Head dipped in submission, palms up, knees spread wide so I could see every inch of her, she literally took my breath away. I'd never seen anything so gorgeous. On the heels of that came another thought. This was a message—one I wouldn't take lightly. She was giving me exactly what I wanted, showing me that she was precisely what I needed. The fact that she was willing to do this for me hit me hard.

Realizing I was standing there like an idiot, I stepped inside and closed the door behind me. Still not fully in control of my body, I leaned back and rested against the cool wood for a moment, reveling in the perfection of the moment.

I couldn't tell for sure, but I thought I saw a tiny smile tilting the corners of Eva's lips, and I had to fight one of my own. There was something about seeing a woman so strong, with so much backbone, bending to a man's will. I never wanted her to lose her fiery independence, but I loved seeing her just like this—ready and waiting for me, and only me.

Pushing off the door, I approached slowly, a predator tracking his prey. I stopped just in front of Eva, the tips of my shoes barely brushing her knees, and I ran a hand over her silky hair. "So beautiful."

"Thank you, sir."

I could tell from her tone that she was pleased with herself, with the situation, and I smiled a little as I continued to stroke her hair. "I love seeing you on your knees for me. Is that pretty little pussy wet?"

Her lips rolled together before she spoke, low and raspy, her voice filled with desire. "Yes, sir."

I moved in a circle around her, trailing my fingers down the side of her face, over her shoulder and across her back. "You've been thinking about me?"

"Yes, sir."

I finished my circuit around her and slipped my fingers under her chin, guiding her gaze to mine. "What have you been thinking about?"

Her eyes met mine, the green of her irises dark with lust. "You. How you feel inside me."

"Is that what you want? Me inside you?"

"Yes, sir." She looked conflicted for a moment, knowing sex was off the table. It only heightened my arousal and anticipation.

I hummed a little sound as I swept my thumb over her lower lip. "I think you should show me how much you like my cock."

Her tongue darted out, sweeping along my thumb, and I pressed it further into her mouth. My cock throbbed, hardening to the point of pain as she suckled the tip of my thumb. With a low growl, I pulled it free and moved my hands to her hair.

"Take it out."

Not pretending to misunderstand, Eva's hands lifted to my belt buckle and pulled it free. Leaving the leather hanging loose, she popped the button of my fly and drew the zipper down with a soft hiss. Slipping her hand inside, she palmed the hard ridge of my erection, and I let out a soft sound of encouragement.

"That's it, angel. I want to feel your mouth wrapped around me."

My pants sagged, drooping down my hips, and she tugged them down, pulling my boxers with them. My arousal sprung free of its confines, and she immediately palmed it, her hot little hand encompassing my hard length. The pressure felt so fucking good, and I let out a sigh as I raked my fingers through her hair.

Her tongue darted out and licked the head of my cock, and my hips jerked forward of their own volition. Wrapping her fingers around the base, she stroked up and down, her lips and tongue teasing the tip. She fitted her mouth around me, taking me into the hot cavern of her mouth, and I let out a garbled groan.

She tightened her fingers around the base, her head bobbing up and down, taking me in as far as she could. Grasping the back of her head, I thrust hard. She gagged as a little as I bumped the back of her throat and tears leaked from the corners of her eyes as she stared up at me, but she kept going, allowing me to fuck her mouth.

"Ah, Christ." I was going to come if she kept it up. "Get on the bed, angel."

She pulled away, a strand of saliva stretching from my cock to her mouth, and the sight made me even harder. I reached down, swiping one thumb over her lips, breaking the thin strand and smearing it over her mouth.

I needed to lie down. Not that I would ever say a word to her, but I felt like I would pass out if I stayed on my feet any longer. Moving to the bed, I stretched out, and Eva moved between my legs. Eyes on me, she lifted a brow. "Lick up every drop."

A tiny smile teased her mouth, and she dipped her head, taking my dick to the back of her throat in one swift stroke. I fisted her hair in one hand, the comforter in the other, as she moved up and down, each pass of her slick tongue curling around me pushing me closer and closer to the edge.

Fire licked through my body, and my stomach muscles contracted under the strain. The stitches along my side pulled tight, and I gritted my teeth against the slight sting of pain. It fueled me, pushing me on, and I gave myself over to the pleasure.

I tightened my hold on her hair, shoving her down on my dick as my orgasm welled and finally released. Throwing my head back, I came on a growl, heat exploding over my skin as her mouth sucked me dry.

"Fucking Christ!"

My body was so drained I couldn't even watch her suck me off. But holy fuck it felt so goddamn good. Her lips continued to move up and down my length, her tongue swirling and sucking as she lapped up every drop. On sensation overload, I pulled her off me.

"Goddamn, woman." My breath heaved in and out of my lungs as I grasped her bicep and yanked her up beside me. "You're going to be the death of me."

Eva chuckled as her head hit the pillow next to mine, a satisfied smile curving her mouth. "As much as I'd like to take credit for that, I seriously doubt that's true."

Huffing out a little laugh at her teasing, I smacked her ass. She jumped, winding herself closer to me. I gently rolled her to her back and loomed over her. "Turnabout's fair play. My turn, angel."

CHAPTER
Thirty-Five

EVA

Dark eyes locked on mine, Fox maneuvered himself between my legs. His knees slipped beneath my thighs, spreading them further and lifting my hips so I was fully open to him. I watched him warily, afraid that he would overexert himself if we had sex. I opened my mouth to stop him, but he silenced me with a single smoldering glare.

He leaned forward, caging me in his arms. I lifted my head for a kiss, but he just quirked a sexy little smirk. Avoiding my mouth completely, he trailed his mouth along my jaw, then down my neck. I jumped as he bit the spot between my neck and shoulder, my hips jerking upward at the sensation of goosebumps exploding over my skin. Though he'd just come, his cock was still thick and hard, and the tip brushed my folds.

Leaving my throat, he kissed his way down my sternum. Plumping my left breast in one hand, he took the sensitive tip between his lips and sucked hard. My breath caught and pleasure shot straight to my core as his tongue swirled around before he gently bit down. I jumped again, and his cock slid right over the sensitive nub between my legs.

"Fox..." I raked my fingers over the short hairs at the back of his head, lifting my hips and grinding against him, but he just chuckled.

"Not yet, angel."

Kissing his way over to my other breast, he performed the same actions, making me senseless with need. He could turn me on with the slightest touch, and by the time he kissed his way down my stomach, his tongue leaving a wet trail along my skin, I was panting with desire.

"Please..." I pressed my head back into the pillow as his fingers slid teasingly over my folds.

"I love when you beg for me."

My next words were stolen as he thrust his fingers deep without warning. He plunged them in and out, fucking me hard with his hand. I grabbed the comforter and held on tight, my face contorting in ecstasy at the exquisite pleasure/pain. Though he filled me, it wasn't nearly enough. I wanted to beg him to fuck me hard, the way we both liked it. I bit down on my lip to keep the words from escaping, feeling like an asshole for even wanting it. Fox was hurt because of me. My thoughts drifted away, back to the office this afternoon. Although Dr. Marlowe and Fox had both tried to tell me otherwise, I read the truth in their eyes. I should have been more careful cleaning and caring for his wound. I should have—

I sucked in a sharp breath as Fox pulled his fingers free and slapped my pussy. "Ow!"

"You back with me?"

He lifted a brow, and I nodded as I bit my lip. "I was... thinking. Of earlier," I added. "I don't want to hurt you."

"I'm fine, angel." He leaned forward and kissed me on the lips. "Now, just lie back and relax."

Shimmying to his stomach in the middle of the bed, he

slid his hands under my thighs and dragged me forward until my knees were hooked over his shoulders. In this position, my pussy was mere inches from his face, and lust shot through me. He'd never gone down on me before, and I watched with anticipation as he dipped his head and licked up my slit.

His mouth was hot, and I let out a little sigh as he tongued my clit. He lapped at me, his tongue spearing deep inside. I clenched the muscles of my thighs in response, holding him close. A sharp hum of pleasure shot through me as he latched onto my clit. He sucked hard, and heat curled in my belly.

One long finger dipped inside, and my walls clenched around him, welcoming him in, never wanting to let him go. Wetness pooled in my core and leaked out of me. I could feel it sliding lower, between my ass cheeks, coating Fox's fingers as he plunged in and out. I was so hot I felt like I would burst into flames. I never felt more whole than I did when his hands were on me, touching me, bringing me pleasure.

He thrust in and out with short, slow strokes, igniting the fire in my core. His tongue swirled around my clit, dragging me closer and closer to the edge of orgasm. I hovered there on the precipice as he pulled his fingers away.

"You want to come?"

"Yes! Oh, God, yes!" I pled incoherently, every inch of me on fire for him. I pressed toward him, searching for release. God, I was so close. He bit the inside of my inner thigh, a warning.

"I want to hear you say it."

His fingers glided through my slick folds, and I ground against him, needing the relief that only he could give me. "Make me come, please!"

Oh, my God. "Oh..." The word bled into a low moan as a delicious burning sensation radiated through my belly.

"That's it, angel. Let go."

He nipped at my clit, and I clawed at the bedspread as the

sensation stole my breath. A second later he was back on me, sucking hard, pulling pleasure from me. Relentlessly, he ate me until I exploded, the graze of his short beard against my sensitive skin pushing me over the edge. I came on a scream, and I bit the back of my hand to stifle the sound. Completely at his mercy, my legs still draped over his shoulders, he licked and teased until my body was completely lax with desire.

"Holy shit," I managed to pant out through heaving lungs as he lowered me back to the bed. "That was…"

I trailed off, and Fox smiled. "I was hoping you would enjoy it."

It was strange. After the sex with Fox, I felt… stronger. More confident. Like he'd awakened something inside me. He'd broken me down, and now I was being rebuilt, better than before.

"So much." I curled into him when he lay down next to me. "I'd ask where you learned that, but I'm not sure I want to know."

His chest lifted slightly as he shrugged. "Beginner's luck."

My brows drew together as I tipped my head up to look at him. "What does that mean?"

Even in the waning evening light, I swore I saw a hint of red sweep over his cheeks. "I've never done that before."

"You've never…?" Seriously? The man who dominated me every way known to man had never gone down on a woman before? I studied him for a long minute, watching him tense like he was embarrassed or uncomfortable.

"Well," I said as I lay down again. "It was amazing. Thank you."

There was a moment of silence, then he dropped a kiss on the top of my head. "You're welcome."

We lay there in the quiet solitude, wrapped around each other, but my mind spun. Finally, I could hold back no longer. "Why me?"

"What do you mean?"

"Why was I your first. To… you know."

Though I didn't look at him, I imagined his intense, dark eyes as he spoke. "I don't like to touch people or be touched."

Not at all expecting his response I froze, wondering if I was pushing the boundaries lying next to him like this. "Oh. I didn't realize."

I shifted slightly in an attempt to pull away, but he caught me and pulled me back. "Not you, angel. You're… different."

The way he said it didn't exactly sound complimentary. I wanted to ask whether it was a good thing or not, but part of me was afraid of his response.

Luckily, he continued. "It's strange," he mused. "I've never really felt like I fit in anywhere. I've never been good with other people, never comfortable around them. But you…" He hesitated for a long moment like he was trying to gather his thoughts. "I've never actually enjoyed spending time with anyone until you came along."

Deep in my heart, despite all the warnings, I knew I was starting to fall for him. He was crass and harsh and controlling… but also charming, protective, and attentive. I would never call him sweet, but he cared for me in his own way. I wanted to believe that he was, at least part of him, good. He had the ability to be bad—but didn't everyone? Everyone was capable of both good and evil. Did it make me a bad person to want to love and be loved by a man like Fox?

One thing I was absolutely sure of was that Fox would never hurt me. Punishment aside, he would never hit me out of anger.

"I think you have a soft side," I teased gently.

He let out a little snort and lightly smacked my bottom. "We both know better."

"I don't know," I said. "I'm seriously starting to doubt you're the bad guy everyone believes."

Fox turned to look at me. "I'm everything they say I am,"

he warned, sending a chill down my spine. "Don't make me out to be a hero, angel. I'll only disappoint you."

I pondered that for a moment. I'd always wondered what made men like Fox tick—why they were the way they were. "Tell me about yourself."

He cocked a brow. "Not a chance. You already know some of the horrible things I've done."

"I don't," I argued. "And that's not what I'm talking about. I want to know about you. Where you grew up, what your life was like."

A mirthless laugh left his throat as he turned his face toward the ceiling. "That's not a good story."

"Tell me. Please."

"Why?"

"Because…" I felt my cheeks heat. "I want to know you."

His face softened a bit, then he turned away again. "It's not pretty."

"It doesn't have to be. I just want to know about you."

He exhaled, long and slow, gaze fixed on the ceiling. "My earliest memories are from an orphanage back home. I was maybe three, four at the time?"

"Back home? You're not from here?" He had no accent, and it surprised me that he wasn't born and raised in America. Come to think of it, though, I did know he was multi-lingual. He'd spoken in another language a couple times that I'd heard, but I just assumed it was the result of an extensive education pertaining to his business dealings.

He shook his head. "Romania. My mother was an addict, and I never knew my father. I doubt she did, either. If she did, she never admitted it before her death."

"Is that how you ended up in an orphanage?"

He paused for a moment. "No, she was still alive then. She just couldn't take care of me, so she gave me away."

"I'm sorry." I cuddled closer, wanting to hold him tight and take all the bad memories away. It was strange, me wanting to save this big, bad man from hurt, but I would do whatever I could for him.

He brushed his fingers through my hair. "It was dreary. Dismal. There were too many children and too few caretakers. We slept three or four to a bed, never had enough to eat, weren't taught to read or write."

That surprised the hell out of me. Fox was one of the smartest men I knew. "But you've done so well. How did you learn?"

His eyes darkened. "I learned later, when I was an... apprentice, of sorts. I was brought to the States when I was eight."

"Were they good to you?"

I somehow already knew the answer, even before he shook his head. "No, Eva. There are many horrible people in this world, and the man who raised me was one of them. He was responsible for making me the way I am."

Whoever he'd been with had stripped a young boy of his innocence, and Fox wholly believed he was a monster because of what he'd endured. I wanted to show him that there was good inside of him. Just as he was capable of evil, he could be good, too. "If you want to talk—"

"No." His voice was fierce, and he clutched at me before gentling his touch. "It's best left in the past. Trust me on this, angel. He's gone, and that's all that matters."

I forced one more question from my throat. "Did he hurt you?"

"Pain is relative, angel. Each trial makes us stronger, teaches us a lesson."

"And what lesson did you learn?"

His eyes were wide, unblinking as he stared at the ceiling. "To never trust anyone but myself."

Fierce protectiveness welled up. "You can trust me."

Slowly, he turned to look at me. His hand moved to the

back of my head, and his thumb stroked along my temple. "I know, angel."

He brushed a soft kiss over my lips, then tucked my head into the crook of his neck. I draped one arm over his chest, careful to avoid the wound along his side. Resting my fingers at the base of his neck, I felt the thrum of his blood pulsing against my fingertips. Moving my hand lower, I splayed my fingers wide over his chest. There was a heart deep inside him —a good one—and I was determined to find my way into it, no matter what it took.

CHAPTER
Thirty-Six

FOX

I spent the day ensconced in my office, pulling every thread we'd been able to dig up in hopes of tracking down this mysterious Araña. Grigori was correct; no one seemed to know anything. There was no information on where the man was from or who he was, no affiliation to the criminal underworld at all. Everyone had a past—except Araña. It was as if the man was a ghost.

I assumed that orders were passed from Araña to a select few delegates who then hired lower-level associates to carry out whatever the man dictated. The men and women who worked as transporters and handlers were paid well to do their job and ask no questions under the threat of death. In doing so, it kept Araña's identity and whereabouts closely guarded. Though the name would imply he was Latin American, there was no evidence yet to support it. All we'd managed to catch wind of were whispers of a mysterious figure pulling strings from behind the scenes. The man was like the goddamned Wizard of Oz, and I wanted to rip his kingdom apart piece by piece.

Striding down the hall, I caught sight of Eva leaving the living room. Quickening my pace, I caught up to her in less than five seconds. She threw a look over her shoulder, and her eyes went soft as they landed on me. Looping one arm around Eva's waist, I pulled her into the closest room, then pressed her up against the wall. She automatically tipped her head up, and I took her mouth in a hard kiss. I was panting by the time I pulled away, my cock pressing against the fly of my slacks. I leaned down so my forehead was flush with hers. "I can't wait another minute."

Her hands moved to my chest and shoved gently, and I reluctantly pulled back. Straight white teeth cut into her lower lip as she leaned away from me, searching my gaze. "It's only been six days since Dr. Marlowe replaced your stitches."

"Six days too long." I lifted my hand to cup the back of her head. "I'm fine, I promise."

Worry filled her eyes. "I don't know…"

"I do," I said firmly. "Tonight, I want to take my time with you, go slow."

I wanted to spend the next several hours worshipping her, touching and kissing every inch of her, feeling her hands and mouth on me. It'd been torture having her next to me every night, not being able to roll over and slide inside her the way I wanted. I was going out of my mind with need, and I couldn't wait another fucking minute.

A tiny smile curved her lips. "I didn't know the word slow was in your vocabulary."

"Only when it comes to you, angel. I want to spend all night bringing you to the edge over and over."

A shudder racked her body, and I tightened my hold on her. Dropping my head, I spoke low next to her ear. "Go to my room and get ready. I'll be there in fifteen."

"All right. You win." She looped her arms around my

neck and kissed me once more before pulling away and sliding through the open doorway.

I watched her go, a fierce possessiveness rolling through me. There wasn't a single thing I wouldn't do for that woman, and I wondered if she knew it. She hadn't made another attempt to leave, instead spending every night in bed next to me. I wanted her to be free, yet I knew it wasn't safe for her. Not yet. Until I found Araña, she needed to stay here with me where I could keep an eye on her at all times. I knew she didn't like it, but I didn't have a choice in the matter. I wasn't willing to risk her safety, even to give her a sense of freedom.

With a sigh, I pushed off the wall and straightened my jacket before heading into the hallway. Xavier stepped out of a darkened doorway a second later as if he'd been hovering there waiting. "Sir, I have news on Sebastian."

The smile I'd been wearing slipped from my face. Goddamn it. I swear to God, one of these days I was going to have to kill the idiot for hurting Marcella. He'd put her through so much already. I hoped she would find someone else—someone better—before he dragged her down with him.

I changed directions and headed toward my office, motioning with my head for Rodrigo to follow. As soon as we were ensconced in the room, I turned to him. "What's the bastard doing now?"

"According to recent travel logs, he's been to North Dakota twice over the past six months. He contracted a private jet and flew into a small airfield in Bathgate."

North Dakota? What the fuck was in North Dakota? He didn't exactly strike me as a hunter, unless it was big game. There were ski lodges scattered around the north, so perhaps he had a ski bunny waiting for him somewhere up there. "Vacation?"

"The first trip was approximately five days; the second time was three days."

Most guide trips for hunters tended to be a week or so long, so we could pretty safely rule that out. "I assume Marcella wasn't with him?"

Xavier shook his head. "However, I discovered that Masterson traveled with him."

"Both times?" Xavier nodded, and I thought it over for a second. "How close to the border is Bathgate?"

"Extremely."

It wasn't a red flag, exactly, but it was... different. Many ski resorts were open during the fall—but not operable for skiing. That still didn't rule out that Moreau had a mistress tucked away in the mountains. But why would Masterson travel with him? Perhaps as a cover? Almost immediately, I dismissed it. Sebastian traveled whenever and wherever he wanted; he didn't need to use another man as cover. Unless there was something more at play.

"Anything of interest happening around those times?"

"Nothing of significance that I can find."

The prickling at the back of my neck resumed. "And from there—where did they go when they left the airfield?"

"Working on that."

It was no secret that every illegal substance known to man was funneled through obscure places with little to no security. Masterson was heavily into drugs, and I wondered if Moreau was the same. They both ran in the same circles, so it wouldn't be a surprise. "Check into it. See if anyone else has heard anything and let me know. See if you can find anyone else who's been there recently."

"Anything else?"

"Not at the moment. And, Xavier?" I threw a look his way. "No interruptions tonight."

He nodded and left, and my pulse kicked up as I made my way through the house and upstairs. Outside my room, I drew in a deep breath and tried to still my nerves. I couldn't put a finger on why I was so anxious, exactly. I wanted to chalk it up to going without sex for several days, but I knew it wasn't the reason I was so worked up.

Before I'd brought Eva into my life, I'd gone months without sex. She was the first woman to ever touch me, but I knew it was more than even that rare physical connection. It was Eva herself—being with her, spending time with her. I wanted all of her, every way. It physically hurt to be away from her. Noir was fine, but it wasn't lost on me that I hadn't devoted nearly as much time to finding Araña as I should be. While he was important, Eva was more so. I wanted to spend every available moment with her.

I threw open the door, and my breath caught at the sight of Eva on her knees beside the bed. I swore I could see her like this every day for the rest of my life and never tire of it.

Stepping inside, I closed the door behind me and locked it before striding toward her. "You look so beautiful like this, angel. So perfect."

"Thank you, sir."

I brushed one hand over her head, running my fingers through the silky strands of her hair where they draped over her shoulder. "Stand up, angel."

I held out my hand and helped her to her feet, then placed her hand over my heart. "Undress me."

Her eyes flicked to mine, and her hand slid slowly over my pecs to the button at the top of my shirt. She slipped it free of its hole, then continued downward until the fabric gaped open. Slipping her hand inside, she slowly pushed it over my shoulders and down my arms. It fluttered to the floor, and she grasped my belt next, pulling it free and dropping it by our feet.

My cock jumped to attention as she rubbed one hand over my fly, then popped the button and slid my zipper down. A small growl welled up my throat, but I forced myself to remain still as she worked the waistband over my hips and down my legs. Toeing out of my shoes, I stepped out of the pool of fabric. All that remained were my boxers, and she licked her lips as she delved beneath the elastic and pulled them down. My cock sprang free, brushing against her belly.

Completely divested of clothing, I took her wrists in mine, sliding my hands up to her shoulders, then back down again. "Get on the bed, angel."

She did as I asked, crawling to the middle of the mattress and lying back, her pale golden hair spread over the pillow. Taking a step closer, I stroked the bone of her ankle. "Spread those legs, gorgeous. Arms over your head."

She opened for me, spread eagle on the wide bed, and it was almost more than I could take. Reaching under the mattress, I grabbed one velvet lined cuff. "Trust me?"

She lifted her head slightly, a tiny smile on her face. "Of course."

"Relax." It felt like forever since I'd had her like this, open and ready for me. I planned to draw out her pleasure until we were both exhausted.

I snapped the cuffs around her wrists, securing them to the bedposts. In less than thirty seconds, she lay spread eagle in front of me, ready to be devoured. Trailing my fingers up her calf, I smiled as her eyes fell closed and her body gave a little shudder of pleasure. She responded to the tiniest of touches, and I fucking loved it. There wasn't another woman on this planet as passionate and open as Eva. She was everything I'd ever wanted and then some. I didn't want to examine my motives too closely, but I felt the overwhelming need to keep her in my bed, in my life.

Standing at the foot of the bed, I stared down at her as I took myself in one hand. Her tongue swiped over her bottom lip as she watched me drag my hand from the base of my dick to the very tip. I swept my thumb over the tip, smearing the tiny drop of precum over the head, and I could tell by the way her legs shifted restlessly that her gaze was fixed on me. "See something you like, angel?"

"You know I do." Her response was low and thick with need.

Achingly slow, I drew my hand down and back up again, watching as she arched slightly, her breasts thrusting forward. I loved drawing out the anticipation. I loved making her beg for it. "Have you been a good girl, Eva, or have you been naughty?"

"I've been bad," she moaned out. "So bad."

I crawled onto the mattress and knelt between her legs. I could smell her before I even got close to her, and I found her folds drenched when I ran my fingers through them. "Do you know what bad girls get?"

"Show me," she panted, pushing her hips forward, searching for my fingers.

I loved that we had barely gotten started and she was already worked up, already anticipating what was to come. I leaned forward and pressed a kiss under her navel. "I think you need me to fill this pretty pussy."

I kissed my way downward, swirling my fingers over this sensitive bundle of nerves at the apex of her thighs. "I can't wait to—"

My words abruptly cut off as the window to my right cracked, mingling with the unmistakable sound of a rifle discharging. Instinctively, I threw my body over Eva's as another volley of semi-automatic gunfire followed the first. The glass in the windows held as it was meant to, and I rolled off the bed, shoving my feet into my pants and reaching for the pistol in my nightstand.

Eva's eyes were wide and glassy with fear. "W-what's happening?"

My gaze skated over her, still restrained to my bed. Fuck. Tucking the pistol into my waistband, I grabbed up a blanket and threw it over Eva to cover her. I fucking hated leaving her like this, but I had no choice. The panic room was too far away; we would never make it past whoever was infiltrating the house, and I couldn't waste time right now untying her. "I'm sorry."

Her eyes widened further as panic crept into her tone. "What are you doing?"

"Stay here," I cautioned. "I'll be right back."

"You can't leave me like this!" Eva thrashed against her restraints. "Fox!"

"Trust me, angel. You'll be safe here," I promised.

Ignoring her terrified shouting, I locked the door behind me as I flew into the hallway, checking both directions for perpetrators. Whoever was here had a lot of firepower. The report of pistol shots ricocheted through the hallways, echoing up from the foyer. On silent feet, I made my way through the darkened house to the top of the stairs.

Keeping my back to the wall, I crept down, my eyes never resting as I continually scanned the area for movement. The front door had been kicked in, and it gaped open, allowing the cold air to rush in.

A grunt came from the bottom of the stairs, and two dark-clad bodies lay on the floor of the foyer, illuminated by the moonlight streaming in through the jagged glass of the broken windows. A man lay slumped against the post, and he coughed, sending a trickle of blood dripping down his chin. As I moved to his side, I recognized Callum. His gun swung up as I moved into his peripheral vision, then dropped just as quickly when he recognized me.

I nodded to the blood saturating the front of his shirt. "How bad?"

Callum's hand rested over his stomach. "Gut shot when I took out these two fuckers." He coughed again, the sound rattling in his chest. "I think they're headed toward your office."

Tucking the gun in the waistband of my pants, I checked

our surroundings once more. Though sounds of broken wood and shattering glass came from the opposite side of the house, here it was quiet. Grasping Callum under the armpits, I dragged him around the corner where he would be out of the line of fire if the assholes headed back this way.

"Call for help." I slipped the phone from my back pocket and passed it to him, indicating that he should call Dr. Marlowe. "How many are left?"

"Not sure." He grimaced as he gripped the phone. "I think there were about a dozen—minus those two."

I glanced toward the bodies on the floor, and pressed a hand to his shoulder. "Well done. I need to check on the others."

With a nod, he dialed Marlowe's number, and I headed down the hall toward the west wing of the house. I found another eight men down on the way, two of them mine. A man moved out from a darkened doorway, and I pulled the trigger twice, not sparing him another glance as I left him to bleed out. By the time I reached my office, my fury was at full pitch. It grew worse when I peered around the doorjamb.

Two bodies lay on the rug in front of my desk, signs of struggle evident in the overturned furniture. Xavier and Rodrigo knelt on the floor in front of my desk, and a man stood behind them, holding a pistol execution-style.

I lifted my pistol but the motion caught his attention, and the man whirled toward me. He fired, his shot going wide and sinking into the door. Wood exploded as I squeezed the trigger, and I winced as a sharp pain radiated from my temple. The man grunted as my bullet sank into his chest but managed to get off another shot as he stumbled. It hit high on the wall, and I popped off two more rounds, each one ripping through his chest. His mouth twisted, and he lifted his pistol toward me again, but I fired off a fourth round. This one went through his forehead, and exited out the back with an explosion of dark spatter in the silvery moonlight.

He dropped to his knees, then collapsed face first, dark blood pooling around his torso.

Behind him, my men rose shakily to their feet. "Good?"

"Flesh wound," Xavier said, running his hand along his bicep.

"Good," Rodrigo affirmed.

"Callum's wounded, but he put in a call to Doc Marlowe." I glanced around. "Let's sweep the house, then call for cleanup."

I had to get back to Eva. Keeping a trained eye on my surroundings, I moved quickly out of my office and around the corner, taking the back steps two at a time. I'd just crested the landing when a door on the right opened up two rooms ahead. Icy awareness slithered down my spine as I lifted my gun. The man's head swiveled my way, and the muzzle of his pistol flashed as he got off a single shot. I fired off three rounds of my own and watched him stumble backwards through the doorway, leaving a streak of blood on the wall before he collapsed. Moving toward him, I picked up his gun and tucked it in my waistband, my heart threatening to beat right out of my chest. Two more rooms and he would have gotten to Eva.

I hated to be away from her for another second, but I needed to make sure it was safe. Footsteps sounded from behind me, and I tossed a look at Rodrigo, who had followed the sound of the gunshots.

I gestured with my head. "Clear the floor. You take the left side, I'll take the right."

We moved quickly and efficiently, Xavier joining us just as we finished sweeping the second floor. I shoved my pistol in my waistband and met his gaze. "All clear?"

"We lost two, and I counted eleven of theirs. Twelve including that one." He tipped his head toward the man sprawled at the end of the hallway.

"Good." I drew in a deep breath. "Let Marlowe know he's

good to come in. Get yourselves taken care of and call the crew. We need to get these windows replaced."

"You got it."

They dispersed, and I made a beeline for my room, unable to stay away from Eva one more second.

CHAPTER
Thirty-Seven

EVA

My heart thudded against my chest as Fox disappeared, slamming the door in his wake. For a second I just stared at the slab of wood. He'd left me. Cold settled over my body as the realization sank in. A piercing howl welled up and out of my throat.

I thrashed against the ties binding me to the bed, but they became tighter the more I struggled. I screamed out my frustration, then cut off mid-scream. Oh, God. What if they heard me? The sharp retort of gunfire intermittently filled the air, along with the sounds of destruction and angry shouts. What if they killed Fox? They would kill him, kill his men. Then they'd come for me.

I jumped as the report of gunfire came from the hallway just outside the bedroom door. Three shots came in quick succession, followed by a heavy silence. My lungs ached as I held by breath, waiting for something to happen. Nerves twisted my stomach into knots, the silence interminable.

Tears streamed down my cheeks until I could barely breathe, my chest constricted by fear. Suddenly, the sound of a key filling the lock met my ears, followed by the grating sound of metal on metal. Every muscle in my body tensed as the knob turned and the door swung inward.

Fox appeared in the open space, and my fear gave way to relief, immediately followed by anger. "Get me out of here!"

My kicking and thrashing resumed, and Fox lunged toward the bed, yanking on the bonds. "Calm down!"

Ignoring him, I fought harder, and he grabbed my arms, stilling them. "I can't get you free if you keep fighting me. I need you to calm down."

I somehow managed to stay still until the last tie fell free, then I launched myself at him. "How could you?" I beat on his chest. "You left me!"

"You're safe, angel," he said, capturing my wrists. "Everything's fine. They're gone and—"

"Nothing is fine!" I screeched, yanking out of his hold. "How can you say that? Someone shot up the house. You could have been killed. I could have been killed!"

My voice was high, hysterical, but I couldn't help it. How did he live like this? My mind was too muddled to think clearly, and I shoved against him. "You left me!"

"I know, angel. I'm sorry."

Though his apology sounded sincere, it didn't placate me. I punched his chest once. Twice. I pounded him with my fists over and over, venting my anger and worry and frustration as tears poured down my cheeks. He didn't bother to fight back; through it all, he held me in the circle of his arms, just taking the punishment. It only made me angrier. I wanted him as outraged and upset as I was. Instead, he seemed... resigned, like this was nothing new to him.

Realization doused me like ice water, and I dropped my arms away. Maybe he was used to this; maybe this was normal for him. How many times had he been shot at, attacked? God, I couldn't bear to think about it.

Stepping away, I pulled out of his grasp. I couldn't be

around him right now. Without looking at him, I turned and strode into the bathroom, keeping my head down so he wouldn't see the moisture tracking down my cheeks. Moving straight to the sink, I flipped the handle and splashed cool water on my face, obscuring the tears that burned up my throat and spilled over my cheeks. I turned off the water and dropped my head so my chin rested on my chest. A tear dropped from my cheek, and I watched it land on the marble.

So absorbed in my own thoughts, I didn't hear the soft footsteps approach until I felt his hand on my shoulder. "Eva."

Blinking the tears away, I turned my back on him without responding and reached for a towel. I blotted my face dry, taking an inordinately long time before finally tossing it on the counter. Fox's hand slipped around my elbow, and he guided me toward him. I couldn't meet his eyes; instead, I stared at his broad chest, the dark skin peeking out of the open vee of his shirt.

One hand cradled my chin, and he bent his knees to meet my gaze. "Talk to me."

I shook my head, directing my gaze over his shoulder.

"You're worried I won't take care of you?"

I let out an impatient huff but didn't say a word. His lips pursed in irritation, then became pensive. "You're worried about me."

I blinked again, steeling my heart, and both hands moved to frame my face so I had no choice but to look at him. "Nothing will happen to me."

"You can't promise that."

He looked like he would argue, then stopped. "No one has ever cared for my wellbeing." He took me in his arms. "You have a good heart."

Part of me wanted to lean into him, to soak up the warmth and security of his embrace. But I still felt too shattered, too on edge. "Is it always like this for you?"

My voice sounded dull and toneless even to my own ears, and Fox stiffened before leaning away a bit. To his credit, he didn't ask what I meant. "Not usually, no. But something I've been working on has... stirred the hornets' nest."

"Are you ever going to tell me?" He wouldn't even tell me what he was working on. Every time I tried to ask, he changed the subject.

"I just want to protect you," he said. "I never want to put you in harm's way."

"Little late for that, isn't it?"

His hands fell away, and a tic ran along the line of his jaw. "No one will ever hurt you—not while I'm here."

Did he not understand? I shook my head. "I need some time to myself."

"Eva..."

I shrugged out of his grasp when his fingers wrapped around my wrist. "I can't. Not right now."

Maybe not ever. He let me go as I left the bathroom, then escaped to my own room and closed the door behind me. It was a flimsy barrier between Fox and me, but I knew he was noble enough to not breach it. Even after everything, he respected me enough to grant my wish to be alone for the time being.

Feeling cold all over, I crawled into bed and pulled the covers up to my chin, hugging a pillow to me. It felt strange to be back in my own room. Here in the silent darkness, I was left alone with my thoughts and plaguing doubts. I was merely a pawn in a game much larger and more complex than I ever imagined. I no longer believed that he had killed Elle, but that still didn't change the man he was. Fox would never change. I was still furious with him for getting hurt. But I was even more mad at myself for loving him.

Is this what my life would be like with Fox—a man who was always on the receiving end of danger? He doled out punishment and pain, but there was no stopping his enemies from retaliating, just as they'd done tonight. I wasn't stupid. This was a never-ending cycle of violence and death. I couldn't stand by and watch him be hunted and killed; it would destroy me.

I felt so much for him—too much—and I missed him even now. I ached so badly just thinking of him that I wondered how I would ever survive without him. But I knew I had to. Whether it was tomorrow or twenty years from now, I would always be on edge, waiting for that awful moment when one of his men told me he was gone.

I couldn't live like that. Mere hours ago, I was ready to tell him that I was falling for him. But now... allowing myself to love Fox would result in only one thing—heartbreak. It was ironic how things had come full circle in the few months since I'd arrived. I'd vowed then never to give him my heart. Now I remembered why.

Admitting my love for him would strip my soul bare—and I couldn't allow that to happen. If I gave him everything, it would shred me, leave me a mere scrap of humanity. I needed to harden my heart so there would be something left when I finally left this place. It was no longer a question of whether I would leave; I had to. There was no other option.

CHAPTER
Thirty-Eight

FOX

I glanced at the pictures spread across my desk. Though I'd seen them only once, in death, I would never forget the hard lines of their faces. I vividly remembered the men's bodies strewn about the house, blood seeping into the hardwood floors.

I traced a finger over the wood grain of my desk. The rug had been rolled up and burned the night after the assault, but a heavy pall still hung over the house. I lifted my eyes to Rodrigo. "They don't look familiar."

He shook his head. "All independent hires. No known accomplices or affiliations."

That was an awfully coordinated attack for a handful of thugs who'd decided to band together. It didn't seem likely, and I didn't believe in coincidences. Someone had hired them, walked them through exactly what they needed to do. I was certain it was Araña.

"Someone knows who they are." The Capaldi family was a fucking mess right now, too, so I couldn't even reach out to them for information. "I'll check with Nikolai, see if he's heard of them."

"I don't know if it's true," Rodrigo said slowly, "but I heard whispers that Sebastian might be involved."

I lifted a brow. "I doubt a pretty boy like him would want to get his hands dirty, not directly at least."

"He has money." Rodrigo shrugged. "And he's not the most discerning person."

That was true. It made me incredibly uneasy. Human trafficking was a $180 billion dollar business; where greed reined, morals quickly fell by the wayside. "See if you can find anything concrete."

Rodrigo dipped his head and left. With a sigh, I ran one hand over my face. The past four days had been sheer torture, and I'd slept maybe a total of twelve hours, all of them on the couch a few feet away.

Eva had pulled away, and I had no idea how to connect with her again. She hid away during the day, ensconced in some rarely used room while I worked, then retreated to her own bed each night. She was barely eating again, and I could see the dark circles beneath her eyes during our infrequent encounters. I wanted so desperately to grab onto her, hold her, but she wouldn't let me get close enough to speak, let alone pull her into my arms.

Never had I seen her like this, not even in the beginning. The night of the break-in had ripped a hole in whatever bond we'd woven over the past couple of months. I'd experienced the soft, quiet tears from punishment, yes—but not the great, racking sobs she'd uttered that night. They'd shredded my insides, seeing her in pain like that. Worst, I had no idea what to do. I couldn't take it back, couldn't make it better. She was terrified not only for herself, but for me. And she wasn't wrong. If I continued down this path, I would be putting Eva in danger. I couldn't live with myself if something happened, but I couldn't let her go, either. It wasn't safe for her here, but it was even more dangerous for her out there, without my protection. I'd been forced to let her go, unsure of what to do. There was a great divide between us even though she was only one room away.

I couldn't fucking stand it anymore. Pushing to my feet, I strode toward the door. The windows I'd had replaced the morning following the invasion were dark as night settled over the house. Everything looked exactly the same—but it felt like night and day difference. I wasn't certain things would ever go back to the way they were. I needed to bridge the gap between Eva and me, but I didn't have a clue how to even begin to fix things.

Moving slowly through the house, I tried to imagine where Eva might be today. My feet carried me toward the den, and I stopped just inside the doorway, relief filling my chest when I saw her curled up on the couch, reading a book.

Her eyes lifted to mine, and I watched every muscle tense before she dropped her gaze away again. I stepped inside, moving toward the sideboard to pour myself a drink. I'd just lifted the decanter when Eva quietly slid off the couch and started to stand. Setting the bottle down, I turned to her. "You're more than welcome to stay."

"That's okay."

She moved toward the door, but I was faster. Reaching out, I grabbed her arm and pulled her to a stop. "Damn it, Eva. Will you stop?"

She shrugged out of my grasp, her gaze fixed on my chest. "Did you need something?"

Her tone was cool, aloof, and it stoked my ire. "Yes, I need something. I need you to stop avoiding me, hiding away in your room."

"I haven't been hiding."

I gritted my teeth together, determined to have it out with her and clear the air. "Well you've been doing an awfully good job of not being present, either."

She stiffened. "I just wanted a little space. I don't think that's too much to ask, all things considered."

I strove for calm as I spoke. "And I gave you the space you asked for. But it's been four days, Eva. You won't talk to me. You won't even let me touch you!"

"If that's all you want, why don't you go fuck someone else?" Bitter resentment flashed momentarily in her eyes before she averted her gaze again, and I reached out, stroking my fingers down her arm.

"I don't want anyone else. I want you. Only you."

"Fox." She sighed. "I just…"

She trailed off, and I picked up. "I haven't seen you for days, and it's been killing me. Damn it, Eva, I miss you."

She seemed to soften a bit but still wouldn't look at me. "I haven't gone anywhere, Fox. I'm still right here."

"Physically, maybe." I shook my head. "But emotionally, you're a thousand miles away. I know you're scared—and you have every right to be," I said when her face snapped to mine. "But you're safe with me."

"You're right," she responded. "I am scared. Do you know what that was like for me?"

I honestly couldn't. I'd been born for this, but Eva was an innocent. She didn't deserve any of this. "No, I don't. And I'm sorry you had to experience that. But I meant what I said—I will always protect you."

"You can't promise that someday—"

I took her biceps in my hands, imploring her to listen to me. "Today is not someday. As long as there's breath in my lungs, I will be here for you. I will kill a thousand men before I ever let someone harm you. I swear that. Please, Eva… I need you to come back to me. I won't let you run anymore."

"I'm not running. I just…" She looked almost regretful when she spoke. "I need more. I need respect. I need…"

Love. She didn't say it, but it hung in the air between us like poison. I wasn't sure I could ever give her what she needed. I knew lust. I knew desire. But love was a completely foreign concept to me. I couldn't begin to grasp how one loved. What did it feel like? What did it look like? Marcella had told me before that she loved Sebastian, yet she was constantly in pain. Was that love? If that was my future with Eva because of love, then I wanted no part of it.

I couldn't summon a single thing to say in my defense, and the sad, hurt look in Eva's eyes told me she'd read me correctly. "I understand. If you'll excuse me, I'm going to bed. I'm tired."

She tried so hard to keep her expression blank, to appear strong, but there was no hiding from me. Eva took a step to move past me, but I stopped her. Everything I wanted to say congealed on my tongue, and she forced a fake smile to her lips.

"It's okay, Fox. You don't have to say anything." Her gaze dropped to my hand on her arm, and I swore I saw tears swimming in her eyes as she pulled away. "Good night."

I'd caused the hurt she was experiencing, and I felt fucking miserable because of it. I was the source of everything bad in her life, yet I couldn't let her go. I wouldn't. I felt too much for her, though I couldn't begin to put into words exactly how I felt. All I knew was that I needed her. I wanted things to go back to the way they were. I wanted her to be happy again. I wanted her in my bed, her body curled around mine. I wanted her open and talkative, the way she'd been before I fucked everything up. I wanted to go back in time and do it all over again.

"You're right." She stopped but didn't turn, and relief coursed through me. I might not be able to tell her the truth, but I owed her more. She deserved more. "I can't take back what happened, but I want you to know…" I stopped myself, unsure exactly how to continue.

Her head slowly swiveled over her shoulder and met my gaze. I held my breath as silence reigned, my heart thudding against my ribs. "I received an invitation to an engagement party for a business acquaintance this Saturday. I'd like for you to come with me"— I drew in a sharp breath—"as my girlfriend."

After the recent infiltration, I needed to show strength and confidence—not hide away. But all of those reasons fell away as I stared at Eva. She was the only thing that truly mattered. "Please, Eva," I said softly. "There's no one I would rather have by my side."

She blinked, and I could practically hear the wheels turning in her brain, trying to discern my motives. Finally, she gave a little nod. "I would be honored."

Relief filled me. "We'll go shopping tomorrow for a gown."

"Okay." A tiny smile lifted her lips as she moved away from me.

It wasn't perfect, but it was a start. I needed Eva to see how much she meant to me, and if this small measure of freedom would prove it to her, I would gladly give it to her.

CHAPTER
Thirty-Nine

EVA

Fox held out his hand, and I slipped my palm into his, allowing him to help me from the car. Out on the sidewalk, I pulled my coat more tightly around me. Spring had sprung, but the air still held a bitter chill. Fox slipped one arm around my shoulders, pulling me close and blocking the chilly breeze, and I allowed myself to sink into his warm embrace for a moment.

I wanted to fall into his arms the way I had before, but it felt like a wedge had been driven between us. I wasn't stupid; I knew I was to blame for that. I felt like I was being pulled in two different directions, but I had to make a decision, and soon. I wanted Fox, but I couldn't stand to see him slowly destroy himself. Whatever he was chasing would kill him—I knew it would.

I couldn't live life like that. I'd been holding myself back for the past few days, but I still hadn't come to a decision. I loved him—I knew I did. But was it worth the consequences? Was the uncertainty, the terror of not knowing if he would survive, worth it? I hated the distance between us, but I wasn't entirely willing to let down my guard.

Callum moved ahead, holding the boutique door wide for us as we entered. He closed up again behind us, then returned to the car to wait. A beautiful young saleswoman approached, a smile on her face. "Hello, I'm Lena. Looking for anything in particular today?"

I let Fox take charge, since I wasn't sure what the dress code would be.

"We have an engagement party to attend this weekend," he said smoothly. "My girlfriend needs a dress."

Hearing him call me his girlfriend sent a little jolt of pleasure through me, and I fought to slow the rapid tempo of my heart. He tossed a secret little smile my way, and I looked away in the pretense of skimming the shop.

"Black tie?" Lena asked.

"Yes." Fox's arm tightened around me. "Have you seen anything you like yet?"

My eyes roved the mannequins dressed in long, crystal studded gowns, and I gave a slow shake of my head. "Not yet."

"Did you have a particular color in mind?"

Lena directed the question at me, but I turned to Fox in question. His eyes heated. "Whatever you want, angel."

I turned my attention back to the room. "I'm open. May I look around?"

"Of course." Lena gestured to the far wall, the rack full of glamorous dresses. "Would you like me to pull a few that I think you might like?"

I sent a smile her way. "That would be wonderful, thank you."

Fox dipped his head, his lips brushing my temple, and I froze. He seemed to sense my hesitation, because his arm slipped away, and his eyes filled with something I couldn't quite discern.

"I'll wait over here." Without waiting for my reply, he moved away.

I felt guilty for putting that look on his face, the dejected set of his shoulders as he moved away. How could I care so much about someone yet still feel so uncertain?

"Fox."

He turned, and those dark eyes met mine. For a second, there was a flare of hope, then they became empty once more. "Yes, Eva?"

His efforts showed that he was trying, and I softened a little toward him. "Will you help me pick something out?"

His brows drew slightly together as he studied me. "I thought you'd like to select your own dress."

"I do," I said as I moved toward him. "But I thought we could do it together. You know what looks good on me."

His chin dipped slightly, a new light entering his eyes. "I'm confused, angel. What is it you want?"

My teeth dug into my lower lip as I contemplated my words. We were no longer speaking of clothing, and I couldn't pretend anymore. I hoped that by calling me his girlfriend, Fox meant I wasn't a prisoner anymore.

"I can't stand this." I gestured between us. "I want to be with you, but…" I paused and drew a deep breath. "I don't know if I can go through something like that again."

"I've increased security," he said immediately, and I knew he was telling the truth. I'd seen extra men patrolling the house and grounds over the past few days. "I'll make sure no one ever gets that close again."

"But that's not solving the problem." I stared at him, a pang of sadness ricocheting through my heart. "I couldn't stand it if anything ever happened to you."

He opened his mouth to speak, but immediately fell silent under my sharp look. "I can't guarantee that things will always be… calm. But trust me when I say this is the first and last time something like that will ever happen."

I tipped my head. "What does that mean?"

"Things aren't normally this bad. But what I'm working on right now…" He gave his head a little shake. "It's sensitive."

I stared at him. "Are you ever going to tell me what it is?"

"Yes," he responded immediately. "Soon, angel. I…" He ran one hand through his hair, then met my gaze. "I'm looking into Spencer Masterson."

Shock rooted me to the floor. "Elle's husband? What does he have to do with anything?"

"I'm not sure yet." He looked truly remorseful when he spoke. "I'll tell you everything, I promise. I just want to make sure I have all the facts first."

I nodded slowly. "Okay. I can respect that. I want you to know that I'm here because I want to be." His dark eyes stared into mine, focused as he listened intently. "Promise me you'll never let anything happen."

"Never." His gaze was fierce, his tone low and harsh. "I'll never let anyone take you from me."

"Good."

His hand slipped from my chin to the back of my head and he kissed me once, hard, before meeting my gaze again. Things were far from resolved, but it was a start.

Slipping my hand into the crook of his elbow, I steered his toward the gowns. Together, we selected several for me to try on, and Lena led me to a dressing room in the back of the store.

I discarded several dresses before I pulled on an emerald cocktail dress and stepped out for Fox to see. His eyes lit with lust and pleasure, and he settled his hands on my hips. "Is this the one?"

"I think so."

He pulled me close, his gaze dropping to my mouth, and I tipped my head up. He kissed me, a sweet, almost chaste brush of his lips against mine. It was over much too soon, and he stared at me for a few seconds, his thumb sliding over my cheekbone.

"I want to go away with you—just the two of us."

His words surprised me, and it took me a moment to respond. "Okay?"

"I have a place in the Caribbean. There's... something I want you to see. I want to take you there. I want to lie on the beach with you and not have to worry about anything else."

I leaned into him. "I think I'd like that."

I still wasn't sure exactly where we stood, but things were beginning to look up. If he could come halfway, then so could I. I'd never met anyone who made me feel the way Fox did, and it was worth fighting for, no matter what.

CHAPTER
Forty

FOX

The soft glow of street lamps strobed over the inside of the car, and I turned, taking in Eva's profile as she stared out the window. Her hands rested in her lap, and I reached over, slipping my fingers around hers. She threw me a look, her mouth curling into a soft smile as I tugged on her hand. She leaned toward me, offering her lips, and I stole a kiss, careful not to smear her lipstick.

As I pulled away, Eva grabbed my lapel. Tossing a look over her shoulder at Rodrigo in the driver's seat, she bit her lip before slowly releasing me. I knew she was worried about what my men thought of us. Personally, I didn't give a single fuck. She was mine, and I wanted to show the whole goddamn world. Tonight was a step in that direction. In doing so, I was inviting trouble. But I would choose Eva over everything and everyone else—always.

Sliding my hands under her legs and bottom, I scooped her up and settled her over my lap. She let out a little squeak and pressed one hand to my chest.

"What are you doing?" she hissed.

"You were too far away." I grinned at her, and I watched the corners of her mouth twitch even as she tried to hold back her smile.

"You're ridiculous."

My hand curved around her hip, and my erection swelled at the feel of her bottom nestled over my lap. "I think the word you're looking for is desperate."

"One more day."

I'd reopened the wound on my side the night of the invasion, and I was infuriated that it had pushed my recovery —and my time with Eva—back even further. The new stitches along my side felt tight and itchy, and I couldn't fucking wait to get them out. Marlowe was scheduled to stop by tomorrow, but I couldn't wait another day to have Eva. Through the fabric of her dress, I cupped her breast, and she let out a soft whimper against my lips.

She pulled away just far enough to whisper, "Not here."

Drawing in a deep breath, I leaned my forehead against hers. For her, I could be patient. Maybe.

Less than two minutes later, Rodrigo pulled up in front of an old brownstone. I waved Rodrigo off, instead unfolding from the car on my own, then helping Eva from the back seat. Tucking her arm into the crook of my elbow, I led her up the stone steps and into the large older home. A table in the corner of the foyer displayed rows of name cards for dinner, and I collected ours, then slipped them into my pocket without bothering to look at the seating chart. All around us, women in stunning gowns laughed and mingled, some tossing speculative glances my way. But all I saw was Eva.

Taking her hand in mine, I walked as sedately as possible, pulling Eva along with me as I made my way down the hall.

Eva nodded to a couple as we passed, then leaned into me, her voice low. "Where are we going?"

"Patience." I didn't know if I was speaking to her or

myself; all I knew was I couldn't wait one more second to have her. She looked so damn beautiful, and she was all mine.

I wanted to tell her everything. It was a huge relief but it also scared the shit out of me. There wasn't a single person—not a living person, anyway—who knew the truth of my sordid past. But I wanted Eva to know. I wanted her to understand, and I wanted her to choose me. I wanted to take her home, make love to her, beg her to stay with me—because she wanted to, not because she had to.

Glancing around, I looked for someplace quiet and secluded. My gaze landed on a door about halfway down the hallway, and I tugged her that direction. Throwing the door open, I peeked inside. A closet. Perfect. I ushered her inside, then closed the door.

"Fox, what—"

Her words abruptly cut off as I pushed her back against the door and slammed my mouth over hers. For a split second, she resisted, then she threw herself into the kiss. Winding her arms around my neck, she leaned into me, giving me everything I wanted.

"I need you, angel."

Hiking up the skirt of her cocktail dress, I reached between her legs and cupped her. Even through the fabric of her skimpy underwear, she was hot and soaking wet. I let out a low growl, my body humming with need. "Don't make me wait anymore."

Her nose brushed mine as she shook her head. I couldn't see her in the near-dark, but I imagined the look on her face, the lust in her eyes as she spoke. "No more waiting. I want you."

"Spread your legs." She did as I asked, her foot bumping mine as she opened for me. Yanking her underwear to the side, I slipped my fingers into her hot passage. She was slick with arousal and ready for me—always ready.

Pulling my shirt free, I flipped open the fly of my trousers and shoved them down. Palming Eva's ass, I lifted her to my chest, pinning her to the cool wood of the door. My cock jutted upward, automatically seeking out the folds shielding her womanhood. I slid in to the hilt with one hard thrust, and I felt our chests rise at the same time we sucked in a sharp breath. It was exquisite, the way I felt with her.

Lifting and lowering her on my shaft, I took her hard, driven by need and something else I couldn't quite explain. No, that wasn't true. My conversation with Carmen from weeks ago filtered through my mind, and suddenly I knew exactly what this was.

Eva's body wrapped around mine, I poured every ounce of emotion into my movements. She buried her face in my neck as she came, her pussy clenching around me and spurring my own release. I came hard deep inside her, filling her with my seed. For what felt like forever, I held her there, both of us breathing hard, my mind a blank void. I'd never felt better in my entire life that I did when I was with her. I wanted this every single day.

Lowering my head, I dropped a kiss on her temple and spoke low next to her ear. *"Inima mea îți aparține, îngeraș."*

My heart is yours, angel.

CHAPTER
Forty-One

EVA

He lowered me to my feet, then framed my face with my hands and took my mouth in a hard, passionate kiss.

I was breathing hard when we finally broke apart. "What did..." I inhaled deeply, trying to force my heart rate under control. "Those words—what do they mean?"

I could almost hear the smile in his voice when he spoke, his thumb gently sweeping over my cheek. "I'll tell you at home."

Fox's huge hand slipped beneath my chin and tilted my face to his, then slanted his mouth over mine in another possessive, scorching kiss. He broke away, leaning his forehead against mine, his hands slipping down my body to rest along the curve of my waist. He squeezed, keeping us pressed close together for a moment before straightening.

The soft rustle of fabric filled the air as we tugged our clothes back into place, and a few seconds later, a soft glow appeared as Fox engaged the flashlight function on his phone. A slow smile curved his mouth as the beam of light swept over me.

"You may want to visit the bathroom before you rejoin the party."

I raised a hand to my hair. "Is it bad?"

"You look..." His smile grew as he drew it out. "...like you just got fucked in a closet."

"Fox!" I lightly slapped his chest, and he grabbed my hand.

"You look beautiful. As always." I melted a little bit as he bent to kiss me once more. He looked pensive as he pulled away. "Do you think they'll miss us if we don't go back?"

"Considering the arranged seating, I would say yes."

"Fuck." I laughed as he cupped the side of my face in one hand and let out a little growl. His thumb swept over my lower lip, and I sucked it into my mouth, watching his eyes darken all over again. "Keep it up and I'm going to take you home and fuck you until you can't move."

"After the party," I promised with a grin. "Now go!"

"What happens to little girls who talk back?" He asked, one eyebrow cocked toward his hairline.

"They get spanked?" I asked hopefully as I pressed my breasts against him.

He let out a throaty chuckle and palmed my right cheek. "You're so fucking perfect."

I grinned, a lightness buoying my heart as I stared at him. There was no denying my feelings for him. This overwhelming happiness, the utter rightness... I was completely and totally in love with him. It took everything in me not to say it to him right then, but it was neither the time nor place. I pressed my lips together and straightened his tie. "We better get going."

He studied me for a moment, then gave me one last squeeze. "I'll meet you out there."

He stepped away, opened the door and peeked through the crack before stepping out. He shot a wink my way before closing the door again. I sagged against the wall, a smile creeping over my face as heat assailed me. Fox was everything I wanted and never knew I needed.

Pushing off the wall, I took a step toward the door. A metallic crunch sounded beneath my stiletto as I stepped forward, and I jumped at the sound. Stooping down, I swept my hand over the floor until I encountered the object. I folded it in my palm as I stood and followed Fox's suit, peering out before slipping from the closet.

I made my way down the hall to the bathroom. It was blessedly empty, and I strode to the counter. The metallic object pressed into my hand, and I inspected the small, oval cuff link. I immediately recognized it as Fox's, and I smiled as I tucked it into my clutch. As soon as I got back to our table, I'd give it back to him. Or maybe I'd make him work for it later.

Once I'd freshened my makeup, I took one last look in the mirror. Fox was right. There was a flush in my cheeks, and his scruff had reddened the skin at the base of my neck. It would be obvious to everyone what I'd been doing—but I didn't care. Fox had wanted to show me off; I wanted to wear his marks so everyone knew I was his.

Head held high, I sailed out of the bathroom and down the dim hallway back to the foyer. I crossed to the closest set of huge, carved wooden doors and paused at the edge of the large ballroom, automatically scanning for Fox. My breath caught in my chest as a familiar face came into view, and my feet were carrying me closer before I'd even considered what I was doing.

Blood rushed in my ears, and my vision tunneled. I felt like I was suspended in a strange kind of alternate reality as I drew up short just a few feet from the small group on the fringes of the room. When I was just a few feet away, my father turned, and our gazes collided. He did a double take, and his eyes widened.

"Dad." I breathed the word, and he quickly took a step

toward me before turning back to his acquaintances and murmuring his excuses. My feet felt leaden, my body frozen. He grasped my elbow and practically dragged me into the foyer, then down a side hallway. I couldn't think straight, couldn't even believe what was happening right now.

I was caught somewhere between being elated and confused. It'd been months since I'd seen my family, and a gamut of emotions roiled within me. I had the urge to pinch myself to see if it was real, but my father still had my arm threaded through his. I watched the patterned carpet swirl beneath my feet as we moved until we were ensconced in the shadows in some seldom-used part of the house.

He didn't look happy; he looked worried. Upset, even. "Dad, what—"

He gave a little shake of his head as he quickly glanced around. "Don't say anything."

"But—"

Again, he cut me off. "Just…" He closed his eyes and swiped one hand over his mouth before staring down at me again. "You're okay?"

"I am." Joyful tears welled in my eyes. I didn't know what had transpired with my family during the time I'd been gone, but there would be time for all of those answers later. I was just so damn happy to see them again, that I threw my arms around my father.

He caught my wrists, shot a quick look around, then gently pushed me away. My heart split in two as he shook his head. "Listen to me. Just… do what he says."

"Who?" Confusion reigned, and my brows drew together as my mind went blank. "I don't—"

"Fox," my father whispered. "He'll kill me if he sees you with me."

I fell back as step, feeling like I'd been hit by a truck. "Wait." Everything seemed to slow around me as I fought the tightness in my chest. "He knew?"

"Yes," he hissed. "He threatened to kill me if I ever stepped in."

Oh, God. Fox had known all along who my parents were. He'd lied to me from the very beginning. Not only that, but my father knew of Fox's reputation. And he'd just... let me go. Like I meant absolutely nothing to him.

Bile burned the back of my throat, and my legs wobbled. I fell back against the wall behind me, and my father stretched out one hand to catch me.

"Eva..." He looked remorseful. "I wish I could help you. I just..."

I extracted myself from his grip and gave a slow nod. "I understand. You... you should get back to your friends."

"You'll be okay?"

I forced a smile to my lips as I looked up at him. "Of course. I just need a minute."

"All right." Reluctantly, he turned to go. He slowed halfway down the hallway, his voice floating softly back to me. "It was good to see you."

I nodded, unable to look at him. I couldn't breathe, couldn't think. The only thing that kept replaying in my mind was my conversation with Fox. My father said Fox had threatened him, yet Fox had acted like no one had ever tried to come for me. Why would he lie?

Like a lightning bolt, the truth slammed into me. He didn't want me to leave. He wanted me all to himself. To control. To own. I was nothing but a piece of property to him, someone with whom to slake his sexual needs and nothing more. I swallowed hard, an urgency clutching at my throat. I needed to get out of there. I frantically looked around, glancing for any exit. Moving quickly, I turned down two hallways and passed through a sitting room before finally coming across a set of patio doors.

I shoved them open and practically threw myself outside. A hand clamped down on my shoulder, and I whirled around with a gasp. My gaze landed on Rodrigo, and I glared at him. "Did you know?"

His dark eyes revealed nothing, spiking my ire. "You knew!" I shoved at him. "You all fucking knew, and you never told me!"

His eyes narrowed, and he grabbed my wrist as I spun away. I slammed my hands into his chest, shoving him back a tiny step. "I hate you! I hate all of you!"

"Then go!" His voice was a harsh whisper, and I could barely understand the words over the blood rushing in my ears, my panting breaths.

I stared at him for a moment, suspicious. "What?"

He released my wrists. "Go." He gestured toward the sprawling garden in the backyard. "I'll take care of it."

I felt rooted to the pavestones as I studied him suspiciously. "Why would you do that?"

He took a threatening step forward, thrusting his face toward mine, and I forced myself not to cower away from him. Rodrigo had always set my teeth on edge, and I didn't trust him as far as I could throw him.

"Because he's better off without you," he snapped.

It shouldn't have hurt as badly as it did, and I swallowed down the spear of hurt. "He's the one who kept me captive, not the other way around."

"He should have listened when I told him to get rid of you. Everything changed the moment you came along. He's losing focus, losing his touch. There's too much at stake for him to give it all up for you."

"So you're just going to let me walk away? What would Fox have to say about that?"

"I'll figure it out." He tipped his chin toward the yard again. "There's a road behind the house. Now go."

Eyes locked on his, I took a step backward. Then another. I was vaguely aware of the cold drizzle that misted against my face as I backed away from Rodrigo. He watched me like a hawk from the shelter of the huge house, never moving a muscle. It was a trap; it had to be. When I was far enough away, I turned and ran. The heels of my shoes sank into the soft earth as I wound my way through the backyard.

I glanced behind me when I reached the gate on the far side of the yard, but the yard was empty. I flipped the latch and escaped onto the sidewalk on the other side. My toes ached already from being pinched inside my shoes, and I paused only for a moment to take them off. The rain increased, the temperature dropping as I started jogging down the sidewalk.

I had no idea how long I ran, a thousand memories flitting through my mind. A sharp stabbing sensation cut through my side, but I forced myself to keep going. Focusing on the pain in my muscles distracted me from Fox's betrayal. No matter how hard I tried, though, I couldn't block his face from my memory. I kept hearing him tell me no one had come for me. That I was his captive. He'd lied. He'd broken his promise to me. He'd had every opportunity to come clean and tell me the truth. Instead, he'd done the very thing he'd promised never to do.

The pain was unlike anything I'd ever experienced. Every moment spent with him crashed over me like a tidal wave. His controlling tendencies, his adamancy that I stay within the walls of the house and speak to no one. I thought things had changed; I thought our relationship had begun to evolve. He was everything I'd ever wanted. But I was only his property.

My stomach flipped at the memory of the night he'd come home from being with another woman. He'd told me I was the only thing he could think about; in truth, it was only because he had full control over me. God only knew how many other women he'd been with since then. Though we'd spent most nights together in bed, sometimes he'd come to me later than others, saying that work had kept him away. I trusted him so much that it had never occurred to me to ask. I wanted to throw up.

A small convenience store came into view, and I followed the fluorescent lights to the parking lot. A shiver racked my body as I leaned against the brick wall of the crumbling old store. I still held my shoes, and the patent leather squeaked as they rubbed together.

I needed to go inside, but my feet ached so badly that I dreaded putting them back on even to walk inside. I needed to call someone. But who? He would track me down wherever I went, and that was the last thing I wanted. I needed to get away from him, put some distance between us. If I saw him right now, I would throw myself at him, beg him to make everything make sense. And he would. I'd fall back into his arms like none of this had ever happened, and I refused to let that happen.

From a few dozen feet away, a man standing beside a tanker truck lifted a hand, his face concerned. "Miss, are you okay?"

I tried to smile but failed miserably as another chill rocked my body. "I..." My teeth chattered, and I clenched them together before speaking again. "I'm fine."

"Are you sure?" He approached cautiously, his gaze sweeping over my pitiful form. "Is there anything I can help with?"

I made a split-second decision as I looked at his truck. "I'm kind of stranded. I hate to ask for a ride, but..."

He nodded slowly. "Where do you need to go?"

"Anywhere but here."

Taking another look at my cocktail dress and shoes, he waved me over. "Hop in and get warm."

The man reached up and held the door open for me as I approached. I'd never hitchhiked before, but I knew how dangerous it could be. At the moment, though, I couldn't summon the energy to care. I stepped up onto the rail that ran along the bottom of the door, trying not to drop my clutch and shoes as I clambered up into the cab of the huge truck.

Once I was inside, the man rounded the vehicle and climbed into the driver seat. The truck shuddered as he cranked the engine, and it came to life with a roar. He reached over and turned up the heat, then turned to me. "I'm Joe."

I offered him a small smile. "Eva."

"Nice to meet you, Eva. Ever been to Omaha?"

"Nope." I shook my head as I settled back against the seat. "But it sounds good to me."

"All right, then."

He shifted the truck into gear, and I tipped my head against the cool glass of the window. Had Fox realized I was gone yet? Would he even care? A dull ache radiated from my chest. I was stupid for even entertaining the idea. Despite knowing better, I'd fallen for him. I didn't honestly know what was worse—that Daddy had left me there, or that Fox had lied to me—about everything.

One thing was for certain—I would never allow someone to control me like that ever again. I watched in the large side mirror as the lights of my hometown grew small and smaller, then disappeared into the darkness. There was nothing left for me there. It was time to start over. Closing my eyes, I promised myself I would never look back.

CHAPTER
Forty-Two

FOX

I walked back toward the ballroom, feeling better than I ever had in my entire life. It was cliché, but I knew what people were talking about now. Happiness was that floating on air feeling, like you were untouchable, indestructible. That's how I felt with Eva. I was no longer the monster I'd been groomed to be. For the first time in forever, I could see the light at the end of the tunnel. And in that light was Eva. She was my salvation, my angel. Once I brought Araña down, I planned to set everything aside—for her. She was all I wanted, all I needed. Everything else was secondary.

Several people stopped me to say hello, and I made small talk as I waited for Eva to join me. Outside the large double doors, I ran one hand down my jacket, smoothing the material before tugging down my sleeves. The cuff around my left wrist hung limply, and I lifted it up to inspect it. Turning my hand over, I immediately noticed the problem. My cufflink was missing, probably somewhere back in the closet. I bit back a smile. I'd sacrifice a thousand cufflinks for a lifetime of moments like that with Eva.

I wished I could have seen her face more clearly before I'd left her. I wanted her to see the intent clearly in my face. I wanted to take her home and spend the rest of the night loving her, tell her how much she meant to me. I planned to devote several hours to that just as soon as we could escape this stupid party.

My gaze roved the ballroom as I stepped inside, and my pleasure from mere moments ago was immediately doused by the presence of a familiar face. I strode toward the man, offering only small nods to acquaintances as I passed, not inviting them to approach me.

Spencer Masterson's eyes widened as they caught mine, and he pasted that stupid fucking politician's smile on his lips as he turned to me. I returned the gesture, mine much more akin to a shark's as I slapped him on the back a little harder than necessary—twice, just for good measure.

He stumbled a little bit and swallowed hard. "Fox. Glad to see you."

"Are you now?" I pinned him with a sharp glare, and his confident façade bled away, though I was pretty sure I was the only one who could read the discomfort in his eyes. "Because I thought I made it extremely clear what would happen if you showed your face around here again."

"But—" He broke off, his gaze darting around the room as he swallowed hard. "It's my cousin's engagement party."

"I don't give a goddamn if it's your mother's fucking funeral," I growled. "You leave tonight, and I don't want to see you again."

Spencer's face fell into a pout. "William is here."

Motherfucker didn't know when to quit. Eva's father, William, was a whole other issue, and one I planned to take care of directly. He knew what would happen if he so much as looked at Eva the wrong way. "He won't be here for long," I promised. "Now. Enjoy what's left of your evening. I have to get back to my girl."

"Oh?" His eyes brightened with interest. "You still keeping Eva on a leash?"

I slanted a look his way, clenching my fists at my sides to keep from laying him out right here in the middle of the room. "She's free to do whatever she wants, as long as she's with me."

"Even speak with her father?"

Except that. "He knows better."

"Well, you might want to remind him of that," he said smugly, "because he walked out with her just a couple minutes ago."

Goddamn it. "Where?"

He started to shrug. "I thought I was supposed to keep—"

I threw a hard look his way, just barely stifling the urge to grab the asshole around the neck and slam him to the floor. "I swear to God I will dismember you right here," I threatened in a low voice. "Tell me where the fuck they went."

"Out that way." He gestured with his head toward a door in the corner.

"Stay the fuck out of my way," I said. "Next time I won't be so amenable."

He nodded but wisely stayed silent, and I skirted the large room until I reached the large set of doors that opened into a long hallway. Quickly scanning both directions, I saw no movement. Taking a gamble, I turned left and headed toward the bathroom. Maybe the asshole was wrong, and she was just tidying her appearance from our romp in the closet.

The memory simultaneously sent fire rushing through my blood and set my teeth on edge. I had to intercept her before that motherfucker who called himself her father found her. A figure came around the corner, and my eyes narrowed when I saw William.

He missed a step as his gaze landed on me, his eyes widening with recognition and wariness. "Fox. I—"

Fisting the front of his shirt, I pushed him around the

corner until we were concealed, then shoved him up against the wall. "Where is she?"

"W-who?"

"Don't play fucking stupid," I warned him. "Tell me now."

"Toward the library." He pointed with one shaking finger. "Take a left down the hallway."

"You tell her anything?"

He shook his head rapidly. "N-no."

I could see the lie in his eyes, the way his Adam's apple bobbed when he swallowed. "I should have cut your fucking tongue out last time. What kind of man begs for his own life, yet sacrifices his daughter's?"

I would never regret the deal I'd made with William, because it had brought Eva into my life. But if she found out he'd practically sold her to me... she would be crushed. I didn't have time to waste. I released him. "Get Masterson and get the fuck out of here."

Without waiting for a response, I took off down the hallway, picking up my pace. I checked the hallway and the library but both were empty. My heart slammed against my ribs as I ran from room to room in search of Eva.

At the back of the house, I saw a set of French doors that led to a terrace, and I flung them open. Overhead, rain fell in a dreary drizzle, soaking the flagstones. To my right, Rodrigo stood beneath the overhang, dragging on a cigarette. He pushed away from the wall, his head tipped to one side as he inspected me. I pointed at him. "Have you seen Eva?"

"Not for about ten minutes," he confirmed, flicking ash on the wet ground before stubbing out the cigarette in a potted plant.

I raked one hand through my hair as I spun in a circle. Where the fuck could she be? "We need to find her," I said to him. "Get the car and—"

"Boss." His dark eyes met mine. "Maybe we should let her—"

"Don't you fucking say it!" I roared, shoving against his chest. "I need to find her."

He gave his head a slow shake. "She's gone."

Ice settled in my bones as I watched him. "What are you talking about?"

"She left through the garden about ten minutes ago."

Rage simmered beneath the surface. "You let her go?"

"You haven't been the same since she showed up," he said stubbornly. "It's for the best."

I straightened. "You think you can make decisions for me?"

"Boss, I—"

His words cut off as my fist collided with his jaw, snapping his head back. He stumbled backward and collapsed onto the pavestones. Lunging forward, I grabbed the front of his shirt and drove my fist into his face over and over until he slumped to the ground, wheezing, shallow breaths leaving his chest. I slapped the side of his face, but he didn't respond. Fury exploded outward, and I dropped him again, not caring that his head slammed into the hard stones beneath us.

I peeled one eyelid back and waited for his pupil to focus on me. "You'll find her, or I'll kill you myself. Do you understand me?"

CHAPTER
Forty-Three

EVA

My eyes popped open as someone gently shook me awake.

"We're here."

Sitting straight up, I glanced around, disoriented, before my gaze landed on Joe in the driver seat. The events of last night came rushing back, slamming into me in rapid succession. The pain. The betrayal. I felt cold all over, completely numb and devoid of emotion.

My gaze skated over the small plaza across from us. "Where are we?"

"Just outside of Omaha."

I threw a tiny smile Joe's way. "Thank you for doing this, I said softly. "If you write down your address, I promise I'll send some money—"

"You don't owe me anything," he said with a wave of his hand. "You just take care of yourself."

"I'll try." Resting my hand on the door handle, I turned back to look at him one last time. "Most people wouldn't have done this... Picking up a stranger, then driving them halfway across the US."

The corners of his mouth tipped up in a smile. "It was only a couple states."

"You know what I mean. I just... Thank you. For everything."

He nodded. "Glad I could help. You know," he said hesitantly, "the past has a way of catching up with us. Sometimes it's better to face it head on and lay your demons to rest."

I studied him for a long moment. From the shrewd look in his eyes, I had a distinct feeling that he was speaking from experience. After everything that happened between Fox and me, though, I wasn't sure I would ever be ready to revisit it. "Sometimes," I returned quietly, "it's best to leave skeletons in the closet where they belong."

He gave a little nod. "You just be careful."

"I appreciate it." With that, I opened the door and slid from the cab, holding the hem of my skirt in one hand to keep it from riding up, my clutch in the other. I stumbled briefly as the heels of my shoes landed with a wobble on the cracked asphalt, then I turned my gaze back to Joe. "Be safe."

"Same to you," he returned.

I shut the door and stepped back, lifting a hand to wave as the truck slid into motion with the squeak of metal and hiss of steam. It was still early afternoon, and though the sun shone brightly overhead, the air was still cool, and I wrapped my arms around myself to keep warm. With no phone and no idea of who to contact at the moment, my first order of business was to get inside and get warm.

I spied at a restaurant on the corner, its fluorescent sign blinking in the window. Almost immediately, I discarded it. I was already out of place in my cocktail dress and heels; I didn't need to draw more attention to myself. I glanced around for a pawn shop, wondering if I could trade my eveningwear for something more appropriate. As I skimmed the names of the businesses, my eyes lit on a small hole-in-the-wall bar tucked away between a travel agency and a law office.

Making a quick decision, I crossed the street and tugged gently on the door. Though it was still a little bit early, I hoped they would be open. I was gratified when the door swung open easily under the pressure, and I stepped inside, my gaze sweeping over the dim and mostly empty interior. A handsome man stood behind the bar drying a glass, and he lifted his chin in greeting as I made my way toward him.

His gaze slid over me from head to toe then back up again, and he set the glass aside. "What can I get you?"

"I'm new here," I said as I leaned my elbows on the bar. "I was hoping you could help with something. I'm looking for a pawn shop, consignment shop, anywhere I can find a change of clothes."

"There's a Salvation Army a couple of streets over. Make a right out of here, then take a right at the first intersection. It's about two blocks down. Can't miss it."

"Thanks." I tapped my fingers on the bar and took a step backwards, then paused. "Do you know if anyone is hiring around here?"

"Maybe." His eyes bored into mine as if trying to read me. "What are you looking for?"

"Anything that pays," I said honestly.

"Can you pour drinks?"

I stared at him, interpreting the question. "Never done it before, but it can't be that hard."

He gave a little shake of his head. "Most of my clientele drinks from the tap."

"I could handle that."

"How soon can you start?"

"Uh..." I flicked a glance around the bar. "Shouldn't I talk to the boss?"

He smirked and held out one hand. "Bryce Warren. Owner, operator."

"Nice to meet you. I'm Eva." I slipped my hand into his, pulling away almost as soon as my palm came into contact with his.

Those piercing eyes watched my every move. "What do you say we meet back here around four?"

I drew in a breath, completely unsure of what I was about to do. "Works for me."

He reached beneath the bar, then grabbed a handful of black fabric and tossed it to me. I caught it to my chest, then slowly opened the T-shirt with the bar's name across the chest in white. It was much too big, but I didn't care. Dropping my gaze to the floor, unable to speak over the emotion clogging my throat, I started to turn away.

"Hey." The man's voice drew me back to him. "Do you have somewhere to stay?"

Immediately, I stiffened. "If you think you're going to offer me a job and a bed to sleep in in exchange for sex, you can forget it."

"Never crossed my mind."

We stared at each other for nearly a minute before I finally nodded. "I could use somewhere to stay for... a while," I finally conceded.

"I've got a friend who has a duplex a couple of blocks from here. He's been looking for somebody responsible to rent it, and I'm sure he'd love to have you."

"It sounds great, but I don't have any money," I said baldly.

"I know," he replied just as succinctly, his gaze sweeping over my cocktail dress again. "We'll work it out."

He looked at the man sitting on the stool a few feet away. "Dale, keep an eye on the place for me, would you?"

The man on the stool nodded, and Bryce slipped around the bar to come meet me. I gestured toward the guy on the stool, my voice low. "You're just gonna leave him in charge of your bar?"

Bryce smiled. "He'll take good care of it."

Keeping a good amount of distance between us, he gestured toward the door, and I preceded him onto the sidewalk. The cold air hit me, and I shivered. Bryce shrugged out of his zip up sweatshirt and threw it around my shoulders. "Oh, I can't—"

"Come on," he said, cutting off my protest. "We'll take my car."

I started to automatically fall into step beside him, then drew to an abrupt stop. "Why are you being so nice?"

He slowed to a stop, then turned to face me squarely. His eyes roved over me before meeting my gaze. "You show up here dressed like that, asking for a job and a place to stay. I'm guessing you don't have anything other than the clothes on your back." I shook my head at the rhetorical statement, and he sighed. "Sometimes you just do something nice for somebody because it's the right thing to do."

Tears burned my eyes, and I fought to keep them from falling. "Thanks."

Bryce gave a slight dip of his chin, and I followed him around the corner to a small silver car parked along the side street. I climbed inside and watched as Bryce slid behind the wheel then cranked the engine. He turned up the heat, then shifted into drive and pulled away from the bar. As we drove, he made a call to his friend, the one I assumed owned the duplex.

By the time we pulled into the parking lot of the Salvation Army, he was saying goodbye to his friend. "It's all settled," he said as he hung up. "Let's get you some clothes."

Two hours later, laden down with bags, we entered the front door of the small duplex. "Laundry room is through there," Bryce said as he pointed down a hallway. "Do you need me to come back and pick you up?"

I shook my head. "No, I can walk. I'd like to wash a load of clothes first, if you don't mind."

Bryce nodded. "Take your time. I'll see you at the bar later."

With that he was gone, and I checked the front door to make sure it was locked before heading to the laundry room. I dumped the clothes in, then added some detergent and closed the lid.

Back in the bedroom, I kicked off my heels and settled on the edge of the mattress. The clutch on the nightstand caught my eye, and I picked it up. I flipped the clasp open and dumped the contents onto the bed. Lipstick, powder. Nothing of value or importance. A small metal object tumbled out, and I picked up the silver cuff link. Turning it over in my fingers, I let the memories of Fox rush over me. It was my last link to him, the last tie to my old life. I curled up in a ball, clutching it tightly to my chest, and let the tears fall.

Epilogue

FOX

SIX WEEKS LATER

"Boss."

"What?" I couldn't keep the agitation out of my voice as I shot a dark look at Rodrigo. He stood before my desk, his back stiff. The scar over his eyebrow was still bright pink, but the motherfucker was lucky to be alive.

"We got a lead."

"Great. Leave it here, and I'll take a look."

My guys had been chasing leads on the trucks bringing the children across the border, but nothing definitive had turned up on Araña. Ever since Eva had left, though, my search for him had taken a back burner to more pressing issues. I'd reached out to everyone I knew, asking if anyone had seen her. No one had. It was as if she'd disappeared into thin air.

I was furious. I was hurt. I wanted to drag her ass back here and punish her for leaving me.

"I think I might know where Eva is."

My gaze snapped to his, and I practically jumped out of my chair. "What the fuck are you talking about?"

Rodrigo tossed a grainy black and white picture on the desk. In the background, a young woman was climbing into the cab of a large box truck. There was no mistaking my girl. "Whose truck is this?"

"Registered to a Joseph Strahovski. He came through here the night Eva went missing. According to dispatch records, his next drop was in Omaha."

"Omaha." I picked up the picture. "See what you can find out."

With a nod, he disappeared out the door, and I sank back into my seat. It'd been so long—too long. But we finally had a clue as to where she might be. Studying the photograph, I traced Eva's beautiful face.

"I'm coming for you, angel."

Sinful Sacrament

Turn the page for a sneak peek at the conclusion of Fox and Eva's story!

Prologue

"The strength of a kingdom comes from its king; the strength of a King comes from his queen."
~Cody Edward Lee Miller

FOX

Anger. Relief. Desire. They all mingled in my chest, the emotions fluctuating so rapidly I could hardly keep up.

Forty-seven days had passed since I'd last seen her, and it seemed as if everything had changed. At the same time, everything remained exactly the same. From my concealed spot where I'd been watching her for the past four days, I studied Eva as she moved behind the bar.

I clamped down on the urge to stalk inside and force her to come with me. I wanted nothing more than to drag her back home, back to my side where she belonged. Instead, I closed my eyes briefly and drew in a deep breath, then focused once more on her beautiful features. Even though she was too far away to see clearly, I vividly remembered the slope of her jaw, the satiny softness of her skin beneath my fingertips. The slight dusting of freckles across her nose and cheeks, and that stubborn little chin. Those pretty green eyes that flashed with fire when she defied me.

Most of all, I remembered the way she made me feel. Whole. Content. Like my entire existence revolved around her. Just seeing her again, knowing that she was safe and hale, eased the pressure on my chest. Immediately on the heels of the intense relief came the anger. She'd run from me without a single word. I wanted to know why—and very soon, I was going to find out.

I turned the black king over in my hands, the carved ridges of the crown familiar beneath my fingertips. My queen had fled, putting miles between us like the spaces on a board. She'd made her move—but now it was my turn.

A slow smile curved my mouth. "Checkmate, angel."

Chapter One

EVA

"Last call."

I held back a yawn as I cleared the sticky, empty glasses from the table, then wiped it down before heading back to the bar. I dunked the glassware into the tub of sudsy water and threw a look down the bar to the handful of men still seated on the stools as I scrubbed the glasses and set them aside to drain.

From his spot in front of the tap, Bryce glanced over his shoulder at me. "Can you get the trash together?"

"Sure. If you want, you can finish up and I'll take it out."

One honey-colored brow lifted. "You sure?"

I nodded, deeply appreciative of his concern for me. He knew how much I hated being alone outside in the dark. But I was a thousand miles from home—and *him*. It was time to move on. I forced a smile. "I'll be fine."

"All right."

After the whole ordeal with Fox a month and a half ago I had disappeared from Chicago with literally only the clothes on my back, hopped into the cab of the semi, and hitchhiked to Omaha. Bryce had welcomed me in with open arms and given me solace working in the bar and staying in his friend's duplex. He watched over me like a big brother and had never made a single untoward comment. There would never be anything romantic between us, and if it bothered him at all, he never said a word.

My heart still felt bruised, and my mind was even worse. I stayed mostly behind the bar, away from the patrons, where I could avoid the flirtatious remarks occasionally flung my direction. If anyone ever came on too strong, Bryce stepped in, always my savior. He had deemed himself my protector, and I appreciated it immensely. I owed him so much for helping me to get back on my feet.

For the first several weeks after I'd first arrived, alone in my small, dark duplex where no one could see, I cried myself to sleep each night. Even though Fox had betrayed me, even after everything, I still missed him. What we'd shared had felt real. Despite the fact that he had initially taken me captive, in the end it had seemed like a real relationship, a connection born of mutual attraction and desire. There'd been plenty of those—but no trust to speak of. Against all odds I'd gambled and put my faith in him—and lost. I still felt the sting of hurt down into the marrow of my bones.

I wasn't sure I could ever get over the fact that he lied to me. He had every opportunity to tell me he knew who my parents were, but he'd chosen to keep that from me. I wasn't sure whose betrayal hurt worse—Fox's or my father's.

My father, who I assumed would have been beside himself with grief and worry, had apparently known where I was all along. He'd willingly handed me over to Fox and cut all ties with his only remaining daughter. Part of me wanted to ask him why he'd done it; the other part of me wanted to cut him as ruthlessly from my life as he'd done to me.

I felt alone and adrift in the world with no one to turn to. Outwardly, I was moving on. Inside, I still felt stuck in the past. I missed Fox, missed the way he made me feel. I had even debated several times reaching out to him or going back, but I could never quite bring myself to do it. Fox had attempted no communication, and I wasn't sure if that dismayed me or not. He had connections all over the US; I was fairly certain that he would have found me and dragged me back to Chicago if he'd wanted to. I could only surmise that he'd decided he had better things to do than track down the errant woman who'd run from him. I'd escaped my captor; it was exactly what I'd wanted. But then why did I feel so empty?

I finished drying the glasses, then wiped my hands on my apron before untying it and setting it aside to toss in the laundry later. Making my way through the bar and kitchen areas, I collected the bags of trash, then glanced at the clock. Bryce had yelled for last call fifteen minutes ago, and now only two men lingered at the bar. As I twisted up the bags, they downed their drinks then pushed the empty glasses toward Bryce, who collected them and dumped them into the soapy water.

An older man who went by the name Tyrone lifted a hand my way. "Have yourself a good night."

My mouth automatically formed a smile, though I didn't feel a flicker of happiness. "See you tomorrow."

With a nod, he turned and loped out the door. He was a perpetual fixture in Bryce's bar, and he sat in the same seat every day from seven o'clock in the evening until we closed at two in the morning. I felt bad for him, having learned a few weeks ago that, after forty-two years of marriage, he'd lost his wife to pneumonia two winters ago. He had no one to go home to, no one to take care of him. I often slid him extra food, and I comped it by covering the cost of the meal with my own tips. I had a feeling Bryce knew, because occasionally my pay would be a little higher to compensate for the difference.

Once I had gathered all the trash bags together, I pushed out the back door into the alley. A security light to my left illuminated the dumpster, and I used a brick to prop the door open before carrying the bags over and tossing them in, one by one. The lid shut with a bang, and I dusted my hands on my jeans before drawing in a deep breath of the muggy early summer air.

A soft scuffle behind me had the hairs on the back of my neck lifting, and I whirled around, immediately on edge. My eyes scanned the dark alley but found nothing. I replayed the sound in my mind over and over, trying to place exactly what it sounded like, where it'd come from. It had sounded almost like a… footstep. I slowly began to edge my way toward the door, scanning in all directions. Suddenly, a clatter rose from a steel trashcan of the travel agency next door, and a scream caught in my throat. I slapped one hand over my heart as a mangy black cat hopped down and strode forward, a scrap of food clenched between its teeth.

Breathing heavily, I collapsed against the jagged brick wall and blinked back the tears that had sprung to my eyes. God, I needed to get a grip. Because on the heels of the initial fear I'd felt, hope had welled up. Hope that he'd found me. Hope that he'd cared enough to come for me. But he didn't. Forty-seven days had passed since I'd walked away from him. Forty-seven days without a single word, without any indication that he wanted me back. He wasn't coming.

Shaking off my wayward thoughts, I strode back into the bar then closed up behind me, making sure that the door was securely locked. By the time I made it back to the bar, Bryce had already washed the remaining dishes and set them aside to dry. He threw a look my way. "Ready to head out?"

"Yep." I grabbed my purse from under the bar. "Trash is taken care of."

"Awesome, thanks." Bryce reached over and flipped a switch that turned off the neon lights in the windows displaying the names of various brands of beer, then grabbed up the deposit envelope to drop off at the bank on his way in tomorrow.

"Come on." He dug his keys from his pocket as he rounded the bar. "I'll drive you home."

It was a nightly routine for us, and though I'd told him a hundred times he didn't have to do it, Bryce insisted on making sure I got home safely every night. I didn't bother to argue with him, just fell into step as we locked up and headed to his car. The duplex I currently rented was only a couple of blocks away, and five minutes later, I climbed out of Bryce's car, gave him a little wave, then headed into the house.

Once I was inside, I watched through the window as he pulled away from the curb and headed home to get some sleep before he had to be back at the bar by noon tomorrow. As soon as his taillights disappeared down the street, I prepared for the night ahead. A small table stood against the wall just inside the entryway, and I pulled it in front of the door, effectively blocking the entrance. A vase took up residence in the middle of the table, and I slid it forward, balancing it precariously close to the edge. The table itself wouldn't stop someone from getting in, but if the door was opened, it would hit the table and send the vase crashing to the floor. Since there was no security system, the noise would at least give me some warning if someone decided to break in.

As soon as everything was in place, I made my way to the bedroom and kicked off my shoes. My hand automatically went to the pocket of my jeans, where I fingered the small silver cufflink within. I'd carried it with me every single day, like a talisman of sorts. My heart ached as I set it on the nightstand next to the bed. Even if Fox wasn't physically here with me, I still had a piece of him.

I shook off my melancholy and strode to the bathroom,

stripping my clothes off as I went. My shirt reeked of beer, and the perpetual scent of greasy fried food clung to my hair. I flicked the handle of the shower faucet over to its hottest setting and waited for a moment as the old pipes warmed up. Soon, steam rose into the air and I gratefully climbed beneath the spray.

Tipping my head back, I allowed the hot water to wash over me, and I reveled in the feeling. I scrubbed at my skin, washing away the grime of the day and leaving the fresh scent of eucalyptus in its place. I poured shampoo into my palm, then lathered and rinsed my hair. A subtle shift in the air had goosebumps sprouting along the backs of my arms, and I froze. The apprehension I'd felt in the alley came back full force, sweeping over me like a tidal wave and rooting my feet to the floor of the tub. Slowly turning my head, I glanced through the translucent curtain. The room beyond was hazy, but I saw nothing out of the ordinary. I leaned forward slightly and peered around the edge of the shower curtain, my eyes scanning every inch of the tiny room. The door stood open exactly as I'd left it, but I heard no movement from the hallway.

I let out the breath I'd been holding and tried to steady my nerves. What was wrong with me? Tonight especially I'd felt particularly on edge, but I couldn't pinpoint the reason why. Nothing out of the ordinary had happened. No one had come on to me, no one had even looked at me sideways. So I couldn't quite tell why I felt like there were eyes on me at all times. Maybe it was a manifestation of my own feelings presenting themselves.

Part of me was still conflicted about the situation with Fox, but I knew I'd done the right thing. Had I never spoken with Daddy, Fox probably would never have told me the whole story. I'd still be there, playing house with a man who'd withheld the truth—that he'd practically stolen me from my father.

That knowledge had plagued me every day for nearly the past seven weeks. Part of me wanted to demand every detail. But the other, far more rational part of me told me it was better this way. My father and Fox were men cut from the same cloth. They were both manipulators who did what was best for them; to hell with whoever or whatever got in their way. The two men I'd cared for most had both betrayed me in some fashion—and I would never let it happen again.

Keep reading Sinful Sacrament!

Also by Morgan James

QUENTIN SECURITY SERIES

Twisted Devil – Jason and Chloe
The Devil You Know – Blake and Victoria
Devil in the Details – Xander and Lydia
Devil in Disguise – Gavin and Kate
Heart of a Devil – Vince and Jana
Tempting the Devil – Clay and Abby
Devilish Intent – Con and Grace
*Each book is a standalone within the series

RESCUE AND REDEMPTION SERIES

Friendly Fire – Grayson and Claire
Cruel Vendetta – Drew and Emery (Fall 2022)

RETRIBUTION SERIES

FROZEN IN TIME TRILOGY

Unrequited Love – Jack and Mia, Book One
Undeniable Love – Jack and Mia, Book Two
Unbreakable Love – Jack and Mia, Book Three
Frozen in Time: The Complete Trilogy

DECEPTION DUET

Pretty Little Lies – Eric and Jules, Book One

Beautiful Deception – Eric and Jules, Book Two

*Each book can be read as a standalone, but are best read in order

SINFUL DUET

Sinful Illusions – Fox and Eva, Book One

Sinful Sacrament – Fox and Eva, Book Two

*Books should be read in order

BAD BILLIONAIRES

(Radish Exclusive)

Depraved

Ravished

Consumed

*Each book is a standalone within the series

STANDALONES

Death Do Us Part

Escape

About the Author

Morgan James is a USA Today bestselling author of contemporary and romantic suspense novels. She spent most of her childhood with her nose buried in a book, and she loves all things romantic, dark, and dirty. She currently resides in Ohio and is living happily ever after with her own alpha hero and their two kids.

Made in the USA
Middletown, DE
31 May 2022